Back by Popular Demand

A collector's edition of favorite titles from one of the world's best-loved romance authors. Harlequin is proud to bring back these sought after titles and present them as one cherished collection.

BETTY NEELS:
COLLECTOR'S EDITION

A GEM OF A GIRL
WISH WITH THE CANDLES
COBWEB MORNING
HENRIETTA'S OWN CASTLE
CASSANDRA BY CHANCE
VICTORY FOR VICTORIA
SISTER PETERS IN AMSTERDAM
THE MAGIC OF LIVING
SATURDAY'S CHILD
FATE IS REMARKABLE
A STAR LOOKS DOWN
HEAVEN IS GENTLE

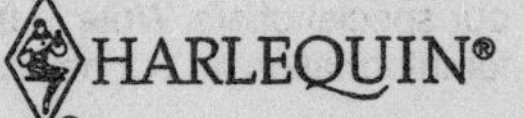

Betty Neels spent her childhood and youth in Devonshire before training as a nurse and midwife. She was an army nursing sister during the war, married a Dutchman, and subsequently lived in Holland for fourteen years. She now lives with her husband in Dorset, and has a daughter and grandson. Her hobbies are reading, animals, old buildings and, of course, writing. Betty started to write on retirement from nursing, incited by a lady in a library bemoaning the lack of romantic novels.

Mrs. Neels is always delighted to receive fan letters, but would truly appreciate it if they could be directed to Harlequin Mills & Boon Ltd., 18-24 Paradise Road, Richmond, Surrey, TW9 1SR, England.

Books by Betty Neels

HARLEQUIN ROMANCE

3355—DEAREST LOVE
3363—A SECRET INFATUATION
3371—WEDDING BELLS FOR BEATRICE
3389—A CHRISTMAS WISH
3400—WAITING FOR DEBORAH
3415—THE BACHELOR'S WEDDING
3435—DEAREST MARY JANE
3454—FATE TAKES A HAND
3467—THE RIGHT KIND OF GIRL
3483—THE MISTLETOE KISS
3492—MARRYING MARY
3512—A KISS FOR JULIE

BETTY NEELS

SATURDAY'S CHILD

COLLECTOR'S EDITION

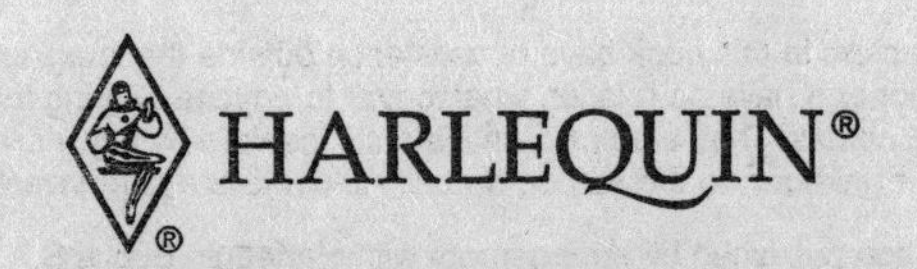

TORONTO • NEW YORK • LONDON
AMSTERDAM • PARIS • SYDNEY • HAMBURG
STOCKHOLM • ATHENS • TOKYO • MILAN • MADRID
PRAGUE • WARSAW • BUDAPEST • AUCKLAND

ISBN 0-373-83394-6

SATURDAY'S CHILD

First North American Publication 1998.

This edition published by arrangement with Harlequin Books S.A.

Printed in U.S.A.

CHAPTER ONE

THE room was chilly and severe, as was the woman sitting behind the desk in one of its corners. The desk lamp, which only partly held at bay the fog of the darkened January sky outside, also served to illuminate her features, and the girl who had taken the chair on the opposite side of the desk in answer to the woman's brisk nod occupied herself in giving her interviewer a softer hair-style, appropriate make-up and a more becoming dress. These alterations, mused Miss Abigail Trent, as she admitted to that name, would take away at least ten years from the age of her unconscious interviewer, who looked up and repeated, 'Your age, Miss Trent?'

'Twenty-four.'

'Your education?'

Abigail murmured the name of a well-known girls' boarding school. When her father had been alive there had been money enough. . .

'You are State Registered?'

Abigail nodded and when asked to give the name of her training school mentioned a famous teaching hospital in London.

'Have you family ties?'

She thought of the two cousins in Canada; they sent her Christmas cards each year, but they could hardly be described as ties, nor, for that matter, could Uncle Sedgeley, her mother's brother, married to a peer's sister and landed gentry, and totally disapproving of her father, her mother's marriage to him and to Abigail herself. She said quietly in her pleasant voice: 'No,' and when she was asked what branch of nursing she had most recently been in, said: 'Surgery—the operating theatre, too.'

'You're willing to travel?'

It sounded like the beginnings of an advertisement

in the Personal Column of *The Times*. She said, 'Certainly,' and smiled at the woman, who didn't smile back but looked at her watch as though time was rationed for her interviews and she had used it all up on Abigail. She got up briskly and went across to the filing cabinet against one wall and started pulling out its drawers. Presently she came back with a small folder and sat down again. 'I think we could offer you a post immediately if you are prepared to take a medical case. A patient in Amsterdam—an American woman staying with friends there, in their flat. She has been in hospital with severe gastric symptoms and is now back with them—still in bed, of course, pending the doctor's decision. She didn't care for the hospital, for she speaks no Dutch and found the regulations a little trying. She is, I gather, rather. . .' She wisely left the sentence unfinished and went on: 'You will be paid twenty pounds a week and receive your board and lodging, and she is prepared to pay your fare at the end of a fortnight. The flat is, I believe, in one of the best parts of the city. You will have two and a half hours free every afternoon, and such other times as you can arrange for yourself. Should you take the post, you will pay this agency twelve and a half per cent of your salary until such time as you leave.'

She finished speaking and sat, tapping her ballpoint on the blotting pad in front of her. After perhaps half a minute she enquired, 'Well, Miss Trent, do you care to take the case?'

It wasn't quite what Abigail wanted, although she hardly knew what she did want—only to get away from London—from England, for a while, so that she could adjust herself to a future which no longer held her mother. And she needed the money. She got to her feet. 'Yes, I'll take it,' she said. 'When do you want me to go?'

'Please sit down again.' The woman looked more severe than ever. 'I'll give you the patient's name and address and advise you on the easiest way of getting to the case. I suggest that you fly over early tomorrow, so that you will arrive in Amsterdam by lunch time—that should give you time to unpack, see your patient and begin your duties without delay.'

Abigail blinked the fine silky lashes of eyes which were her sole claim to beauty in an otherwise ordinary face. They were brown and large and the brows above them were silky too. But her nose was too short, her mouth too wide and her hair too mousy to give her even a modicum of good looks. She wasn't sure at this moment if the change would be for the better; probably not, but she could always go back to hospital again. She held out a hand in its slightly shabby glove and took the papers which the woman was holding out to her.

Two minutes later she was outside in the street, standing rather uncertainly on the pavement while the passers-by pushed and jostled her first one way, then the other; not meaning to treat her roughly, but intent on getting to wherever they were going as quickly as possible. Presently she crossed the road, drawn by the cheerful lights of a Golden Egg restaurant, and went inside. It was almost twelve o'clock on this damp and foggy day in the first week of January; lunch in a pleasant warmth seemed a good idea. She chose egg and chips and coffee and while she was waiting for them got out her little notebook and started doing sums. Twenty pounds a week would be a godsend; she hadn't earned any money at all for three months now. When her mother had fallen ill, she had given up her job at the hospital and stayed at home to nurse her, because the doctor had told her that her mother had only a few months to live anyway, and Abigail couldn't bear the thought of her living out those last few weeks in some strange hospital bed. She had gone home for almost three months, and her mother had had every small comfort and luxury she wished for or needed, and Abigail had spent what money she had saved, which wasn't much, to pay for them. Her mother's pension had paid the rent of their small flat and the household expenses, but when she had died there had been nothing left at all. The furniture went with the flat, her mother's jewellery, never very valuable, had been sold over the last five years, and Bollinger, who had served her father faithfully until his death and had refused to leave them after it, was owed almost a year of his low wages. The funeral had taken almost all the money she had, and now today, barely a week later, she had gone out to get a job, and it had had to be private nursing—that way she would get her board and lodging free and would get paid sooner.

The egg and chips arrived and she ate them, still doing sums in her head. She would just about be able to get to Amsterdam and have a pound or two in her purse until she was paid. Two weeks wasn't long to wait, and anyway it didn't look as though she was going to get much free time in which to spend her money. Even when the twelve and a half per cent had been deducted, she would still be able to send Bollinger some money. He would retire now, she supposed, but he would only have his old age pension, and that wouldn't go far in London. She began to worry about where he would live; after that night they would have to leave the flat and she wasn't going to leave him to struggle on his own after the years of service he had given them, and he had been so kind and helpful to her and her mother. The food on her plate became dimmed by the tears in her eyes, but she fought them back and doggedly went on eating the chips on her plate and drinking the coffee she didn't want any more.

She took a bus back to the flat, the small top flat just off the Cromwell Road where they had lived since her father died and Abigail had started her hospital training. As she put her key in the front door at the top of the long flights of stairs, she could hear Bollinger in the kitchen; he came to its door as she went inside and said comfortably:

'There you are, Miss Abby, the kettle's on and I treated us to some crumpets. Nothing like a nice hot crumpet.' He went back to the gas stove. 'How did it go?'

'I've got a job, Bolly—twenty pounds a week, in Amsterdam, nursing an American woman. I'm to go tomorrow, and isn't it lucky I've still got my passport from that trip we had to Ostend? So everything's going to be OK.' She cast her coat and hat over the back of one of the wooden chairs at the table and went to get the teapot from the dresser. 'Now, about you—did you manage to find anything?'

'I did—the woman at the paper shop, remember her? She's got a daughter with a house just round the corner from here. I can have a room and me meals with her and her husband. Four pounds and fifty pence a week—leaves me plenty, so don't you worry your pretty head about me.'

She looked at him with deep affection, loving him for the cheerful lie. He was almost seventy, she knew, and he had worked very hard around the flat since they had moved into it, shopping and cooking and repairing fuses and waiting on her mother hand and foot. It was impossible to repay him, but at least she would see that he got the money which they owed him and then a small weekly pension after that so that he could find a proper home and not some small back room where he would be lonely. Years ago he had been her father's gardener and odd job man, and when her father had died he had somehow stayed on with them, smoothing her mother's path, offering practical advice when it was discovered that there was no money at all, and Abigail had never quite discovered how it was that he had persuaded her mother to keep him on at such a ridiculous wage.

She made the tea and they sat down together with the plate of crumpets between them. 'I'm glad you've got somewhere to go for the present,' began Abigail. She opened her handbag. 'They gave me five pounds in advance on my salary,' she went on mendaciously. 'I've got more than enough and this'll help you to get started, then each week, once I get my pay, I shall send you some money,' and when he began to protest, 'No, Bolly dear, you're my friend and you were Mother's and Father's friend too—I can well afford to pay you back the wages we owe you and then pay you a little each week. It won't take me long, you see, for I get my room and my food for free, don't I? And in a little while I'll get a hospital job again and perhaps we can find a small place and you can come and run it for me while I work.'

She smiled at him, trying not to see that he was getting quite elderly now and wouldn't be fit to do much for many more years—something she would worry about when the time came, she told herself vigorously. She poured more tea and said cheerfully: 'How funny Uncle Sedgeley was yesterday. I wonder what he and Aunt Miriam would have done if I'd accepted their invitation to go to Gore Park and stay with them? They hated Father, didn't they, because he was a Methodist parson and hadn't any worldly ideas and they hadn't been near. . .' She paused, unable to bear talking of her mother. 'Aunt Miriam told me how fortunate I was that I had a vocation, for all the world as though I'd taken a vow not to marry.'

'Of course you'll marry, Miss Abby,' said Bollinger, quite shocked.

'That's nice of you to say so, Bolly, but I'm afraid she may be right, you know. I'm twenty-four and I've never had a proposal—nothing even approaching one. I'm a sort of universal sister, you know, because I'm plain.'

'You're talking nonsense, Miss Abby. You just haven't met the right man, that's all. He'll come, don't you fret.'

'Yes? Well, when he does I shan't marry him unless he lets you come along too,' she said firmly. 'Now let's go and see this room of yours and then I'll treat us to the pictures.'

A remark which would have shocked Uncle Sedgeley if he could have heard it; to go to the cinema barely a week after her mother's funeral—unthinkable! She could just hear him saying it, but it didn't matter what he thought; her mother would have been the first one to suggest it. Life went on and you didn't forget someone just because you sat in the stalls and watched some film or other without seeing any of it, and at least it would be warm there and infinitely better than sitting in the little flat talking, inevitably, of old times with Bolly, something she couldn't bear to do.

She said goodbye to him the next morning and started her journey. She had booked her flight when she had left the agency, obedient to the severe woman's instructions, and had packed her case with the sort of clothes she considered she might need, adding the blue uniform dresses and caps and aprons she had been forced to buy, and now on the plane at last, she got out her little notebook again and did some anxious arithmetic. With luck she wouldn't have to spend more than the equivalent of a few shillings; stamps for her letters to Bollinger, small odds and ends for herself. She hoped that her patient might need her for more than two weeks—three, or even four weeks at twenty pounds a week would mount up nicely, and they were going to pay her fare too. She closed the little book, opened the newspaper the air hostess had handed her and read it with grave attention, fearful of allowing her thoughts to wander, and was surprised when far below she saw the flat coast of Holland, glimpsed through the layers of cloud.

Schiphol, she discovered, was large, efficient and pleasantly welcoming. With hundreds like her, she was passed along the human conveyor belt which eventually spilled her into the open air once more, only to be whisked up once more into the waiting bus which would take her to Amsterdam. It covered the ten miles to the capital with a speed which hardly gave her time to look around her and she got out at the bus terminus, still not quite believing that she was in Holland. It seemed such a very short time ago since she had said goodbye to Bollinger, as indeed it was.

Mindful of her instructions, she took a taxi to the address in the Apollolaan. It was, she quickly discovered, away from the centre of the city, for they quickly left the bustling, older part behind, to drive through modern streets lined with blocks of flats and shops. When they stopped half way down the

Apollolaan, she got out, paid the driver from her small stock of money and crossed the pavement to enter the important-looking doorway of the building he had pointed out to her. It was of a substantial size, and from the cars parked before it, inhabited by the well-to-do, and inside the thickly carpeted foyer and neatly uniformed porter bore out her first impression. He greeted her civilly, and when she mentioned her name, ushered her into the lift, took her case from her and escorted her to the fourth floor. Here he abandoned her, her case parked beside her, outside the door of number twenty-one—occupied, according to the neat little plate at the side of the door, by Mr and Mrs E. Goldberg. Abigail drew a heartening breath and rang the beautifully polished bell.

The door was opened by a maid who, in answer to Abigail's announcement of her name, invited her to enter, waved her to a chair, and disappeared. Abigail looked at the chair, a slender trifle which she felt sure would never bear the weight of her nicely rounded person, and stood looking around her. The hall was carpeted even more lushly than the foyer; the walls were hung with what she considered to be a truly hideous wallpaper, embossed and gilded, and as well as the little chair she had prudently ignored, there was a small settee, buttoned fatly into red velvet, and another chair with a straight back and a cane seat which looked decidedly uncomfortable. A wall table of gold and marble occupied the space between two doors, burdened with a French clock and matching vases. Abigail, who had a nice taste, shuddered delicately and wished that her mother could have been with her and share her feelings. For a moment her opulent surroundings faded to give place to the little flat in the Cromwell Road, but she resolutely closed her mind to her memories; self-pity helped no one, she told herself firmly, and turned to see who was coming through the door on the other side of the hall.

It had to be Mrs Goldberg, for she looked exactly like her name. She was middle-aged, with determinedly blonde hair, blue eyes which were still pretty and a baby doll face, nicely made up, which, while still attractive, had lost its youthful contours. She smiled now, holding out her hand, and when she spoke her voice was warm even though its accent was decidedly American.

'Well, so you're the nurse, my dear. I can't tell you how glad we are to have you.' She added dramatically, 'I am exhausted, absolutely exhausted! Night and day have I been caring for our dear Clara—she is so sensitive, you know, we couldn't leave her in hospital, although I'm sure they were kindness itself to her, but she's used to the little comforts of life.' The blue eyes looked at her a shade anxiously. 'We hope that the worst is over; Doctor Vincent will be in after lunch and this evening he'll bring a specialist—the very best to be got, I assure you—to see dear Clara, and he'll decide whether to operate or not.' She paused to take breath and Abigail asked quickly: 'You'd like me to take over immediately, I expect? If I could go to my room and change. . .'

Mrs Goldberg smiled widely, showing a hint of gold tooth. 'My dear, will you? I simply must rest. We lunch at half past twelve—so early, but when in Rome, I always say—If you could get into your uniform and make poor Clara a little more comfortable?'

'Of course.' Abigail smiled understandingly, hoping at the same time that Mrs Goldberg might suggest a cup of coffee or tea. Half past twelve was an hour away and she was, while not exactly tired, in need of a few minutes to collect herself, but Mrs Goldberg made no such offer, but followed her from the hall and into a short passage and so to her room. It was nice, with a view over the Apollolaan and comfortable anonymous furniture so often found in guest rooms, and it had the added attraction of a bathroom next door. As soon as she was alone Abigail unpacked her uniform, washed her face and hands, put her mousy hair up into its tidy bun, perched her frilly cap on top of it, buckled her belt around her trim waist and with a nicely made-up face, went back into the hall.

Mrs Goldberg must have been waiting for her; she appeared suddenly, like a cheerful outsize fairy, from one of the doors and said approvingly:

'My, how quick you've been, and what a quaint outfit—that cap, it's not a bit like our nurses wear back home.'

Abigail explained quickly that her hospital took pride in allowing its trained nurses to wear that particular headgear—it had been worn for a very long time and no one, least of all the nurses, wanted it changed.

'Mighty becoming,' commented Mrs Goldberg, 'it sure will tickle poor Clara pink.'

Abigail, following her companion through another door, wondered if her patient felt well enough to be tickled by anything. At first sight it seemed not. Mrs Clara Morgan lay uncomfortably hunched against far too many pillows. Some of these she had tossed to the floor, the remainder were crowding into her back, which probably accounted for her petulant expression. She acknowledged Mrs Goldberg's introduction languidly and said tiredly, 'I'm glad you've come, Nurse, I'm very poorly and I need a great deal of skilled care and attention.'

Abigail murmured suitably and enquired if the doctor had left any message for her.

'No,' said Mrs Goldberg, 'because he'll be here in a couple of hours. Clara will tell you all about herself, won't you, Girlie?'

Abigail judged it a good idea to get her oar in before her patient did, for she looked ill and tired and that was probably why she looked peevish. Her voice was persuasive. 'Would you like me to give you a bed-bath and a fresh nightie and make you more comfortable? You'll feel better for it.'

Her patient agreed, and while she submitted to Abigail's kindly hands, discoursed at length upon her condition, its seriousness, the possibility of an operation, the need for her to return to the States as soon as she could, and the kindness of her friends the Goldbergs. That there was a thick thread of self-pity winding through her narrative was natural enough; it hadn't taken Abigail long to gather that her patient was rich, spoilt and self-indulgent. She had, it transpired, been widowed twice, and, a still attractive woman in her early forties, was prepared to marry again should she find someone she liked sufficiently. Abigail listened without envy, because it wasn't in her nature to be envious, and a certain amount of pity, because it seemed to her that Mrs Morgan was lonely too, despite her silver-backed hairbrushes and silk nighties and enormous bottles of perfume. But talking cheered her up, and by the time Abigail had smoothed the last wrinkle from the sheets, she declared that she felt a new woman.

'I do believe we're going to get on just fine,' she declared. 'I must admit that the idea of an English nurse didn't appeal to me, but I'll admit to being mistaken, though your uniform is pretty antiquated, isn't it?'

Abigail admitted that perhaps it was. 'They're trying to change the uniforms in England, but you see, some of the hospitals are very old and they like to keep their own, however old-fashioned. Especially the caps—it's like a regimental badge, everyone knows which hospital you were trained at just by looking at your cap.'

'Well, I must say whoever thought of yours had a nice eye for something sexy.'

Abigail was folding towels neatly. No one had ever called her cap sexy before! She remained silent, nonplussed, and then said:

'I think a nice milky drink, don't you? I'll go along and see about it.'

Milk and water, in equal proportions with afters of Mist. Mag. Tri., were her patient's portion for lunch. Abigail measured carefully, arranged the two glasses on a little tray with a pretty cloth and bore them away to the sickroom, where she put the tray on the bed table, together with a selection of novels, the daily paper and a handful of glossy magazines, and then, quite famished, found her way to the dining room.

Mr Goldberg had come home to lunch. A small fat man with large glasses and a fringe of greying hair, possessed of a charming smile. Abigail liked him at once and wasn't surprised to hear that he was something important to do with a permanent trade mission—anyone with a smile like that deserved to have a top job! They sat her between them at a large rectangular table and plied her with food. It was cold and grey outside, but here in the warm, over-furnished room, there was no need to think about the weather. She drank her soup, accepted a glass of wine and embarked on beef olives while she listened to her host and hostess and made polite replies to their questions whenever they asked them, which was frequently. She would have liked to have lingered over coffee with them, but she was on a job, after all. She excused herself and went back to her patient to find her asleep.

It seemed a good opportunity to unpack her few clothes and scribble a quick note to Bolly; most likely she would have the chance to post it before bedtime; if not, surely the hall porter would do it for her. She wrote the address with a little lump in her throat, because Bolly would probably be sitting by himself in that dreadful little back room with no other view than the house behind.

Dr Vincent came shortly afterwards. He was a tall man in his thirties, with regular features and an excellent command of the English language. He was obviously relieved to see Abigail and after he had examined Mrs Morgan and talked to her for a little while, he retired to the sitting room with Abigail so that he might discuss their patient. They sat opposite each other, on the edge of over-stuffed and very large easy chairs, because to sit back in them would have meant a complete loss of dignity on both their parts and the doctor was nothing if not dignified. He took her carefully through the ins and outs of Mrs Morgan's illness. 'This evening a specialist will come, Nurse—I shall of course accompany him. He is a consultant surgeon at several of our big hospitals and very well known. I feel that his opinion will be invaluable. It would be a pity for our patient to undergo an operation unless it is absolutely necessary. If we can get her well enough, she would much prefer that she should return to the United States with all speed. You are prepared to stay here until she returns, I hope?'

Abigail said that yes, she was. 'What have they in mind?' she wanted to know. 'A gastrostomy? Surely if it's a bad ulcer they'll have to do an end-to-end anastimosis.'

Dr Vincent eyed her warily. 'I think, Nurse, that we must leave such things for Professor van Wijkelen to decide.'

With a name like that, Abigail thought flippantly, a man ought to be able to decide anything. He would have a beard and begin all his remarks with -er. She would probably dislike him. Dr Vincent was speaking again, so she listened carefully to his instructions and forgot about the professor.

He came that evening, an hour or so after her patient had had another glass of milk and water with its attendant powder, and Abigail herself had had a short break for her own tea. Mr and Mrs Goldberg were out, and it had been brought to her on a tray in the sitting room. It had been pleasant to sit down for a little while on her own, while she had it, and then have the time to tidy herself, powder her ordinary nose and put on more lipstick. The results weren't very encouraging, she considered, looking in the bedroom mirror. She had gone back to her patient's room and taken her temperature and pulse, and sat her up more comfortably against her pillows, and was on a chair in her stockinged feet, reaching for a vase of flowers which someone had placed out of reach, and which, for some reason, Mrs Morgan had taken exception to, when there was a knock on the door and Doctor Vincent came in. The man who came in with him eclipsed him completely. He was a giant of a man, with a large frame which radiated energy despite the extreme leisureliness of his movements. He was handsome too, with pale hair, thickly silvered at the temples, a high-bridged nose and a well-shaped, determined mouth. His expression was one of cold ill-humour, and when he glanced up at her, still poised ridiculously on the chair, Abigail saw that his eyes were blue. It struck her with something of a shock that they were regarding her with dislike.

She got down off the chair, the flowers clutched in one hand, hastily put them down on one of the little tables which cluttered the room, crammed her feet into her shoes and reached the bedside at the same time as the two men. Doctor Vincent introduced the professor, adding a corollary of his talents, and Mrs Morgan, suddenly interested, shook hands. 'And our nurse,' went on Doctor Vincent, 'arrived from England today and is already, I see, attending to the patient's comfort. Miss Trent, this is Professor van Wijkelen, of whom I spoke.'

She held out her hand and he shook it perfunctorily and said nothing, only looked at her again with the same cold dislike, before sitting on the side of Mrs Morgan's bed and saying, 'Now, Mrs Morgan, will you tell me all your troubles, and perhaps Doctor Vincent and I can help you to get well again.'

His voice was charming, deep and quiet and compelling, and Mrs Morgan was nothing loath. Her recital, with various deflections concerning her own personal courage in the face of grave illness, her fears for the loss of her good looks and the fact that she had been twice widowed, took a long time. The professor sat quietly, not interrupting her at all, his eyes upon her face while she talked. He seemed completely absorbed and so, to his credit, did Doctor Vincent, who, Abigail guessed, must have heard the tale at least once already. She herself stood quietly by the bed, a well-trained mouse of a girl, her eyes, too, on her patient, although she would very much have preferred to fix them upon the professor.

Mrs Morgan finished at length and the professor said, 'Quite, Mrs Morgan,' and went on to ask her several questions. Finally, when he was satisfied with the answers, he turned to Abigail and asked her to prepare Mrs Morgan for his examination. He asked courteously in a voice of ice; Abigail wondered what had happened to sour him and take all the warmth from his voice as she bent to the task of getting Mrs Morgan modestly uncovered while the two men retired to the window and muttered together in their own language.

'He's ducky,' whispered Mrs Morgan, and then sharply, 'Don't disarrange my hair, honey!'

She lay back, looking, to speak the truth, gorgeous. Abigail, obedient to her patient's wish, had been careful of the hair; she had also arranged her patient's wispy trifle of a bedjacket to its greatest advantage. Now she stood back and said briskly, 'Ready when you are, sir,' and watched while the professor conducted his examination. He prodded and poked gently with his large, square hands while he gazed in an abstracted fashion at the wall before him. At length, when he had finished and Abigail had rearranged Mrs Morgan, he said: 'I think that there will be no need for an operation, but to be quite sure there are several tests which it will be necessary to do, and I am afraid that they must be done in hospital.' He paused to allow Mrs Morgan to pull a pretty little face and exclaim:

'Oh, no, Professor—I was so utterly miserable when I was there just a week ago, that's why I engaged Nurse Trent here.'

'In that case, may I suggest that you take her with you to hospital? She can attend you during the day and I am sure that we shall be able to find an English-speaking nurse for night duty. I should suppose that three or four days should be sufficient, then you can return here to await the result of the tests. If they are satisfactory, a week or so should suffice to see you on your feet again and well enough to return home.'

'If you say so, Professor,' Mrs Morgan's voice was just sufficiently plaintive, 'though I'm sure I don't know how I shall get on in that hospital of yours. Still, as you say, if I take Nurse with me, I daresay I'll be able to bear a few days.'

She smiled at him after this somewhat frank speech, but he didn't smile in return, merely inclined his head gravely and offered his hand.

'You'll come and see me again, Professor?' Mrs Morgan was still smiling. 'I sure feel better already, you've a most reassuring way with you.'

If the professor was flattered by this remark he gave no sign. 'Thank you, Mrs Morgan. I think that there is no necessity to see you again until you enter hospital. I will arrange that as soon as possible and you will of course see me there.'

'I look forward to that—and be sure that I have a private room. I'm so sensitive, I can't bear the sights and sounds of hospital, Professor.'

He walked to the door and then turned to face her with Doctor Vincent beside him. 'I feel sure that Doctor Vincent will arrange everything to your liking, Mrs Morgan, and you will have your nurse to shield you from the—er—sights and sounds you so much dread.' His smile was fleeting and reluctant, a concession to good manners, and it didn't last long enough to include Abigail. He nodded curtly to her as he went away.

Surprisingly, he came the following day, late in the afternoon when Abigail had returned from her few hours off and was sitting with her patient, reading the *New York Herald Tribune* to her. She read very nicely in her quiet voice, sitting upright in a truly hideous reproduction Morris chair. She had enjoyed her afternoon off, and wished that her patient lived in one of the old houses beside the canals, because she would have dearly loved to see inside one of them. The flat in the Apollolaan was comfortable to the point of luxury, but all the same, she wouldn't have liked to live in it for ever, but the brick houses with their gabled roofs reflected in the still waters of the *grachten*—they were a different matter; it would be wonderful to live in their serene fastness.

The morning had been successful too; Mrs Morgan seemed to like her, for she had chatted animatedly while Abigail performed the daily nursing chores, talking at great length about Professor van Wijkelen. 'A darling man, Nurse,' she mused. 'I must find out more about him—such good looks and such elegance.' She smiled playfully at Abigail. 'Now mind, dear, and tell me anything you should hear about him. You're bound to find out something in the hospital, aren't you?'

Abigail had said that probably she would, provided she could find someone who could speak English. She had gone to lunch with Mr and Mrs Goldberg after that, and they had asked her a great many questions about her patient and seemed, she thought, a little relieved that dear Clara was to leave them for a day or two. Without someone in constant attendance, she must have put quite a strain on their good-natured hospitality.

Mrs Goldberg had asked her kindly if she had everything she needed and to be sure and say if she hadn't and then told her to hurry out while she had the chance. And Abigail had, wrapped in her well-cut but not new tweed coat against the damp cold winds of Amsterdam. She hadn't been able to do much in two hours, but at least she knew where she would go when next she was free; the complexity of *grachten*, tree-lined, their steely waters overlooked by the tall, quaintly shaped houses on either side of them, needed time to explore. There was no point in looking at the shops, not until she had some money to spend, but there was enough to see without spending more than the price of a tram fare.

The knock on the bedroom door had taken them both by surprise. Mr and Mrs Goldberg were both out, neither Abigail nor her patient had heard the maid go to the front door. She came in now and said in her basic English, 'A person for the *Zuster*.'

Abigail put down the paper, which she was a little tired of anyway, saying: 'Oh, that will be instructions from the hospital as to when we're to go, I expect. I'll go and see about it, shall I?' and followed the maid out of the room. The visitor was in the sitting room. Abigail opened the door and went in and came to a standstill when she saw the professor standing before the window, staring out.

'Oh, it's you!' she declared, quite forgetful of her manners because of her surprise, and was affronted when he answered irritably:

'And pray why should it not be I, Nurse? Doctor Vincent has been called out unexpectedly and finds himself unable to call, and I had to come this way.'

'Oh, you don't have to explain,' Abigail said kindly, and went on in a matter-of-fact voice, 'You'll want to see Mrs Morgan.'

'No, Nurse, I do not. I wish merely to inform you that there will be a bed in the private wing tomorrow afternoon. Be good enough to bring your patient to the hospital at three o'clock. An ambulance will fetch you—you will need to bring with you sufficient for three days, four perhaps. Be good enough to see that Mrs Morgan fasts from midday tomorrow so that no time is wasted.'

He spoke shortly and she wondered if and why he was annoyed, perhaps because he had had to undertake Doctor Vincent's errand, although surely he had a sufficiency of helpers to see to such mundane things as beds. . . He looked very arrogant and ill-humoured standing there, staring at her. She said briskly, 'Very well, sir—and now if you'll excuse me, I'll go back to my patient.'

He looked faintly surprised, although he didn't bother to reply. Only as she started for the door did he ask, 'What is your name?'

She barely paused. 'Trent, sir.'

He said impatiently, 'I am aware of that—we met yesterday, if you care to remember. What else besides Trent?'

It was on the tip of her tongue to tell him to mind his own business, but she wasn't given to unkindness and perhaps he had some very good reason for looking so irritable all the time. 'Abigail,' she offered, and watched for his smile; most people smiled when they discovered her name; it was old-fashioned and quaint. But he didn't smile.

'Why?'

'I was born on a Saturday,' she began, a little worried because he wasn't English and might not understand. 'And Abigail. . .' She paused. 'It's rather a silly reason and I don't suppose you would know. . .'

He looked more annoyed than ever, his thick almost colourless brows drawn together in a straight line above a nose which to her appeared disdainful.

'You should suppose nothing. I am sufficiently acquainted with your English verses—Saturday's child has to work for her living, eh? and Abigail was a term used some hundreds of years ago to denote a serving woman, was it not?'

'How clever of you,' said Abigail warmly, and was rewarded with another frown.

'And were your parents so sure that you would be forced to work for your living that they gave you this name?'

She said tight-lipped, because the conversation was becoming painful:

'It was a joke between them. You will excuse me now, sir?'

She left him standing there and went back to her patient, who, on being told who the visitor was, showed her displeasure at not receiving a visit, although she brightened again when Abigail pointed out that she would see a good deal of him in hospital once she was settled in there. They spent the rest of the day quite happily, with Abigail opening and shutting cupboards and drawers in order to display various garments to her patient, who, however ill she felt, intended to look as glamorous as possible during her stay in hospital. It was much later, when Abigail had packed a few things for herself that, cosily dressing-gowned, she sat down before her dressing-table to brush her hair for the night. She brushed it steadily for some time, deep in thought, and she wasn't thinking about herself, or her patient or Bollinger, but of Professor van Wijkelen. He was the handsomest man she had ever seen, also the most bad-tempered, but there had to be a reason for the look of dislike which he had given her when they had met—as though he had come prepared to dislike her, thought Abigail. She finished plaiting the rich thickness of her mousy hair and stared at her face in the mirror. Plain she might be, but in an inoffensive manner—her teeth didn't stick out, she didn't squint, her nose was completely unassuming; there was, in fact, nothing to cause offence. Yet he had stared at her as though she had mortally offended him. She put the brush away and padded over to the bed, thinking that she would very much like to get to know him better, not because he was so good-looking; he looked interesting as well, and for some reason she was unable to explain she found herself making excuses for his abrupt manner, even his dislike of her. She got into bed wondering sleepily what he was doing at that moment—the idea that he was a happily married man dispelled sleep for a few minutes until she decided that he didn't look married. She slept on that surprisingly happy thought.

CHAPTER TWO

THE hospital was hidden away behind the thickly clustered old houses and narrow lanes of the city. It was itself old, although once inside, Abigail saw that like so many of the older hospitals in England, it had a modernised interior despite the long bleak corridors and small dark passages and bare enclosed yards which so many of its windows looked out upon. Mrs Morgan's room was on the third floor, in the private wing, and although small, it was well furnished and the view from its window of the city around was a splendid one. Abigail got her patient safely into bed, tucked in the small lace-covered pillows Mrs Morgan had decided she couldn't manage without, changed her quilted dressing-gown for a highly becoming bed-jacket, rearranged her hair, found her the novel she was reading, unpacked her case and after leaving the bell within reach of her, went to find the Ward Sister.

Zuster van Rijn was elderly, round, cosy and grey-haired, with a lovely smile and a command of the English language which Abigail found quite remarkable. They sat together in the little office, drinking the coffee which one of the nurses had brought them, while Zuster van Rijn read her patient's notes and charts and finally observed:

'She does not seem too bad. Professor van Wijkelen never operates unless it is necessary—he is far too good for that, but she must have the tests which have been ordered—she can have the X-ray this afternoon and the blood test—tomorrow the test meal—just something milky this evening for her diet. You're to stay with her, the professor tells me.'

'Yes, Mrs Morgan is a little nervous.'

Zuster van Rijn smiled faintly. 'Yes,' her voice was dry. 'There's a room ready for you in the Nurses' Home—would you like to go there now? There is nothing to do for Mrs Morgan for half an hour and one of the nurses can answer the bell. I will tell Zuster de Wit to go over with you.'

Abigail went back to her patient, to explain and collect her bag, and then followed the nurse down one flight of stairs, over a covered bridge, spanning what looked like a narrow lane of warehouses, and so into the Nurses' Home. Zuster de Wit hurried her along a long passage and then a short one to stop half way down it.

'Here,' she said, and smiled as she flung open a door in a row of doors. The room was comfortable although a little dark, for its window overlooked another part of the hospital, but the curtains were gay and it was warm and cheerful. Abigail smiled in return and said, 'How nice. Thank you,' and Zuster de Wit smiled again, said '*Dag*' and hurried away. Obviously she had been told to waste no time. Abigail, listening to her rapidly disappearing feet, hoped that she would be able to find her own way back to the ward again as she began to unpack her things. She had bought only a modicum of clothes—mostly uniform and her thick winter coat and a skirt and sweater, boots and the knitted beret and scarf she had made for herself during the weeks she had nursed her mother. It took only a few minutes to put these away and another minute or so to powder her nose and tuck her hair more tidily under her cap. It was almost four o'clock, as she shut the door she wondered about tea—perhaps they didn't have it; there were several things she would have to find out before the day was over. She went back over the bridge and found her way to her patient's room, to find her asleep.

Working in an Amsterdam hospital was almost exactly the same as working in her own London hospital; she had discovered this fact by the end of the day. Once she had become used to addressing even the most junior nurses as '*Zuster*' and discovered that she was expected to say '*Als t'U blift*' to anyone she gave something to, and '*Dank U wel*' each time she was given something, be it instructions—mostly in sign language—or a thermometer or a holder for the potted plant someone had sent her patient, she felt a little less worried about the problem of language. She had had to go without her tea, of course—they had had it at three o'clock, but she went down to supper with the other nurses at half past six; a substantial meal of pea soup, pork with a variety of vegetables, followed by what Abigail took to be custard and as much coffee as she could drink.

She went back to the office to give her report and then returned to sit with Mrs Morgan who was feeling a little apprehensive about the test meal. At half past eight, just before the night nurse was due on duty, a house doctor came to see the new patient and a few minutes later Doctor Vincent. He listened patiently to her small complainings, soothed her nicely, recommended her to do as Abigail told her, and went away again, and presently when the night nurse came and Abigail had given her a report too, she went herself, over the bridge to the Nurses' Home and to her room.

She hadn't been in it for more than a minute when there was a knock on the door and the same nurses she had seen at supper took her off to their sitting room to watch TV which, although she was tired, Abigail found rather fun because Paul Temple was on and it was amusing to watch it for a second time and listen to the dubbed voices talking what to her was nonsense. For so the Dutch language seemed to her; she had been unable to make head or tail of it—a few words and phrases, it was true, she had been quick enough to pick up, but for the most part she had had to fall back on basic English and signs, all taken in very good part by the other nurses. It had been a great relief to find that the night nurse spoke English quite well; enough to understand the report and discuss Mrs Morgan's condition with Abigail, and what was more important, Mrs Morgan seemed disposed to like her.

After Paul Temple she was carried off once more, this time to one of the nurses' rooms to drink coffee before finally going to her own room. She slept soundly and got up the next morning feeling happier than she had done for some time; it was on her way down to breakfast that she realised that the uplift to her spirits was largely due to the fact that she would most probably see the professor during the course of the day.

Her hope was to be gratified; he passed her on the corridor as she made her way to her patient's room after breakfast. She saw him coming towards her down its length and watched with faint amusement as the scurrying nurses got out of his way. When he drew level with her she wished him a cheerful good morning and in reply received a cold look of dislike and faint surprise, as though he were not in the habit of being wished a good day. Her disappointment was so sharp that she took refuge in ill temper too and muttered out loud as she sped along, 'Oh, well, be like that!'

She found her patient in good spirits; she had slept well, the night nurse had understood her and she had understood the night nurse, and the Ryle's tube had been passed and the test meal almost finished. The night nurse, giving the report to Abigail in the privacy of the nurses' station further down the corridor, confided in her correct, sparse English that she herself had enjoyed a quiet night and had got a great deal of knitting done. She produced the garment in question—a pullover of vast proportions and of an overpowering canary yellow. They had their heads together over the intricacies of its pattern when the professor said from behind them:

'If I might have the attention of you two ladies—provided you can spare the time?' he added nastily.

The Dutch girl whipped round in much the same fashion as a thief caught in the act of robbing a safe, but Abigail, made of sterner stuff and unconscious of wrongdoing, merely folded the pullover tidily and said: 'Certainly, sir,' which simple remark seemed to annoy him very much, for he glared at her quite savagely.

'You are both on duty, I take it?' he asked.

'No, me,' said Abigail ungrammatically in her pleasant voice. 'We've just discussed the report and Night Nurse is going off duty.'

'When I need to be reminded of the nurses' routine in hospital, I shall say so, Nurse Trent.'

She gave him a kindly, thoughtful look, her previous temper quite forgotten. Probably he was one of those unfortunate people who were always ill-tempered in the early morning. She found that she was prepared, more anxious to make excuses for him.

'I didn't intend to annoy you, sir,' she pointed out to him reasonably, and was rewarded with a sour look and a compression of his well-shaped mouth.

'The test meal,' he snapped, 'when is it complete?'

She looked at her watch. 'The last specimen is due to be withdrawn in fifteen minutes' time, sir.'

'If the patient doesn't tire of waiting for your return and pull the Ryle's tube out for herself.'

'Oh, no,' said Abigail seriously, 'she'd never do that—you see, I explained how important it was for her to do exactly as you wish. She has a great opinion of you.'

Just for a moment she thought that he was going to laugh, but she must have been mistaken, for all he said was, 'I want Mrs Morgan in theatre at noon precisely for gastroscopy. The anaesthetist will be along to write her up. See that she is ready, Nurse Trent.'

He turned to the night nurse, who had been silent all this while, and spoke to her with cold courtesy in his own language. She smiled at him uncertainly, looked at Abigail and flew off down the corridor, leaving behind her the strong impression that she was delighted to be free of their company. Abigail picked up the report book and prepared to go too, but was stopped by the professor's voice, very silky.

'A moment, Nurse Trent. I am interested to know what it was you said in the corridor just now.'

She wished she could have looked wide-eyed and innocent, or been so pretty that he really wouldn't want an answer to his question. She would have to tell him, and probably, as he seemed to dislike her so much already, he would say that he wanted another nurse to work for him and she would have to go back to England. Did one get paid in such circumstances? she wondered, and was startled when he asked, 'What are you thinking about? I assure you it is of no use you inventing some excuse.'

'I'm not inventing anything. What I said was,' she took a deep breath, ' "Oh, well, be like that." '

'That is what I thought you said. May I ask if you are in the habit of addressing the consultants in your own hospital in such a fashion?'

She considered carefully before she answered him. 'No, I can't remember ever doing so before, but then, you see, they always said good morning.'

She studied his face as she spoke; perhaps she had gone a little too far, but she didn't like being treated in such a high-handed fashion. He looked very angry indeed—she waited for the outburst she felt sure would come and was surprised when all he said, through a tight mouth, was:

'Young woman, you disturb me excessively,' and stalked away, leaving Abigail with her eyes opened very wide, and her mouth open too.

She didn't see him again until she entered the theatre and she thought it unlikely that he would notice her, disguised as she was in theatre gown of voluminous size and nothing visible of her face, only her nice eyes above the mask.

The morning's work had gone exactly to plan. It was precisely noon. Theatre Sister and two nurses were there and of course the anaesthetist—there was to be no general anaesthetic, but Mrs Morgan had had a pre-med and would need a local anaesthetic. He was a nice sort of man, Abigail thought; his English was fluent if a little difficult to understand and he had smiled kindly at her. Mrs Morgan, her hand held in Abigail's comforting grasp, was dozing in her drug-induced sleep; she had joked a little about it before they went to theatre because she would miss seeing Professor van Wijkelen, and Abigail had consoled her with the prospect of further visits from him, for there were still one or two more tests to carry out, though once the professor had done the gastroscopy and had made up his mind whether he needed to operate or not, there wasn't much more to be done.

Abigail arranged the blanket over her patient, turning it down below her shoulders so that it wouldn't get in the surgeon's way once he started. Mrs Morgan made a little whimpering sound and opened her eyes, and Abigail said instantly in a soothing voice, 'It's all right, Mrs Morgan, the professor is just coming.'

He was in fact there, standing behind her, talking quietly to Sister. He finished what he was saying and went closer to his patient, ignoring Abigail completely—something she had expected.

He spoke quietly to his patient. 'You feel sleepy, don't you, Mrs Morgan? We are going to spray your throat now and it will feel numb, but you will feel nothing else—a little uncomfortable perhaps, but that is all. It will take only a short time. Your head will be lifted over a pillow now and I am going to ask you to open your mouth when I say so.'

The small examination went well and Mrs Morgan, whom Abigail had expected to be rather difficult, didn't seem to mind at all when the professor inserted the gastroscope and peered down it, his great height doubled, his brows drawn together in concentration. At length he said, 'That will do. Kindly take her back to the ward, Nurse.'

Which Abigail did, to spend a rather trying few hours because Mrs Morgan was under the impression that the local anaesthetic would wear off in ten minutes or so, and when it didn't she was first annoyed and then frightened. Abigail, explaining over and over again that the numbness would disappear quickly and that no, Mrs Morgan couldn't have a drink just yet, longed for an hour or so off duty. It was already three o'clock; she had been relieved at dinner time, but no one had said a word about her off-duty. Probably the Ward Sister thought that she wouldn't mind as long as someone relieved her for a cup of tea.

The door opened and she looked up hopefully, unaware that her face plainly showed her disappointment at the sight of the professor standing there, for he certainly hadn't come to release her from her duties. She got to her feet, wondering why he stared so, and fetched the chart for him to study. He hadn't spoken at all and since he seemed to like it that way, she hadn't either. She had half expected to hear more about their morning's meeting, but now she rather thought that he wasn't going to do anything more about it. She took the chart back again and stood quietly while he spoke briefly to Mrs Morgan. Presently he turned away from the bed. 'Nurse, I shall want another blood count done and the barium meal will be done tomorrow at two o'clock. Attend to the usual preparations, please. I can find nothing very wrong, but I shall need confirmation of that before I make my final decision.'

She said, 'Yes, Professor,' and admired him discreetly. Forty or more, she concluded, and unhappy—though I don't suppose he knows it.

His voice, cutting a swathe through her half-formed thoughts, asked:

'You are comfortable here, Nurse? Everyone is kind to you? You have your free time?'

'Yes, thank you,' she answered so quickly that he said at once, 'Today?'

'Well, not yet, but I'm perfectly all right. Mrs Morgan is my patient, isn't she, and the ward is very busy. I'm quite happy.'

He said surprisingly, 'Are you? I should have supposed otherwise, although I daresay you do your best to disguise the fact.'

She was appalled, and when had he looked at her long enough to even notice? 'I—I. . .' she began, and was instantly stopped by his bland, 'No need to excuse yourself, Nurse Trent—we all have our worries and sorrows, do we not—and never as important as we think they are.'

Abigail went brightly pink. She blushed seldom, but when she did, she coloured richly from her neck to the roots of her hair. He watched her now with a detached interest, nodded briefly, and went away.

She was relieved shortly after that and after a cup of tea in the dining room she tore into her clothes and went out into the city. The night nurse had explained how she could get to the shops in a few minutes; now she followed the little lanes between the old houses, pausing frequently to make sure that she could find her way back again, and came all at once into a brightly lighted street, crowded with people and lined with shops. She spent half an hour peering into their windows, working out the prices and deciding what she would buy when she had some money. That wouldn't be just yet; as soon as she had her first pay she would have to send it to poor old Bollinger. She wasn't happy about his room—it had looked cold and bare and although the landlady seemed kind enough she hadn't looked too clean, and supposing he were to become ill, who would look after him? She stood in the middle of Kalverstraat, suddenly not sure if she should have left him.

Mrs Morgan stayed in hospital for another three days, becoming progressively more cheerful because it seemed unlikely that she would need an operation after all. Besides, the professor visited her each day and she made no secret of her liking for him. He spent ten minutes or so listening gravely while she explained some new symptom she feared she might have, and then courteously contradicted her, impervious to her undoubted charm and quite deaf to her suggestions that he might, in the not too distant future, pay her a visit at her Long Island home. He seldom spoke to Abigail and when he looked at her it was with a coldness which she admitted to herself upset her a great deal more than it should have done.

They went home on the sixth day, this time in Mr Goldberg's Buick motor car; the professor had paid a visit the evening before and had stayed a little longer than usual, reassuring Mrs Morgan as to her future health, and had bidden her goodbye with his usual cold politeness, nodding briefly to Abigail as he went away. On her way off duty, half an hour later, she had seen him in the main ward, doing a round with his registrars and housemen, Sister and attendant satellites of students, nurses, physiotherapist and social worker. He looked very important but completely unconscious of the fact, an aspect of his character which she found strangely endearing.

The days following passed pleasantly enough. Mrs Morgan was out of bed now, although she preferred to keep to her room, walking a little and talking incessantly about her flight to the States, which she anticipated with all the impatience of someone who always had what they wanted when they wanted it. Abigail was impatient too—although she damped it down—for pay-day. She had had several letters from Bolly and from the sparse information they contained as to how he fared, she guessed that life was being difficult for him. She had already decided that she would send almost all her money to him, for she was almost certain that Mrs Morgan would ask her to stay another week, perhaps longer, and she didn't want him to wait any longer for it. The moment she got back to London she would go to the agency again and ask for another job. She reviewed her plans almost daily, and behind all this careful scheming was the thought that she would never see the professor again once she had left Holland. A ridiculous thing to worry about, she told herself scornfully, for she very much doubted if he would notice if she were there or not. She dismissed him firmly from her thoughts and went out each day, exploring Amsterdam.

It was on the morning that she was due to be paid that Mrs Morgan asked her if she would stay another week. 'I know I don't really need you, honey,' she said, 'but you are such a comfort to have around, and Dolly and Eddy don't need to worry about me at all. I've booked a flight for next week—a week today—if you would stay and see me safely away?'

She opened the crocodile handbag with the gold fittings which looked almost too heavy for her to carry and took out an envelope. 'Here's your salary, honey—I got Eddy to see to it for me. You'd rather have the cash, I'm sure. I bet you've got your eye on something pretty to buy with it.'

Abigail agreed pleasantly. She had grown quite fond of her patient while she had been looking after her and she saw no point in disturbing her complacent belief that the rest of the world lived in the same comfortable circumstances as herself. She put the envelope in her pocket and picked up the guide book of Holland which she had been reading to Mrs Morgan. Later, when she was free that afternoon, she would go to the post office and send the money to Bollinger, and perhaps now that she knew when she would be finished with the case, she should write to the agency and ask if they had anything else she could go straight to. The problem remained at the back of her mind while she read aloud about the delights of Avifauna and the best way of getting there, she was interrupted half way through by her companion telling her with enthusiasm that she intended to return. 'Because,' said Mrs Morgan, 'this is a sweet little country and I must say some of the people I've met are well worth cultivating.' She giggled happily and Abigail, who knew that she was talking about Professor van Wijkelen, smiled politely and wondered what success she would have in that quarter.

With her patient tucked up for her afternoon nap, Abigail was free to go to her room and open the envelope. There was two weeks' salary inside and her fare—but only her single fare. She had expected to be given the return fare and had neglected to ask anyone about it. Perhaps she was only entitled to half her travelling expenses; on the other hand, Mrs Morgan might give it to her with her next week's pay. She put the fare away in her bag, popped the rest into the envelope she had ready and got into her outdoor clothes.

It was cold outside and bleak with the bleakness of January. The clouds had a yellow tinge to them and the wind was piercingly cold. She hurried to the post office some streets away, where there were clerks who spoke English and would understand her when she asked for a registered envelope.

The post office was warm inside. The walk had given her eyes a sparkle and put some colour into her cheeks. She had perched her knitted beret on top of her head and wound its matching scarf carelessly round her throat. She took her gloves off and blew on her cold fingers and went up to the counter.

It took a little while to understand the clerk and then she was so disappointed that she could hardly believe him. She had taken it for granted that she could send either the cash or a money order to Bolly and it seemed she had been hopelessly at fault—she could do no such thing. Go to a bank, suggested the clerk helpfully, where there would be forms to be filled in and a certain amount of delay. But she wanted Bolly to have the money now—within the next day or two. If she waited until she went back herself that was a whole week away—besides, she had promised Bolly. She sighed and the clerk sighed in sympathy and she said, 'Well, thank you very much for explaining. I should have found out earlier, shouldn't I?'

'Can I help?' The professor—she would have known his icy voice anywhere. She whirled round to face him.

'Oh, how funny to meet you here, sir. I don't think so, thank you. It's just something that was my own silly fault anyway.'

'Why should it be funny, Nurse Trent? I also write letters, you know.'

'Yes, I'm sure you do, only—only I should have thought that you would have had someone to post them.'

'Indeed? I am not particularly interested in your suppositions, but I find this one extraordinary. How can I help you?'

Persistent man, he wasn't going to take no for an answer. She explained in a matter-of-fact voice and apologised again for being stupid.

'Why should you be stupid?' he asked irritably. 'You were not to know before you asked. How much money did you want to send?'

'Forty pounds. No—I've got to take some off. . .' she began to reckon twelve and a half per cent of forty pounds in her head and the amount came different each time she did it. Finally she asked, because he showed signs of impatience, 'How much is twelve and a half per cent of forty pounds?'

'Five pounds. Why?'

'Well, that's what I have to pay the agency for as long as I work for them.'

'Iniquitous! It so happens that I am going over to London this evening. I will take the money, since you seem so anxious to send it.'

She stared at him, astonished. 'But you don't even. . .you're very kind, but I couldn't trouble you.

I shall be going back myself in a week's time.'

The professor tweaked her out of the queue forming behind her.

'Ah, yes—I should be obliged if you would remain in Amsterdam for a further few weeks. I have a patient upon whom I shall be operating in ten days' time, and he will need a special nurse in hospital and probably to accompany him home when he is sufficiently recovered. Your usual fee will be paid you.'

Abigail's voice sounded a little too loud in her own ears. 'But you don't. . .' She stopped—what had his personal opinion of her got to do with it anyway? He wanted a nurse and she was available. She answered him with her usual calm good sense, 'Yes, Professor, I should be quite willing to stay on for as long as you require me.'

He nodded carelessly, as though he had known all along that she was going to say yes.

'Very well, we will consider the matter settled,' and when she looked at him it was to find him smiling. Perhaps it was because she had never seen him smile that her heart lurched against her ribs and her breath caught in her throat. It transformed his handsome face into one of such charm that if he had at that moment suggested that she should remain in Holland for the rest of her life, she would probably have agreed without further thought. But her idea wasn't put to the test; the smile vanished, leaving him looking more impatient than ever.

'Give me the address of the person who is to receive the money,' he suggested, 'and I will see that it reaches him—or her.'

'Him,' said Abigail, and would have liked to tell him about Bolly, but quite obviously her companion was anxious to be gone. She handed him the envelope with the letter inside and the forty pounds hastily pushed in with it. She had forgotten about the agency fee, but he hadn't.

'Twelve and a half per cent?' he wanted to know.

He really was in a hurry. 'I'll—I'll take it out of my pay next week. You're sure. . .?'

He interrupted without apology, 'Stop fussing, Miss Trent.' He stuffed the envelope into a pocket with a nonchalance, Abigail thought vexedly, of a man who found forty pounds chicken feed, wished her a curt goodbye and walked away. She began to walk back to the flat, her head bent against the sneering wind, telling herself that the reason she felt so happy was because Bolly would have the money by the following evening, or at the very least, the morning after.

The professor came to see Mrs Morgan three days later. He paid his visit while Abigail was out for her afternoon walk and left no message for her at all. It wasn't until the evening previous to Mrs Morgan's departure that he came again. Abigail was packing her patient's clothes, surrounded by tissue paper, orderly piles of undies, innumerable hats and an assortment of suitcases. Evidently Mrs Morgan never worried about excess baggage. That lady was reclining on the couch, directing operations; she looked very well and remarkably attractive, which was more than Abigail felt, for her head ached and her usually neat hair was a little untidy, nor had she had the time to do anything to her face for some time, and over and above these annoyances she was worried about Bolly; she had had a cheerful letter from him, thanking her for the money, but she sensed that he was hiding something from her. She was thinking about it now and frowning—she was still frowning when there was a knock on the door and Doctor Vincent and the professor walked in. They both wished her a good evening and she flushed a little under the professor's brief, unfriendly glance, very conscious that she wasn't looking her modest best. They stayed perhaps ten minutes, made their farewells and started for the door. But this time Professor van Wijkelen made a detour and came to a halt by her and her pile of luggage.

'I understand that you will be taking Mrs Morgan to Schiphol tomorrow morning. You will be fetched from there and taken straight to the hospital. Perhaps you can arrange to have your luggage with you.' His eyes strayed over the ordered chaos around them. 'I trust you have a good deal less than this.'

'One case,' Abigail told him briefly, and he nodded. 'I will leave a message for you at the hospital tomorrow,' he stated. 'Good evening, Nurse.'

He had gone before she could thank him for posting her letter.

Mrs Morgan was actually bidding Abigail goodbye at Schiphol when she interrupted herself to exclaim, 'There, I knew there was something, honey! I've clean forgot to give you your money.' She made to open her unwieldy bag, but it was too late; a smiling official indicated the passenger conveyor belt which would take her one stage nearer the plane. 'I'll post it to you,' she called, waved and smiled and nodded, and was borne swiftly away; so easy for her to say it, thought Abigail a little forlornly, but where would she send the money to? Mrs Morgan knew that she was going to another job, but she hadn't asked for any details and Abigail hadn't volunteered any. Perhaps she would send the money to the agency. If so, would the severe woman who had interviewed her send it on, or would she keep it and expect Abigail to call for it? And what about the rest of her fare—she hadn't had it yet.

She stood pondering, pushed to and fro by the hurrying people around her. She had been silly; she should have asked for her salary and her fare sooner. But she hadn't liked to, even though the money was rightly hers. And now she had landed herself with only a few pounds. Supposing the professor had changed his mind about employing her for his next patient? She had been rash enough to buy herself a pair of shoes the day before, and now she was left with less than her fare to England. She moved at last, back to the reception area to fetch her case. She had been foolish twice over; the professor had said that she would be fetched from the airport, but how was she to know who was looking for her? Supposing they couldn't find her and she was left—supposing they forgot all about her, supposing. . . Her gloomy thoughts were cut short by the professor's voice. She hadn't seen him, but here he was beside her, taking her case from her as relief as well as delight flooded through her, although her quiet 'Good morning, Professor,' was uttered in her usual voice. She received an ill-tempered grunt in reply and a brief, 'Come along, Nurse,' as he made for the door.

She trotted beside him because otherwise she could never have kept up with him, and to lose him now would be unthinkable. There were a great many cars outside and she wondered which of them was his.

He stopped in front of a black Rolls-Royce Silver Shadow, sleekly and unobtrusively perfect among the other cars, opened its doors, told her to get in with the cold courtesy she had come to believe was the only alternative to his ill-humour, and went to put her case in the boot. He didn't speak when he got in beside her, and was still silent as he edged the car away from the crowded bustle of the airport and on to the main road. They were tearing along the motorway to the capital when she ventured helpfully:

'I expect you came yourself so that you could save time telling me about the patient.'

She looked at him as she spoke and he turned to meet her gaze briefly. She wished that he would smile again, but he didn't, although when he did speak she had the impression that somewhere, deep down inside him, he was laughing. Imagination, she told herself roundly; why should he laugh?

'A doctor,' he stated flatly. 'Professor de Wit, seventy years old. He's to have a gastroenterostomy—CA, of course, but everything's in his favour, he's got a sound heart and chest and a great desire to live. He is to have a room in the private wing and you will be working under Zuster van Rijn with whom you will arrange your off-duty, please.'

Having thus given her the bare bones of the case he fell silent once more, and Abigail, not knowing if he was occupied with the intricacies of the day's operating list, forbore from disturbing him. It was only when he drew up in front of the hospital entrance and called to the porter to come and collect her case that she said:

'Thank you for posting my letter. I heard from—that is, it arrived safely. I'm very grateful to you.'

He looked at her with quick annoyance. 'There's no need to say any more about it,' he stated with such finality that she felt snubbed, so that she too was annoyed. 'I shan't,' she told him crisply. 'Obviously gratitude and thanks are wasted upon you, sir.'

She walked briskly into the hospital, not waiting to see what the porter was going to do about her case. She was half way across the width of the entrance hall when she was amazed to hear the professor laughing. It was a deep bellow and sounded perfectly genuine.

It was surprising to her how quickly she slipped back into the routine of hospital. She had been given the same room again and this time it was so much easier because she knew some of the nurses and they greeted her as an old friend. Zuster van Rijn seemed glad to see her again too; they were short-staffed on the surgical side, she told Abigail, and specialling could be awkward unless there were enough nurses.

'Will you work as you did before,' she asked, 'and take an afternoon off? I know it's not quite fair that you shouldn't work shift hours as the other girls do, but that way I can spare a nurse to take over while you're off duty. There will be the same night nurse as you have already worked with, and you shall have your days off, of course, but how or when I do not know at the moment. You are content?'

'Quite content,' Abigail told her. Days off didn't matter, not for the first week at any rate, for she hadn't any money to spend. The problem of how to get the money over to Bolly was looming heavily again too; she had done nothing about it because she had expected to return to England, now she would have to start all over again. She dismissed her problems and followed Sister, prepared to meet her patient.

She liked him on sight. He was lying in bed and

although his face was pinched and white with his illness, he was still a remarkably good-looking old man. Excepting for a thick fringe of white hair, he was bald, but the fringe encircled his face as well in rich profusion and his blue eyes were youthful and sharp. She shook his hand—gently—because she could see that he was an ill man, and despite his alert expression and merry eyes, probably in pain as well.

Zuster van Rijn left them together after a few minutes and Professor de Wit said, 'Pull up a chair, my dear, and let us get to know each other. I believe Dominic wishes me to spend a week in bed before he operates, physiotherapy and blood transfusions and all the other fringe benefits of his calling which he so generously offers.'

Abigail laughed with him. So the professor's name was Dominic—she stored the little piece of information away, though what good it would do her she had yet to discover. She listened to the old man's placid talk in his slow, almost perfect English and by means of gentle questions of her own found out that he slept badly, ate almost nothing, had lost his wife twenty years previously, had a doting housekeeper to look after him, and a dog and a cat to keep him company, as well as a half-tamed hedgehog, a family of rabbits and a pet raven. They were discussing a mutual dislike of caged birds when Professor van Wijkelen came in.

The two men, she saw at once, were old friends. It was also apparent that the older man trusted the younger completely. He lay listening quietly while the professor told him exactly what he was going to do and why.

'It sounds most promising, Dominic. I gather I am to be a new man by the time you have finished with me.'

'Shall we say soundly repaired, and fit for another ten or fifteen years—and that's a conservative estimate.'

'And what does Nurse say?' It was her patient who spoke.

Her smile lighted her ordinary face with its gentleness and sincerity.

'I never think of failure—Professor van Wijkelen will operate and it will be a complete success, just as he says.' She looked across at him as she spoke and found him staring at her, and there was no mistaking the faint sneer on his face, but because she liked him, she saw the hurt there too. Someone at some time had turned him into a cold, embittered man; she wondered who it was and hated them. Once, just once, he had smiled at her and she wanted him to smile like that again, but that, at that moment, seemed unlikely.

She settled down to a steady pattern of work, the same work as she would have been doing in a London hospital, even though the language was different, but all the doctors and a good many of the nurses spoke English and she herself, with the aid of her dictionary and a good deal of good-natured help from everyone else, managed to make herself understood. The days passed quickly. Under her patient's kindly direction she went each afternoon to some fresh part of the city, sometimes to a museum, sometimes to gaze at the outside of some old house whose fascinating history he had described to her delighted ears while she was fulfilling the various duties which made up her day. He was looking a little better, mainly due to the blood transfusions, to which he submitted with an ill grace because they interfered with his movements in bed. He was a great reader and an even greater writer and a formidable conversationalist. Abigail became fond of him, as indeed did anyone who came in daily contact with him. The day before his operation he paid her, handing her an envelope with a word of thanks and a little joke about him being strong enough to do it the following week, which touched her soft heart because although she had complete faith in Professor van Wijkelen, things quite outside his control could go wrong. She tucked the envelope away under her apron bib and as she did so wondered for the hundredth time why Bolly's last letter had been so strange; asking her not to send him any more money for at least another week. A good thing in a way, because she had not yet discovered the best way of sending it to him, all the same, she felt a vague disquiet.

Professor van Wijkelen came each day, treating her with his usual polite chill, at direct variance to the obvious regard he had for his patient. She stood quietly by while they talked together and longed for the warmth of his voice to be directed just once at herself. A wish which was most unlikely to be fulfilled, she told herself wryly, handing him charts and forms and reports and at the end giving him her own report very concisely in her clear precise voice. He liked to take her report outside the patient's room and did her the courtesy of giving her his full attention. And now, on this day before he was to operate, he listened even more carefully than usual. When she had finished he said, as he always said: 'Thank you, Miss Trent,' and proceeded to give her detailed instructions as to what he wished her to do on the following day.

The operation was a success, although only the next few days would show if the success was to be a lasting one. Abigail had taken her patient to the theatre and remained there to assist the anaesthetist. For a good deal of the time she was free to watch the professor at work. He was a good surgeon completely engrossed in his work and talking very little. When at length he was finished, he thanked the theatre sister and stalked away without a word. He was in his old friend's room within minutes of his return to it, though. Abigail was still getting the old man correctly positioned and adjusting the various tubes and drip when he came silently through the open door.

'I don't want him left, Nurse. I have spoken to Sister—if you wish to go off duty, she will send someone to take over. Is that clear?'

'Perfectly, thank you,' said Abigail, and because she was checking the closed drainage, didn't say any more. She had no intention of going off duty; she had promised Professor de Wit that she would stay with him and she could see no reason why she shouldn't do just that. She was, when all was said and done, his special nurse. Professor van Wijkelen said abruptly:

'He'll do—with careful nursing,' and turned on his heel and left her.

She didn't leave her patient again, only for the briefest of meal breaks and the professor came in twice more as well as his registrar, a portly little man whom Abigail rather liked. He spoke a fluent, ungrammatical English and she got on famously with him and she was grateful to him too, because he came often to check on the patient's condition and cheer her with odd titbits of gossip so that the day passed quickly. It was half an hour before she was due off that Zuster van Rijn came rustling down the corridor to tell her that the night nurse had been struck down with a sore throat and a temperature and wouldn't be able to come on duty, and there was no one to take her place. 'I can put a nurse on until midnight, though, and then she need not come on until the noonday shift. Could you possibly. . .?'

'Yes, of course,' said Abigail. 'I'll go off at eight, have supper and a sleep and come back here at twelve.'

Zuster van Rijn looked relieved. 'That is good—tomorrow morning I will get someone to take over while you go to bed for a few hours.'

So it was that when Professor van Wijkelen came at one o'clock in the morning, it was Abigail who rose quietly from her chair near the bed. His glance flickered over her as he went to look at his patient; it was only when he was satisfied as to his condition that he asked curtly:

'Why are you on duty? Where is the night nurse?'

'It's quite all right, sir,' said Abigail soothingly. 'Nurse Tromp is off sick and there wasn't time to get a full-time night nurse. I've been off duty, I came back at midnight.'

'Until when?'

'Until I can be relieved. Zuster van Rijn will arrange something.'

'Have you had your days off?'

'I'd rather not have them until the professor is better.' She spoke uncertainly because he was looking annoyed again. 'I imagine that my days off can be fitted in at any time, as I'm not a member of the hospital staff.'

'You have no need to state the obvious, Nurse. You must do as you please and I daresay Zuster van Rijn will be glad if you remain on duty for a few days until Professor de Wit is on the mend.'

He spoke carelessly as though he didn't mind if she had her days off or not, and indeed, she thought wearily, why should he?

He went away then and she spent a busy night, because there was a lot of nursing to do and the professor had regained consciousness and wished to be far too active. But presently, after an injection, he dropped off into a refreshing sleep and Abigail was free to bring her charts up to date, snatch a cup of coffee and then sit quietly between the regular intervals of checking one thing and another. It was, she mused, a splendid opportunity to think quietly about the future, but perhaps she was too tired, for when she tried to do so, she seemed unable to clear her mind. She gave up presently, and spent the rest of the night idly thumbing through her dictionary, hunting for words which, even when she found them, she was unable to pronounce.

The professor came again at seven o'clock. Abigail, with the help of another nurse, had made her patient's bed and sat him up against his pillows; she had washed him too and combed his fringe of hair and his whiskers and dressed him in his own pyjamas. He looked very old and very ill, but she had no doubt at all that he was going to pull through, for he had a good deal of spirit. She was drawing up an injection to give him when Professor van Wijkelen arrived; he looked as though he had slept the clock round, and now, freshly shaved and immaculately dressed, he sauntered in for all the world as though he were in the habit of paying his visits at such an early hour.

His good morning to her was brief; so brief that it seemed pointless, but she answered him nicely, smiling from a tired face that had no colour at all, unhappily aware that there was nothing about her appearance to make him look at her a second time.

He didn't say much to his patient but motioned her to give the injection, walked over to the window and sat down at the table there and began to study the papers she had laid ready for him. He had given her fresh instructions and was on the point of leaving when he remarked:

'You look as though you could do with a good sleep, Nurse.'

'Of course she needs a good sleep,' Professor de Wit's voice was testy even though it was weak. 'Just because you choose to work yourself to death doesn't mean that everyone else should do the same.'

'I have no intention of working anyone to death. Nurse is doing a job like anyone else and she has a tongue in her head. If she cannot carry out her duties, she has only to say so.'

He didn't look at her but flung 'I shall look in later,' over his shoulder as he went.

'Such a pity that...' began her patient, and fell asleep instantly just as Abigail was hopeful of hearing why something was a great pity—something to do with Professor van Wijkelen, she felt sure.

The next few days were busy ones. Her patient continued to improve, but there was a great deal of nursing care needed and Abigail was a conscientious nurse. She took her daily walk because she knew that she needed the exercise in the fresh air, despite its rawness and the bitter wind which never ceased to blow, but her days off she saved up; she would take them when the case was finished. There had, as yet, been no talk of sending Professor de Wit home although it had been made clear to her that she was to accompany him. They would be in hospital another week at least—two probably; if it hadn't been for the niggling worry about Bollinger, she would have been happier than she had been for a long time. She had made some friends in the hospital by now and she was battling on with her Dutch, helped a great deal by her patient, who now that he was feeling better spent a fair proportion of his waking hours correcting her accent and grammar.

It was the day after the drip came down for the last time and the old man had walked a few steps on her arm that Professor van Wijkelen had come to see him and on his way out again had said in his usual austere way:

'Nurse, if you are free tomorrow afternoon, I wish you to come with me—there is someone who wants to meet you.'

'Who?' asked Abigail, who liked to know where she was.

'Shall we say you must wait and see?' he enquired silkily, and then suddenly, as though he sensed that she was about to refuse, he smiled with such charm that she would have agreed to anything he wished. 'Please,' said the professor.

She nodded, knowing that when he looked at her like that she wanted nothing more than to please him. She was thoughtful after he had gone and Professor de Wit said nothing, although she had expected him to. When she saw that he didn't intend to discuss it with her, she launched into an argument on the subjunctive in the Dutch language, concentrating fiercely upon her companion's learned comments, because Professor van Wijkelen was taking up much too much of her attention these days.

CHAPTER THREE

THE professor was waiting for her when she reached the hospital forecourt the following afternoon. He greeted her with unsmiling courtesy as he opened the car door for her to get in, and because he so obviously didn't want to talk, she remained silent as he took the car through the gates and into the narrow streets beyond.

'You don't want to know where I am taking you?' he enquired blandly.

'Yes, of course I do, but I daresay you wouldn't choose to tell me, so I shan't ask.' Abigail spoke matter-of-factly and without rancour.

'We are going to my house.'

That startled her. 'What ever for?'

'There is somebody you should meet—it seemed the best place.'

'Oh, I see.' She didn't see at all and she was longing to ask him who it was and didn't because he would be expecting it.

'Very wise of you,' he commented silkily, answering her unspoken thought. 'I've no intention of telling you. How do you find Professor de Wit?'

She obligingly followed his lead. 'Determined to get well as soon as possible.'

'Yes—I have every hope that he will. The operation wasn't quite straightforward.' He launched into details and then said to surprise her:

'He likes you, Nurse Trent. I hope that you will be prepared to go home with him for a few days?'

'Certainly,' said Abigail. There was nothing she would like better, for a variety of reasons, which for the moment at least, she didn't intend to look into too deeply. She looked about her. They were travelling along the Herengracht, beautiful and picturesque with its old houses on either side of the tree-lined canal. Some way down its length the professor turned the car into a short arm of the canal—a little cul-de-sac, spanned by a narrow footbridge half way down its length. Houses lined the cobbled streets on either side of the water and across its far end, and trees, even
in their winter bareness, crowded thickly along its banks.

The Rolls slid sedately along its length and came to a halt outside one of the houses at the end, facing the canal. It was a very old house, with double steps leading to a great door and another, smaller door tucked away under those same steps. The windows were high and narrow and climbed up the front of the house. The higher they climbed the smaller they became, until they terminated in one very large one, heavily shuttered under the steep gable of the house. There was a tremendous hook above it, because that was the only way to get anything in or out of the houses' top floors.

It was peaceful in the small backwater, away from the traffic, with only the wind sighing around the steeple roofs. Abigail got out and looked around her while the professor opened his house door, and then at his bidding went inside.

It was all she had expected and hoped for, with its black and white tiled floor, its plasterwork ceiling and plain white walls, upon which were hung a host of paintings, and its carved staircase rising from one side.

The furnishings were in keeping—a heavy oak table along one wall, flanked by two carved oaken chairs which Abigail thought looked remarkably uncomfortable, while the other wall held an oak chest upon which reposed a great blue and white bowl, filled with spring flowers.

Abigail rotated slowly, trying to see everything at once. 'How absolutely beautiful—it's quite perfect,' she said, and was instantly sorry she had spoken, because when she looked at her companion he was looking down his long nose at her as though she had been guilty of some offending vulgarity. She went a faint, angry pink, which turned even brighter when he remarked austerely:

'I feel sure, from the ferocious expression upon your face, that you are on the point of bidding me not to be like that, or some such similar phrase, Miss Trent. May I beg you not to do so—I am easily irritated.'

'So I've noticed,' Abigail told him tartly. 'The smallest thing. . . And now, Professor, if I might meet this person.' Her eyes swept round the empty hall;

the house was very quiet, she allowed her thoughtful gaze to rest upon the man beside her and was on the point of speaking when he interrupted her:

'No, Miss Trent, I can assure you that there is nothing of sinister intent in my request to you to accompany me here.' He smiled thinly. 'You surely could not have seriously supposed that?'

It was annoying to have her thoughts read so accurately. Abigail said crossly, because that was exactly what she had been thinking, 'No, of course not. I'm not such a fool—you have to be joking.'

He said nothing to this but opened a door and said: 'Perhaps you would like to wait in here?'

She went past him into a small panelled room, warm and snug in the light of the fire burning in the steel grate. It was furnished in the utmost comfort with a number of easy chairs, leather-covered; a charmingly inlaid pier table against one wall, I small round table, inlaid with coloured mosaic work, conveniently close to the hearth, a revolving bookcase filled with books and a small Regency work-table. The professor pressed a switch and a number of table lamps bathed their surroundings in a delicate pink, highlighting the walls, which she could see were covered with red embossed paper, almost hidden along two sides of the room by the pictures hung upon it, and completely hidden on its third side by shelves of books. The room called for comment, but this time she held her tongue, walking to the centre of the room and standing quietly, waiting for him to speak first.

He didn't speak at all, but went out of the room, shutting the door behind him, and Abigail for one split second fought an urge to rush to the door and try the handle. Instead, she turned her back on it and went to examine the paintings on the walls. Mostly portraits of bygone van Wijkelens, she decided, who had undoubtedly passed on their good looks with an almost monotonous regularity. She was peering at a despotic-looking old gentleman in a tie-wig, when the door opened behind her and she turned round to see who it was.

Bollinger stood there. She cried on a happy, startled breath: 'Bolly—oh, Bolly!' and burst into tears. He crossed the room and patted her on the shoulder and said: 'There, there, Miss Abby—I gave you a shock, eh? Thought you'd be pleased and all.'

'Oh, Bolly, I am! I'm so happy to see you, that's why I'm crying—aren't I a fool? But how did you get here?' A sudden thought struck her. 'In the professor's house?' She whisked the spotless handkerchief he always carried out of his pocket and blew her nose and wiped her eyes. 'Does he know?'

'Course he knows, love. It's him as thought to do it. You see, he comes along one night and gives me your letter and the money, and I asks him to have a cuppa, seeing as it's a cold night, and we gets talking and I tells him a bit about us, and he says to me, "Well, Bollinger, seeing as how Miss Trent's going to be in Amsterdam for a week or two yet, why don't you get yourself a little job and be near her?" '

' "Well," I says, "that's easier said than done," and he says: "I'm looking for a gardener and odd job man for a week or two while my man has his bunions done—how about it?" So here I am, Miss Abby, came yesterday. He paid me fare and I'm to get my wages, so I'm in clover, as they say—no need for you to give me any more money.'

'It's fantastic,' declared Abigail. 'I simply can't believe it—do you like him, Bolly?'

'Yes, that I do, Miss Abby—a bit of a toff, you might say, but a gent all right.'

Abigail blew her nose again to prevent herself from bursting into another bout of tears. 'Oh, Bolly, it's like being home again. And of course I shall go on paying you your money—have you any idea how much it is we owe you? Don't you see, Bolly, I must pay you back now that I know about it and can afford to do so?'

'Well, if it makes you happy, Miss Abby. How long do you think you'll be here?'

'I'm not sure. Another two weeks, perhaps three. What have you done about your room?'

'I give it up, it wasn't all that hot. This professor, he says he knows someone in London lets rooms, very nice—a bit more than I got, but if I save me wages. . .'

'And I pay you each week while you're here, and by the time I get back to London and you're running a bit low, I'll be in another job and be able to send you something each week.' She hugged him. 'Oh, Bolly, it's all so wonderful, I can't believe it. Are you happy here? Where do you live?'

'Here, of course, Miss Abby. I got a room at the top of the house—very snug and warm it is too.'

'You don't have to work too hard?'

'Lord love you, no, Miss Abby—nice little bit of garden behind, and I does the odd job—and I'm to go to his other house in the country once a week and see to the garden there.'

Abigail stood silent, digesting this new aspect of Professor van Wijkelen. 'Well. . .' she began, and was interrupted by the door opening to admit a small round dumpling of a woman with a pleasant face. She shook Abigail by the hand and said in very tolerable English, 'The housekeeper, Mevrouw Boot,' and Abigail, mindful of her Dutch manners, replied: 'Miss Abigail Trent.'

Mevrouw Boot eyed her with kindly curiosity as she spoke. 'The professor begs that Miss will return to hospital when she must. There is a car at the door in five minutes. He excuses himself.'

She smiled again and went quietly out of the room, and Abigail looked at Bollinger and said with unconscious sadness, 'He doesn't like me, you know,' and had this statement instantly repudiated by Bolly who exclaimed in a shocked voice:

'That I can't believe, begging your pardon, Miss Abby—a nice young lady like you. . .'

'Well, it doesn't matter in the least,' said Abigail with such firmness that she almost believed what she was saying—but not quite, because it mattered out of all proportion to everything else. 'I'd better go, I suppose it's a taxi and I oughtn't to keep it waiting. Come to the door with me, Bolly.'

They crossed the hall, lingering a little. 'The professor says you're to come whenever ye're inclined,' Bolly explained, 'but not the days I go to the country.'

She nodded and stopped. 'All right, Bolly, I'll remember. I'm very grateful to him. Do you suppose I should write him a letter?'

He looked astonished. 'You see him, don't you, can't you do it then?'

She shook her head. 'I told you he doesn't like me,' and as if to underline her words one of the doors opened and Mevrouw Boot came into the hall and before she closed the door behind her, Abigail and Bollinger had an excellent view of the professor sitting at a desk facing it—the powerful reading lamp on it lighted his face clearly; he was staring at Abigail with no expression, giving her the peculiar feeling that she wasn't there, and then lowered his handsome head to the papers before him. The door closed and when the housekeeper had gone, Abigail said softly:

'You see, Bolly? He doesn't even want to see me, let alone speak.'

She smiled a little wanly, wished him a warm goodbye and went outside. The Rolls was before the steps, an elderly man at the wheel. He got out of the car when he saw her and opened the door, smiling nicely as he did so although he didn't speak, and she returned the smile, for he had a kind face, rugged and lined—like a Dutch Bolly, she thought as she settled herself beside him for the journey back to the hospital. During the short ride she tried her best to reconcile the professor's dislike of her with his kindness to Bollinger. There had, after all, been no need to offer the old man a job, even a temporary one. She hoped that Bolly hadn't told him too much, although she discounted as ridiculous the idea that he might have acted out of sympathy to herself as well as Bollinger. It was all a little mysterious and she gave up the puzzle and began to ask her companion some questions about Amsterdam, hoping that he could understand. It was an agreeable surprise to find that he could, and moreover, reply to them in English.

At the hospital, she thanked him for the ride, wondering who he was and not liking to ask for fear the professor would hear of it and consider her nosey. She went back to her patient with her curiosity unsatisfied, to find him feeling so much better after a refreshing nap that he wanted to know what she had been doing with her afternoon. She told him, skating over the more unexplainable bits, and rather to her surprise he made very little comment, and that was about herself and Bollinger. About the professor he had nothing to say at all.

The days slid quietly by, each one bringing more strength to Professor de Wit. He was to go home in a week's time, said Professor van Wijkelen when he called one morning soon after Abigail had been to his house, and as he had said it, both he and his patient looked at her.

'You'll come with me, Abby?' asked her patient, who considered himself on sufficiently good terms with her by now to address her so. The professor's cool, 'I hope you will find it convenient to go with Professor de Wit for another week, Nurse Trent,' sounded all the more stilted. She said that yes, of course she would, hiding her delight at the idea of seeing the professor, even if he hated her, for another few days, and the lesser delight of knowing that she would be able to repay Bolly quite a lot of money. She went away to fetch the latest X-rays the professor decided to study, walking on air.

She told Bollinger about it the next day when they met, as they often did, for a cup of coffee and half an hour's chat. Bollinger, she was glad to see, looked well, and he was happy with his gardening and the odd jobs he was doing around the house. He had been to the country too, but Abigail didn't press him with questions about this; somehow she felt that the less she knew about the professor's private life, the better it would be.

She hadn't been back to the house on the *gracht*—not since the time when he had looked right through her, as though she were someone he didn't want to see there. Each time Bollinger suggested it, she had some excuse, but when she went home with Professor de Wit, she would have to do better, for she discovered that the older man had a small house within walking distance of the professor's home, and Bolly would expect her to go and see him quite often and she could think of no good reason why she shouldn't. The professor had even told Bollinger to use the small sitting room where they had met, and offer Abigail tea if she wished, which, considering the lack of friendliness he showed towards her, puzzled her very much.

She took care during the next few days to keep herself busy, both in her work and her leisure; under her patient's tuition, she was beginning to make a little headway with her Dutch, and because it pleased him excessively and kept him interested in something while he struggled through the unrewarding days of convalescence, she spent a good deal of time outside her working hours with him, not admitting to herself that it served her purpose very well and gave her a real excuse for not going to the house on the *gracht*.

The professor came daily, sometimes twice, but beyond wishing her a good day and asking her in a strictly professional manner how his patient did, he made no effort to talk to her. About Bollinger he had said nothing at all, and the short, painfully careful note she had sent him had been ignored.

But she was not able to follow this rather cowardly scheme for any length of time; Professor de Wit took her to task for not going out enough, and dispatched her to Kalverstraat on her next free afternoon to fetch him some books he had ordered. She knew her way about by now and hurried down the narrow lanes, wrapped warmly against the snarling wind and the first powdering of snow from a heavy sky. There were several ways in which she might reach the bookshop; she chose the longest of them, because although it didn't pass Professor van Wijkelen's house, it went close to it, which, she told herself sternly, was the silliest reason for taking it.

There were several alleys connecting one *gracht* with the next. She went down one of them now, her head bent against the quickening snow, her feet sounding loudly on the uneven cobbles and echoing against the silent warehouses, leaning, crooked with age, against each other on either side of her. She was nearly at the end when a movement in the gutter drew her attention—a slight movement, made without sound. She slowed her pace to investigate, crossing the road gingerly; it might be a rat, and she was afraid of rats. But it wasn't a rat, it was a kitten, a very small one, its dirty black and white fur clinging wetly to its bony body, a few drops of blood on its filthy white shirt-front. She stooped and picked it up with care, fearful of hurting it, and exclaimed with pity at its pathetic lightness. It was an ugly small creature, with a large nose; even when clean and well fed, she doubted if it would be worth a second glance. It gave her a penetrating glance from blue eyes and mewed, and all thought of fetching her patient's books went out of her head. She wrapped the waif in the ends of her long scarf, cradled it against her and hurried on. The professor's house was only around the next corner. She would go there and get Bolly to take care of it after she had examined it to see where it had been hurt.

At the house she hesitated. To ring the front door bell and ask to go in so that she might attend to a stray kitten seemed to her to be taking advantage of the professor's message that she might stay for tea with Bolly—and probably it had been mere civility on his part, with no thought of her accepting. She didn't think he was at home—there was no car to be seen and the house stood silent in the snow. She knocked on the little door beneath the steps and waited.

Bollinger opened the door, his face lighting up at the sight of her. 'There, Miss Abby,' he exclaimed, 'I knew you'd be along—on such a nasty day too. Come in and we'll have a cuppa.' He opened the door wider, saying: 'But I don't know if you should come in this door. The one above's for you.'

'Well, no—I shouldn't think so,' Abby stated. 'I haven't been invited you know—besides, I've got something—look.'

They carried the kitten to the kitchen at the back of the house, a surprisingly bright room overlooking a small walled garden, now shrouded in snow. There was no one there; Bolly explained that Mevrouw Boot had gone out to see some relative or other and the daily woman who came in to do the rough work had gone home. 'Let's put the little beggar in front of the stove,' he suggested, 'get him warm, then we can have a look.'

Which they accordingly did, to be rewarded after a few minutes by a faint movement from the small creature, who put out a pink tongue and weakly tried to lick its fur. 'There,' said Bolly, who knew every old wives' tale and believed them all, 'she'll get better—she's licked herself.'

Looking at the bedraggled kitten, Abigail refrained from saying that she considered that a too optimistic statement. Nevertheless, they must try to do something. Because there had been nothing else, she had wrapped it in her scarf; now she produced a handkerchief and started to clean its dirty fur. She did it very gently because she was afraid of hurting it, but she managed to get off enough of the muddy wet to discover where it was hurt. There was a cut on its puny chest, not a large one, but probably deep.

'If I had a pair of scissors. . .' she began.

Someone had come into the kitchen and joined them. 'If I might take a look?' the professor enquired almost apologetically.

It was Bolly, who had gone to the stove to warm some milk, who answered him. 'Ah—good thing you've come, sir—this here beast don't look too good, Miss Abby found him in one of them alleys round the back.' His tone implied that the alleys in question failed to win his approval. 'She brought him here.'

'And quite right too.' The professor was on his knees beside the scrap stretched on Abigail's scarf, his capable hands busy. 'I didn't hear the house door bell,' he commented mildly, and looked at Abigail.

'No—well, I didn't come in through the big door.' At his raised eyebrows she hurried on, 'I—I had to take the kitten somewhere and I was close by and I thought that Bollinger might help—so I rang the bell of the little door under the steps.'

He had picked the kitten up and was inspecting the cut. 'It is, of course, no concern of mine, Miss Trent,' his voice was smooth, 'but I can assure you that you have no need to—er—creep in the tradesmen's entrance of my house.'

'I didn't creep. . .' began Abigail indignantly. 'I didn't know you were here.'

'And if you had known?'

She went pink, longing to tell him that ringing the door bell of his house was something she would never willingly do, knowing herself unwelcome in it. She said nothing, but took the saucer of milk from Bolly. She asked:

'Can it have this? Is it likely to need an anaesthetic?'

His mouth twitched, but he said gravely enough, 'I think there will be no need of that. Give him a little of the milk and I'll put a stitch in. He'll be all right in a day or so—he's nearly starved to death.'

He got to his feet and went away, to return presently with a needle and gut, scissors and a spray of local anaesthetic. 'Bring him over here,' he commanded Abigail, 'and hold him still on the table. Bollinger, turn on the light, if you please.'

He was very quick and the kitten lay still, licking the last drops of milk from its small chops. When he had finished, the professor unbent himself and gathered up his odds and ends.

'And now what is to become of the creature?' he wanted to know blandly. 'You intend to take him back with you, Miss Trent?'

Abigail removed her finger from the kitten's clutches and stared down at it. It was unthinkable that it should be turned into the streets; she would have to take it with her, and heaven knows what they would say about it in hospital—perhaps she could keep it in her room and take it back to England when she went. . . Her thoughts were interrupted by the professor's voice. 'No doubt you think that he should remain here?'

She looked at him then. He had never been particularly pleasant to her, but she refused to believe that he was an unkind man. 'I don't think you would turn anyone or anything away if they needed help,' she stated flatly, and added, 'That's if you don't mind.'

The stare from his blue eyes was shrewd; when he didn't answer she went on quietly, 'It's quite all right if you don't want to be bothered. I'll manage. Thank you very much for being so kind.' She smiled at him and the plainness of her face was changed to a kind of beauty. She picked up her scarf and began to arrange it around the kitten, then buttoned up her coat. Her fingers faltered at the top button when the professor spoke.

'I beg your pardon for teasing you. Of course the animal shall stay here.' His manner changed to a fierce mockery. 'In any case, how could I refuse after your pretty speech?'

'I meant it,' said Abigail, trying to keep the hurt out of her voice. 'Thank you, Professor. It won't be any trouble to you, I know Bollinger will keep it out of your way, won't you, Bolly?' she besought the old man, who said at once, 'Of course I will, Miss Abby, don't you fret your pretty head, I'll do me best—you won't know him when you come.'

'Your thoughtfulness does you credit, Miss Trent, but I assure you that the kitten will be welcome. I have a dog who will be delighted to have company when I am not here, and as the kitten is a female,

I foresee no difficulties.' He started for the door. 'Bollinger, perhaps you would be so good as to make a pot of your excellent English tea and bring it to my study. Miss Trent, be so good as to accompany me.'

Abigail was astonished to a state of speechlessness. 'Me?' she wanted to know, and then, remembering, 'But I can't—I've got to go to the Kalverstraat and get Professor de Wit's books.'

Her host's eyes flickered to his watch. 'No matter, I have to go there myself this afternoon—I'll bring them with me when I call in later.'

He held the door open for her, so certain that she would do as he wished that she saw no other course open to her. She went past him and up a few steps, old and worn uneven by countless feet over the years. There was a door beyond them which he pushed open and they were, as she had guessed, in the back of the hall, which they crossed to enter a room she took to be his study. The walls were lined with books, a large circular table standing in the centre of the room held more books as well as papers, unopened letters as well as opened ones, several copies of *World Medicine* and *The Lancet* and a great many journals in the French and German tongues. She turned, round-eyed, from this businesslike disorder, to view the desk in one corner, very tidy, although there was a sheaf of papers pushed to one side as though he had risen from his chair in haste. That same chair was tall and straight and definitely not for lounging, but there were two leather armchairs on each side of the brightly burning fire, and a table lamp beside one of them cast an inviting glow. It was a well-lived-in room; she could imagine the professor sitting here working and reading; the thought conjured up a picture of a lonely, bookish life, which she felt sure was quite erroneous; with his good looks and unmarried state, not to mention the fact that he was undoubtedly wealthy, he would be much in demand among his friends and acquaintances. She frowned because it was foolish of her to speculate upon his private life, but the frown turned to a delighted smile as a Great Dane came from behind the desk and offered a paw. Abigail shook it and hugged him as well. 'Beautiful,' she addressed him, 'and so...' she remembered just in time how vexed the professor had looked when she had admired the hall. She said instead, 'What's his name?'

'Colossus.' And she, forgetting to be wary of him, chortled: 'Oh, how apt—Julius Caesar, isn't it? Something about petty men walking under his huge legs,' she added admiringly. 'How very clever of you.'

She smiled at him and encountered a look of such fierce derision that she got to her feet and said instantly, 'I don't think I'll stay for tea, if you don't mind.'

The look had gone. 'I must beg your pardon for the second time this afternoon,' he smiled unexpectedly and she felt her heart tumble. 'Please stay, Abigail.'

She would never understand him; it was like going along a winding road wondering what would be around the next corner. She sat down in one of the chairs and asked in a voice which forgave him, 'What will you call the kitten?' She pulled Colossus's ear and heard the dog sigh with pleasure, and at that moment Bollinger came in with the tea-tray and the professor said:

'We want a name for the kitten, Bollinger. Any ideas?'

Bollinger put the tray down by Abigail, smiled at her and then frowned in thought. 'Well,' he said at length, 'she's an orphan, isn't she? So she'll be Annie.'

He looked at them hopefully. 'Little Orphan Annie,' he explained, and beamed at the professor when he declared: 'A splendid name for her, Bollinger. Annie it shall be. When she's a little more herself, Colossus shall go down to the kitchen and make friends.'

'She's having a nap,' continued Bollinger, 'I

haven't moved her, so snug she lies. I'll feed her presently.'

'Every two hours—milk, Bollinger, and not too much of it.'

'OK, boss,' said Bollinger comfortably. 'I'll say bye-bye for now, Miss Abby.' He sounded wistful and she was quick to hear it.

'I'll meet you for coffee—tomorrow, Bolly, and you can tell me about Annie.'

The professor's voice was blandly polite. 'May I suggest that you come here? I shall be away for a couple of days and I think it would be as well if you kept an eye on Annie until I return.'

'Now that's an idea,' said Bollinger enthusiastically. 'No reason why you shouldn't, is there, Miss Abby?'

Abigail said that no, there wasn't, in a rather prim voice which concealed sudden delight. She wanted to come to this old house again; she could think of nothing nicer than living in it for ever and ever. She lifted the teapot and almost dropped it again, struck by the knowledge that the house meant nothing at all without the professor in it—bad temper, frowns, sneers and all. Somewhere behind that forbidding manner must be the man she had fallen in love with—once or twice he had allowed himself to be glimpsed and she dearly wished that he would allow it again. She had no illusions about herself; the professor was as likely to fall in love with her as the moon would turn to cheese, although miracles did happen. . . She handed him his tea and poured some for herself, asking in a matter-of-fact voice whether Colossus found city life a little trying.

'No—not really. He has a good walk each morning and another some time in the evening and he goes with me to Friesland, where I have another home. He can exercise there to his heart's content.'

'Friesland,' wondered Abigail, 'isn't that a long way?'

'No, a hundred and thirty odd kilometres. An hour and a half's driving—less.'

'Is that where Bollinger went?'

'Yes—there is quite a large garden there. He enjoyed himself enormously.'

He handed Abigail a dish of little cakes and she took one and bit into it. It tasted as delicious as it looked. 'Yes, he loves gardening, but I expect you know that. He has green fingers.'

'Green. . .? What does that mean?'

'He can grow things and they grow for him because he understands them.'

The professor sipped his tea. 'How interesting. I shall look forward to a beautiful garden this spring.'

Abigail put down her cup and saucer—delicate, paper thin and transparent with a white and purple pattern; she would make a note of them and ask Professor de Wit about them later on—the teapot too; silver and very plain with a rounded lid. 'I think I'd better go,' she said politely, while she longed to stay, but her companion, while making pleasant enough conversation, had shown no great delight in her company, nor did he press her to stay. He got up as she did and went with her into the hall. There were red tulips, dozens of them on the chest today, she noticed. They were half way to the front door when the professor stopped.

'One moment, Miss Trent—your scarf. You made a bed for the kitten, did you not?'

'Yes, but it doesn't matter. I'm not cold and it's a short walk.'

He ignored this and turned on his heel and went to a pillow cupboard at the back of the hall and came back with a silk square. 'This will do.' He unbuttoned her coat, tied the scarf round her neck and buttoned the coat up again, and when she murmured her thanks made no reply, but went ahead of her to the door and flung it open on to the snow outside. The Rolls was by the steps.

'Jan will take you back. Goodbye, Miss Trent.' As she went down the steps she thought indignantly that he sounded relieved that she was going, and possibly he was, but he might have had the decency to pretend—and he had lent her his scarf, but then he would have lent a scarf to anyone in an emergency. She refused to tease herself any more and began a determined conversation with Jan, which lasted until they reached the hospital entrance.

She had spent two happy afternoons at the house on the *gracht*, playing with a slowly recovering Annie and listening to Bollinger's cheerful talk. She had been able to give him some more money too, which he had refused to take until she had pointed out that the quicker she paid her debt to him the quicker she could make a fresh start.

'There's nothing you can do about it, Bolly,' she told him, 'so don't argue. Besides, I'm to be a week at Professor de Wit's house and I've got my fare back to England and some money besides.' She didn't mention that she had heard nothing from Mrs Morgan—she could always go to the agency and ask what to do about it. The prospect of going back to England depressed her, but she was too level-headed to allow it to dominate her thoughts. She had told Bolly that when she knew for certain when she was leaving, she would let him know and he could either come with her or follow when it was convenient. As far as she could make out, he and the professor had a very easy-going agreement between them, and Bolly had said that the man whose work he was doing wouldn't be well for a few weeks yet; he might stay until he was and that would give her time to find another job, this time where she could live out and get a small home together for them both.

The transfer of her patient went without a hitch. Professor de Wit's house was much smaller than his friend's but just as old. It had no garden though, just a few square feet of paving stones and a high wall, but the rooms were delightful. His bedroom was on the first floor and hers next to it, because, as he pointed out to her, after his stay in hospital he was a little nervous of being quite by himself. His housekeeper, Juffrouw Valk, seemed to Abigail to be a sensible and kind woman and perfectly able to look after the professor once she had been told about his diet and what he might and might not do. She spoke no English, which, Professor de Wit pointed out with some glee, was splendid for Abigail's Dutch. And so it was; by the end of the afternoon Abigail had managed to communicate quite a lot to Juffrouw Valk, who smiled and nodded and encouraged her and went to a great deal of trouble to have things just so.

Abigail and her patient ate their dinner together in the small dining room at the back of the house after she had spent some time in the kitchen showing the older woman what Professor de Wit might eat and how much, and immediately the simple meal was finished, she helped him climb the stairs and got him to bed, for he was tired and happy and exhausted. She had settled him nicely in his bed and was getting his spectacles and newspaper for him when Professor van Wijkelen arrived. He stood in the doorway of the bedroom, looking larger than ever, and, Abigail was quick to perceive, very out of humour. Or perhaps it was only herself who caused that expression on his face, for it cleared as he went over to sit by his patient's bed, and after a minute, seeing that she wasn't needed, she slipped away, downstairs to the kitchen, to help Juffrouw Valk with the washing up and improve her Dutch at the same time. She was forced to go back upstairs very soon, though, because the professor called to her briskly from the head of the narrow little staircase. She followed him into his patient's bedroom and stood, very neat in her uniform, waiting to hear what he had to say.

'We have been discussing you, Miss Trent. Professor de Wit agrees with me that another week of your excellent nursing and he will be able to dispense with your services—with regret, I must add.'

He sounded not in the least regretful himself. Abigail fastened her eyes on the glowing silk of his tie and remembered, for no reason at all, that once, quite by accident, he had called her Abigail.

'This suits me very well, however,' went on the professor, 'for I have another patient in need of your care for a week or so. A Scotswoman who lives in one of the houses in the Begijnhof—you have probably been there?'

Abigail nodded. It was peaceful and beautiful and the little houses couldn't have changed much since they had been built centuries before. 'A week should suffice,' went on the professor smoothly, 'a short delay for you, I know, Nurse, but you would be doing her a great kindness—she is a charming person.'

He smiled at her, and even as she heard her own voice saying that yes, she was quite prepared to take another case for him, she was chiding herself for being a fool. Now that he had got what he wanted he would doubtless be as morose and irritable as before; it was an ever-recurring pattern which she weakly never attempted to alter. She only had to say no. She peeped at him—he wasn't smiling now and she saw that he looked very tired, so that his hair looked more grey than it really was and the lines of his face were etched more deeply. He looked up and his eyes held hers for a brief moment and the smile on her lips froze before their coldness. She looked away quickly and he turned back to Professor de Wit, and presently got up to go. It hardly seemed the right moment to give him back his scarf, but she went and fetched it all the same and handed it to him with a word of thanks, remembering how gentle his hands had been when he had tied it round her neck. He took it carelessly now and stuffed it in a pocket. Abigail went downstairs with him and let him out into the coldness of the winter evening. He didn't reply to her sober good night.

'I shall miss you, Abby,' declared her patient when she went back upstairs, 'but Dominic is quite right, I shan't really need you. I've surprised even him, I believe. But I'm glad you will still be in Amsterdam. You must come and see me when you can.'

'I should like that, though I shall only be here for another week after I leave you, shan't I? I must write to the agency in London and see if they have another job for me.' She smiled at him. 'Otherwise I might have to wait a few days for a case and I should prefer to go straight to a patient.'

'What—no days off, Abby?'

'Yes—that is, no, I can't. . .don't let's talk about me, it's so dull.'

'Dull? My dear Abby, you are the last person I should describe as dull. Tell me, how is that ridiculous kitten you wished on Dominic?'

They spent the rest of the evening talking about nothing in particular and when she had finally tucked the old man up for the night she went to her own room and got ready for bed too. It was marvellous, she told her reflection in the little shieldback mirror on the dressing-table, that she had another patient to go to, and marvellous, said her heart, that she would see the professor for a further week. 'And a lot of good that may do you,' she admonished her mirrored face, 'for he only speaks to you when he's got something unpleasant to say or when he wants something.' Her face reflected sadness; she made a derisive face at it and got into bed and lay awake, thinking about Dominic van Wijkelen. He had looked so very tired that evening, and although the house on the *gracht* was a beautiful home and his housekeeper everything she should be, it surely wasn't quite the same as going home to a wife and children. Even if he were tired to death, he would open the great front door and find them waiting for him. It would be lonely in that house. . .a tear slid beneath her lids and she blinked it away. 'At least he's got Annie,' she reminded herself, and went to sleep on that ridiculous thought.

The week went pleasantly by. Professor de Wit, now that he was home again, began to take up the thread of his life once more; he was still weak, but he managed the stairs on his own now and spent an hour or more each day working on the book he was writing—a lengthy treatise on biochemistry, which Abigail strove to understand, when, carried away by some theory or other, he would talk at great length about the fascinations of cell life. And his friends came; learned gentlemen who spoke kindly to her and drank a great deal of coffee while her patient sipped his milk.

Juffrouw Valk had proved a treasure; not only had she obtained extra help in the house, she had proved a quick and willing learner when it came to Abigail explaining her patient's diet and what he might and might not do. She wrote it all down in laborious Dutch too so that Juffrouw Valk couldn't forget, and that lady, far from laughing at Abigail's efforts, praised her kindly and tactfully pointed out the mistakes. Abigail could see that she would be leaving Professor de Wit in excellent hands.

Professor van Wijkelen came daily, sometimes briefly, sometimes to stay long enough to play chess with his old friend, and each time he came he brought news of Annie and Bollinger—both, it seemed, in the best of health and firm friends. On one of his visits he suggested that she should go to see them and when she replied quietly that she had been that very afternoon he answered dryly, 'Ah, yes—while I was away from home on operating day, as you very well know.'

The afternoon before she was due to leave Professor de Wit's house, she walked round to see Bollinger once more and enquire after Annie. Despite the professor's words, she had formed the habit of ringing the bell of the little door under the steps, with the vague, half-formed idea that if the professor were home she could, if she wished, beat a hasty retreat. But he was out that afternoon, she had a cup of tea with Bollinger, admired Annie, who had turned from the miserable little waif she had been into a plump, enchanting kitten, and petted Colossus, who chose to have tea with them, taking up a good deal of room before the fire. He stretched out now with Annie balanced on his paws while she tidied away her whiskers after the saucer of milk Bollinger had given her.

'So you're off again, Miss Abby,' he commented, and Abigail detected the satisfaction in his voice. 'The boss says it's a Scotch lady this time—very nice too, specially as his gardener ain't going so fast as he might with his bunions.' He sighed happily. '"No hurry," he tells me, "you're far too useful a man to go before you need."' He added proudly, 'I help Jan with the cars—cleaning 'em, you know.'

Abigail hadn't seen him so happy for a long time, not since her father had been alive and Bolly had seen to the garden and driven and serviced their old-fashioned, solid car, and between whiles made himself useful in the house. She wondered how he would like London again; even if she was very lucky and got a job where she could live out, it would have to be a furnished flat, and a small one at that. She said now, her nice voice urgent:

'Bolly, when I go back to London, don't come with me, not if there's still a job for you here. Stay on a little while, until I can get a home for us.'

'And who's going to look after you?' he demanded fiercely.

'I'll be fine, Bolly. I'll get a job where I can live in for a couple of weeks, that'll give me a chance to look round.'

It sounded easier than it would actually be, but it lulled the old man into a sense of security; he needed very little persuasion to do as she asked and she knew that secretly he was happy to be staying.

When she got up to go she said, 'I don't know exactly when I'll be here again, Bolly. I'll have to see how the new patient is, but I'll come as soon as I can.'

'Right, Miss Abby. The boss'll tell me how you go on, he always does.'

Abigail, on her way out, stopped. 'Does he? Does he really? I shouldn't have thought. . .' She walked on again, having uttered these rather obscure remarks, said her goodbyes and went back to her patient.

The professor came early that evening. They had barely finished their simple dinner when he was announced by Juffrouw Valk, who in the same breath offered coffee and perhaps, if the professor was a hungry man, a little something to eat. He declined the little something but accepted the coffee, which

Abigail poured for him, listening with a sympathetic ear to his patient's gentle complaints about not being allowed to drink that beverage. Abigail offered him his milk with such a motherly air, explaining how good it was for him, that he chuckled and said:

'Abby, I find I do a great many things I don't care about, as a consequence of your persuasive ways. I can see that in due course you will wheedle your husband and children most shamefully into doing exactly what you want.'

Abigail laughed at his little joke and hoped that it didn't sound hollow. She saw no prospect of marriage, and even if she did, she only wanted to marry the professor, sitting beside her now, drinking his coffee and taking no notice of her at all. She got to her feet.

'I expect you would like to talk, and there are several things I have to do.'

'Stay where you are,' the professor's voice was a little sharp and when she looked at him in surprise he added: 'Please.'

So she sat down again, looking at him with a calm face, wondering what it was he had to say.

'I shall fetch you tomorrow,' he spoke in a no-nonsense voice. 'Kindly be ready by three o'clock. My patient is nervous of returning home alone, and it seems to me that getting to know each other over a cup of tea might be best for you both. I should imagine that you will be with her for a week or ten days and I have told Bollinger this—he knows that he is free to leave when he wishes. I don't know what arrangements you have made, but he seemed to think that he would stay here while you—er—find a home.'

'Yes,' said Abigail briefly. It was, she told herself, no concern of his.

'Which is no concern of mine, is it?' concluded the professor with uncanny perception. He turned back to Professor de Wit. 'I'll be in to see you each day, but you are making good headway now and you have Juffrouw Valk, who, Nurse tells me, has proved an apt pupil in the compiling of your diet and so on.'

Abigail perceived that he had finished with her. She was still not sure what her patient was suffering from and if he didn't choose to tell her, then she wasn't going to ask. She got to her feet again, and this time no one suggested that she should stay.

She was quite ready by three o'clock, with her case in the narrow hall and her outdoor clothes on. She had said goodbye to Juffrouw Valk, promised Professor de Wit that she would visit him before she went back to England, extracted a promise from him to be good and do exactly what he should and thanked him with charm for the gloves he had given her. They were lovely ones, warm brown leather, fur-lined. She hadn't had such a pair for a very long time. She put them on and declared that as long as winter lasted she would wear them every day, and because he looked so lonely sitting there she put her arms round his thin shoulders and kissed him, just as the professor came into the room.

'Ah, Dominic, envious?'

His visitor smiled bleakly and turned such a look of ice upon Abigail that she blinked under it. He said briefly to his patient, 'Hullo,' and advised him that he would call in later, and then asked, in a voice to freeze her marrow, 'You're ready, Nurse?'

She told him yes, she was, in a voice as cold as his own, though it warmed as she bade her patient goodbye and followed the professor out to his car.

She sat silently beside him because it was obvious that he was in a towering rage about something or other. He had woven the car through the traffic on the Herengracht before he spoke.

'Your patient,' he began, 'Mrs Macklin—she has been ill for some time. A peptic ulcer—I operated some six weeks ago, but she has been slow to recover. She is now much better, but naturally after so long a stay in hospital, she's nervous of going home alone. She has no relations and isn't the type to bother her friends. She has very little money, by the way—you will be good enough to say nothing to her about your fee. If she should ask tell her that it will be settled later. I will see that you are paid.'

Abigail took a quick look at him. He was staring ahead, his profile fierce and unfriendly, as though daring her to make any comment, so she said in a matter-of-fact voice, 'Just as you wish, sir. How old is Mrs Macklin?'

'Sixty-five. She is the widow of a Scottish Presbyterian parson.'

He didn't speak again, even when he pulled up in the Begijnsteeg, got her case from the boot of the car and crossed the quiet Begijnhof to the end house on the semi-circle of quaint dwellings surrounding the church. The steps leading to its door were narrow and worn, and the front door creaked with age as he turned its handle and walked in, saying, 'Hullo there,' in a cheerful voice, the sort of voice he never used towards Abigail. She stifled a sigh and followed him into one of the smallest houses she had ever been in.

CHAPTER FOUR

THE hall contained two doors and a small circular staircase at its end, its wooden steps worn crooked with age, its floor was brick with a hand-made rug upon it, the walls were white plaster, upon which was displayed a fine plate of Delft Blue and nothing else. The professor opened the door nearest him and ushered Abigail inside, into a room which was small, low-ceilinged and rather dark, although the early February afternoon largely accounted for this.

It was an attractive room, though cluttered, with small tables laden with photographs in silver frames, a writing bureau against one wall and a display cabinet on the other. There were footstools and several small comfortable chairs; there was one large easy chair by the small old-fashioned pot stove set in its traditional tiles; the woman sitting in it spoke to them as they entered.

'Dominic, my dear, how punctual. I won't get up—you won't mind? And is this my nurse?'

'It is. Miss Abigail Trent—Mrs Macklin. I'll take the bags up, shall I?'

He went out of the room again and it seemed much larger without his bulk half filling it. Abigail said how do you do and stood quietly while she was inspected, carrying out her own inspection at the same time. Mrs Macklin was tall, though how tall it was hard to say until she stood up, she was also very thin, with a long, sharp-nosed face and bright dark eyes. Her iron grey hair was screwed into an old-fashioned no-nonsense bun, skewered with equally old-fashioned hairpins. After a moment they smiled at each other and Mrs Macklin said, 'You're exactly as Dominic described you. Shall we have a cup of tea together? Could you put the kettle on? The kitchen is behind this room and you'll find the tray already laid. A neighbour kindly did it for me—she was here waiting when Dominic brought me home a couple of hours ago.'

Abigail took off her gloves and unwound her scarf and went to find the kitchen, small and a little old-fashioned, with a gay gingham frill round the mantelshelf above the small electric cooker and a row of pot plants on the windowsill. She filled the kettle and put it on, listening to the creak of the stairs as the professor descended them with measured tread. He had very large feet, thought Abigail lovingly, but then he was a very large man. She could hear the murmur of their voices in the room next door as she made the tea in the brown earthenware pot, put it on the tray and carried it through to the sitting room.

The professor took the tray from her at the door and Mrs Macklin smiled at her and said, 'My dear, there's a fruit cake in the tin on the middle shelf of the cupboard,' so Abigail went back and found the cake, a plate to put it on, a knife and three little porcelain tea plates, all different in design and, she guessed, very old.

They had tea to the accompaniment of cheerful small talk, and Abigail, under the impression that she now knew the professor quite well, discovered another side of him entirely. It was as though Mrs Macklin had charmed away his ill temper and coldness, and although he spoke seldom to her, and then only briefly, she was aware of this. She didn't talk much herself, but sat listening to her new patient and the professor mulling over the city's news.

The professor got up to go presently, saying as he did so: 'Be good enough to come with me to the door, Nurse Trent, I have one or two instructions for you.' He wasn't looking at her and his voice was as cold as ever it had been, but at the door, just as he was going, he halted and said in quite a different voice: '*Hemel*, I forgot the cat—I intended to fetch him...'

'You have enough to do,' called Mrs Macklin from the sitting room, 'you know you haven't a minute to spare this evening.'

'I'll get him,' Abigail offered. 'I know my way around Amsterdam very well now and I'm sure there'll be plenty of time this evening.' She had a sudden unsatisfactory picture of the professor, spending his evening wining and dining some gorgeous girl who could make him smile instead of scowl as he was at that moment.

'I can't allow you to go trudging all over Amsterdam after a cat.' His voice was polite and quite impersonal.

'You exaggerate,' Abigail pointed out reasonably. 'I never trudge anywhere—you make me sound like Little Orphan Annie...' She stopped, because although she wasn't Annie she was an orphan. She fixed her gaze on the fine cloth of his car coat and clenched her teeth to stop the tears coming into her eyes. She gulped back the lump in her throat and said: 'I shall enjoy it.'

'And will you enjoy the shopping and housework and the cooking?' he enquired.

'Yes. There isn't much nursing for me to do, is there? And it's such a tiny house.'

'I will get some kind of household help for Mrs Macklin by the end of the week. In the meantime I should like you to restrain her from doing everything. She has always been a very active woman and likes to have her own way.'

'Most people do,' remarked Abigail, and looked at him, to surprise an expression on his face which set her pulse racing—it was such a peculiar look, half wonder, half amusement, wholly tender. She met his eyes squarely and waited for him to speak.

'I didn't know that there were girls like you left in the world,' he said slowly, and put up a hand and lifted her chin gently with his forefinger and scanned her face as though he hadn't really looked at it before. 'You've almost restored my faith in women, Abigail.'

He dropped his hand, turned on his heel and was out of the door, wishing her good afternoon in a perfectly ordinary voice before she could draw a difficult breath.

She had no time to ponder his remark because she went to fetch Jude the cat soon afterwards, and when she got back and had settled him with his mistress, Mrs Macklin began at once to talk.

'Sit down, my dear. You must be wondering about me and why I should need a nurse, for I'm sure Dominic neglected to tell you anything at all, except the number of pills I'm supposed to take each day. I was his mother's dearest friend, you know, and when she died I promised that I would keep an eye on him, because I've known him ever since he was a baby, but now I'm older and the boot is on the other foot. It's he who keeps an eye on me now, although I will say that he still listens to me with a fair amount of patience and even takes my advice from time to time. When this silly ulcer business started, nothing would do but that I must go into hospital, and when he saw that medical treatment wasn't going to cure me, he operated himself and insisted on me staying there much too long, I consider. He seems to think that I need a nurse for a short time, though I told him that I was as fit as a fiddle, and now he tells me that he's arranging for someone to come each day and help in the house when you go.' She snorted delicately. 'I never heard such nonsense, though I must admit, my dear, that I'm going to enjoy your company—to tell you the truth, I was just a little nervous, and since he tells me that it will cost me nothing. . . I didn't know that the *Ziekenfonds* paid for private nurses, but they've improved these things so much in the last few years, haven't they, and I've never had occasion to make use of them before.'

Abigail made a sympathetic murmured reply. So that was what the professor had told her patient, and that was why she was to say nothing about fees. He was paying them out of his own pocket. She reflected with brief tenderness upon him, then remarked calmly:

'I'm sure the professor knows best; it really does seem a bit strange when one comes back from hospital. We could use this week finding out just how much you can do without getting tired, don't you think? Then if you have someone in to do the housework, you'll be able to cope with the cooking and perhaps the shopping—isn't that a good idea? Now, shall I get some supper for us—and what about Jude, he'll want a meal, I expect—supposing you sit there and enjoy his company for a while and I'll explore the kitchen.'

Mrs Macklin agreed to these suggestions readily enough and Abigail retired to the kitchen; her patient was more tired than she wished to say, and a week of cosseting would do her good. Abigail nodded her neat head in confirmation of her own opinion and began opening cupboard doors and peering at their contents.

She saw her patient into bed quite early that evening, with Jude on his own shawl at her feet and a bell within reach, and then crossed the landing to her own room. It was extremely small and rather sparsely furnished, but the bed and the chest in the window and the chair beside it were very old and glowing with the loving polishing of many decades of housewives. She undressed slowly, despite the chill, thinking about the professor and wondering what exactly he had meant that afternoon. Why had he lost his faith in women in the first place—or had he been joking? That was unlikely—he wasn't a man to make that kind of a joke. She went downstairs, dressing-gowned and slippered, and had a shower in the cubicle squeezed in beside the kitchen, then crept upstairs again and into bed, her thoughts still centred on him. Perhaps he was in love with someone who didn't love him, although this seemed to her to be quite inconceivable—she was still worrying about it when she went to sleep.

She got up early the next morning to find a light powdering of snow once more and a snarling wind whining round the little square. She made tea and took Mrs Macklin a cup, suitably weak, then let Jude out for his morning prowl. Mrs Macklin, sitting up in bed to eat her breakfast, said cheerfully that she had slept like a top and she hoped that Abigail had too. 'And my dear,' she went on. 'I really cannot call you Nurse or Miss Trent—I shall call you Abigail, such a pretty name and seldom heard these days. Was there a reason for it?'

Abigail explained, and her companion said admiringly: 'What a good idea—how imaginative some people are.' She bit into a slice of paper-thin bread and butter with relish. 'I was sorry to hear about your mother, child.'

Abigail almost dropped an empty porridge plate she was removing to the kitchen. 'My mother?' she faltered. 'How could you possibly know?'

Mrs Macklin gave her an innocent look. 'Dominic told me, of course—should he not have done so?'

Abigail shook her head. 'No, it's not that—it's just that I didn't think he knew. . .!'

'Dominic knows everything,' remarked her patient complacently, 'as you will discover for yourself, no doubt.'

She spent the morning tidying the house and shopping and cooking their simple meal, which they had barely finished when the professor arrived. The visit seemed more social than professional; he greeted Abigail with his usual distant manner and then sat for ten minutes with Mrs Macklin, talking about nothing in particular. As he got up to go he remarked to Abigail, 'I see you brought Jude safely back. You had no difficulty in finding the place?'

Abigail said that no, she hadn't, thank you, and forbore from mentioning that she had had to pay a week's board for the animal before they would let her have him. The professor had paid all the previous bills; he had forgotten this, the final one; a mere thirty gulden for him perhaps, but a large slice of the money she had left in her purse. She hoped that he would remember it when he paid her, for she had given Bollinger most of the money she had earned from looking after Professor de Wit. She still had her fare to England, but not a great deal besides.

He nodded carelessly in reply. 'I imagine Mrs Macklin is going to rest for a couple of hours. Get your hat and coat and I will take you along to see Bollinger—and Annie.'

Abigail opened her mouth to refuse this high-handed disposal of her free time, but was thwarted by her patient.

'What a splendid idea!' declared that lady. 'I shall lie down here on the sofa and take a nap until you return. Run along and put on your things, Abigail, Dominic can make me comfortable.'

Abigail, running a professional eye over Mrs Macklin when she came downstairs again, had to admit that he had done his work very well—the old lady looked not only comfortable, but pleased with herself. She wished her goodbye and followed the professor out of the house and walked with him across the cobbled square and into the car. He didn't speak for the entire journey, and she, who had hoped that perhaps his remark of the previous day might have meant a breaking of the ice between them, was disappointed. They got out, still silent, at his front door and went inside, where he cast his coat in an untidy heap into one of the chairs, his gloves after it, and strode across the hall to the room where she had had tea with Bollinger. And all he said was: 'Bollinger will be in directly,' as he went away.

It was nice to see Bolly again—and Annie, tucked cosily under his arm. They sat by the fire and drank their coffee which Mevrouw Boot had brought to them and Abigail listened to Bolly's account of his day in Friesland and saw how happy he was. It seemed a pity that he couldn't stay for always. She voiced the thought. 'Bolly, if the professor asked you, would you stay here? It's just what you like, isn't it, and it suits you, doesn't it? I should be perfectly all right in England—you know what private nursing is, first one place, then the other. I shall be away from home a great deal.'

He looked shocked. 'Miss Abby, what's ever come over you?' he wanted to know. 'I must own it's nice here, but the other bloke'll be back before long anyway and I doubt if the professor would want me. Besides, we want a home, don't we?'

'Yes, of course, Bolly,' she agreed hastily, 'it was only an idea. How's Annie?'

'See for yourself, Miss Abby. Flourishing, and such friends with Colossus; sleeps with him too, and sits in the dining room while the boss has his meals. He's that fond of her.'

'I'm so glad.' She stroked the kitten on her lap. 'I didn't think he would be—I mean, I knew he'd be kind to her and give her a home...'

'Lord love you, miss, the boss ain't a bit like he seems—very soft-hearted, he is. Does a lot, quiet like, so I hear.'

'I'm sure he does, Bolly—and now I must go because I don't want to be too long away from Mrs Macklin. I'll come again very soon. I still think it would be the best thing for me to go back alone and you follow me when I've found something.'

He nodded reluctantly. 'OK, Miss Abby, anything

you say, and you're to go out the front door, the boss says. Real narked, he was, that you should use the servants' entrance.'

Abigail's nice eyes rounded with surprise. 'Was he? I should think that would be the last thing to worry him.' A thought struck her. 'Bolly, did you tell him much about us—I mean Mother and. . .'

'Only a trifle, here and there, so to speak.'

With which remark she had to be content. She wished him a warm goodbye and went, obedient to the professor's wish, through the house door. At the bottom of the steps stood the Rolls with Jan at the wheel. He got out when he saw her and said: '*Dag*, miss. I take you back, the Professor's orders.'

She wondered how long he had been waiting there and why the professor hadn't told her. Probably he hadn't given it a thought after he had given Jan the order. She got in and immediately embarked on a conversation with Jan in her laborious Dutch, without mentioning his master; she knew without being told that Jan would hear no word of criticism against him.

She was out shopping when the professor called the next day. Mrs Macklin told her in a satisfied voice when she returned that he was sufficiently pleased with her progress to allow her to do a little cooking. 'So I shall cook supper, my dear, though I doubt if I shall feel much like washing up the dishes afterwards. And tomorrow if it is fine, I should like to come with you, just to the grocers in the Begijnsteeg. Dear me, how pleasant it is to get back to normal life, and with you here, not nearly as frightening as I had imagined.' She added hastily as if to explain her change of attitude, 'One gets lazy in hospital and too secure.' She smiled at Abigail. 'How pretty you look in that woolly thing, dear, and such pink cheeks. Oh, I nearly forgot to tell you, Dominic has got someone to do the housework, a Mevrouw Rots, she'll be coming in a week's time. What happens to you then, Abigail?'

'I go back to England, Mrs Macklin.'

'You have a home to go to—relatives?'

'No—cousins in Canada and an uncle and aunt

who don't want to know about me. But don't worry, all I have to do is to go to the agency and they'll find me another job—at once, the same day, perhaps.'

'How appallingly efficient,' said Mrs Macklin dryly, 'and how very dull for you. All work and no play. . .'

'Oh, I daresay I'll take a day off.'

'Big deal,' commented her patient unexpectedly, and Abigail laughed with real amusement. 'That's better. You should laugh more often, Abigail.'

Abigail had nothing to say to this and her companion went on in the most casual manner, 'Dominic doesn't laugh enough either. Did you get all the shopping?'

The day passed at a gentle pace, for although Abigail found enough to do in the little house there was no hurry over the doing of it; during the morning Mrs Macklin told her its history and added, 'I was lucky to get it, because they're really almshouses, I suppose. It's so central and the rent is low—besides, it's close to my friends. Are you going to see Bollinger today?'

'I thought I might go and see how Professor de Wit is—he was my last patient, you know.'

'Yes, Abigail, a good idea. He's an old acquaintance of mine too. Dominic has promised to take me to visit him one day soon—he has been very ill, I understand, but you know more about that than I do. Dear me, how dull life would be for us elderlies if we were without Dominic to keep a watchful eye upon us. He has never allowed me to be lonely—he was fond of my husband.'

Abigail made some reply; Mrs Macklin must know the professor very well; perhaps during this week she might tell her a little of his life. It would be nice to know; she mused over the interesting fact that he appeared to be Doctor Jekyll and Mr Hyde, for according to her patient there never was a better man. Undoubtedly there was a great deal more than met the eye. She said now: 'Bollinger thinks the world of him and I can quite understand why, for he made it possible for him to leave the most dreary room imaginable—he was so lonely, too, and here in Amsterdam he's happy.'

'Yes?' Mrs Macklin sounded interested. 'Dominic mentioned in the vaguest way that he had been lucky enough to find someone to take Jaap's place until he got back to work, but he didn't tell any of the circumstances.' She gave Abigail a shrewd glance. 'Sit down, dear, and tell me about yourself and Bollinger, and your parents too, that is if you can bear with an old woman's curiosity.'

It was a delight and a relief to be able to talk to someone about Bolly and her mother and their life in London and how she missed the hospital; she told about the agency too and made Mrs Macklin laugh with her description of the stern woman in charge of it. At length when she had finished, Mrs Macklin leaned back in her chair and sighed. 'You poor child, life hasn't been very kind to you in these last few years.' She studied Abigail's face. 'But you're not sorry for yourself, are you?'

'No—well, almost never. Sometimes when I see a lovely dress or some fab jewellery, or a girl with everything, you know—lovely face and hair and up-to-the-minute clothes and the men looking at her—then I wallow in self-pity.' She laughed as she said it and her companion laughed with her.

'Bunkum,' said Mrs Macklin firmly. 'Go and put on your hat and coat and visit Professor de Wit and give him my best wishes.'

Abigail spent a pleasant hour with the old man; he was as thin as ever and still pale, but he had lost none of his zest for life; he wanted to know exactly what she was doing and if she was happy, and listened to what she had to say about Mrs Macklin. 'She's a dear,' said Abigail. 'You know with some people you can be friends at once, just as with others it's quite impossible.' Of course she was thinking of the professor and her elderly companion gave her such a penetrating look that she went a guilty red, although he had said nothing, and changed the conversation.

'I'm going back to England next week,' she volunteered.

He looked surprised. 'You'll like that?'

'I—I suppose so. I like Amsterdam, though at first I thought it would be a bit difficult and lonely, but it's not—there are Bolly and Annie and you and Mrs Macklin, as well as the nurses in the hospital.'

She omitted the professor and her listener appeared not to notice, for he said jokingly, 'Quite an impressive list! We shall all miss you. And now, my dear, run along to the kitchen and see if our good friend Mevrouw Valk has made that abominable weak tea I am forced to drink.'

Abigail, who liked her tea strong, sipped the tasteless beverage with him and listened intelligently to his theories on cell life, while at the very back of her mind she wondered what the professor was doing. He was, in fact, in the act of pulling the door bell and appeared a moment later before them, dwarfing everything in the room behind him. He greeted his old friend warmly and Abigail with the cold courtesy she had come to expect. She offered him tea and took care not to catch his eye because she happened to know that he detested weak tea, and this was pale and insipid and, what was more, tepid. She sat for another ten minutes for the sake of good manners, then rose to go with the excuse that she should return to Mrs Macklin before that lady, refreshed from her afternoon nap, decided to do something beyond her strength.

The professor got up too, observing that he would show her out, and when she assured him that she was very well able to see herself to the door, he remarked, 'Don't be bird-witted, I have something to say to you.'

She bade Professor de Wit goodbye with the hope that she would see him again before she left Amsterdam, and went out of the room closely followed by the professor. In the dark, panelled hall which was barely big enough for the two of them, he said to surprise her into speechlessness:

'It is the hospital dance in five days' time. I should like you to come—it is to commemorate its foundation.'

Abigail's heart tripped, steadied and turned right over. She spoke quickly before that treacherous organ should make her change her mind.

'Thank you, Professor, but I don't think I'll accept your kind. . .'

'Why not?'

She stared up at him, looming over her in the dimness and much too near for her peace of mind, trying to think of a really good excuse. 'Well. . .' she began, not having the least idea what she would say.

'Don't tell me that you have nothing to wear,' he remarked with faint amusement, and she, who had been on the point of saying just that, exclaimed roundly, 'Certainly not, I have several. . .' She paused, unwilling to utter such a trivial lie to him. 'I don't know anyone,' she offered with sudden inspiration.

'Me?' he queried.

'Oh, don't be ridiculous!' Abigail's voice was a little gruff and she had the uneasy feeling that she was being rude; all the same she went on: 'You're hardly likely to spend the entire evening. . .' She broke off.

'No, probably not,' he agreed with infuriating readiness, 'but my junior registrar professes a desire to get to know you, and Professor de Wit will be there. . .'

'You're never allowing him to dance?' Her voice squeaked in protest.

'I should have thought a woman of your good sense would have known better than to have asked such a silly question.'

It was annoying to be addressed as a woman of good sense; if that was how he thought of her then she would go to this dance and she would find a dress to fit his detestable opinion. Something grey or mousey with a high neck and one of those awful shapeless draped fronts.

He asked sharply, so that she jumped guiltily, 'What are you plotting? You will buy a dress—pink, I think, deep pink and of a style to suit you. I believe that I shall come with you to buy it.'

'Indeed you will not,' declared Abigail, her fevered imagination picturing him selecting delectable gowns without once looking at their price tickets.

'And who will carry all the parcels?' he enquired silkily. 'There will be shoes as well.'

'No, thank you, Professor, I would far rather go alone—it would be distracting.'

'Do I distract you, Miss Trent?'

She fumed silently at his awkward questions. 'No—yes, I don't know—you see, I shall want to have a good look round first.'

'Yes? I should have thought that you could have found what you wanted within minutes at Dick Holthaus or Max Heymans.' Two dress shops which she, after only a short stay in Amsterdam, had discovered matched high prices with high fashions—they were the sort of shops she would have loved to have gone to. She frowned, wondering how it was that the professor knew about them, and then remembered to look casual as she said carelessly:

'Oh, I daresay they have, but I still want to look everywhere first.'

He opened the door for her. 'As you wish, but pink, remember, and pretty.'

She walked back to the Begijnhof with a head full of ideas pushing each other round and round; she would never be able to buy a dress with the money she had. True, she had been paid the day before, but the professor had obviously forgotten about Jude's fees and she wasn't going to ask him for them. And she, like a fool, had given Bolly half straight away. She could borrow on her fare, for she would be due another week's salary when she left Mrs Macklin and there was still the money from Mrs Morgan, surely waiting for her at the agency. She did some rapid sums in her head, and when she got back to Mrs Macklin, asked that lady if she knew of a dressmaker.

'Of course, my dear,' said that lady without hesitation. 'There's Juffrouw Blik, three doors down—a *dominee*'s daughter and crippled in one foot, poor woman, but charming. Don't be put off at the sight of her, Abigail, she's not a very fashionable sort of woman, but she's very good with clothes, especially with something pretty.'

She gave Abigail a questioning look and was instantly told all about the invitation. 'I'd rather like to have the dress made,' said Abigail, 'then I can get exactly the material and shade I want.' Quite unconsciously she spoilt this by adding, 'Is she expensive?'

Mrs Macklin bent her head over her knitting. 'No, dear, about twenty-five gulden, I should think, and for these days it's ridiculously cheap. Why not go to the Bijenkorf tomorrow and see if you find what you want? I know they have a silk sale on, but there'll be other materials, not in the sale.'

They spent the evening discussing the sale, the dance, the dress, the most suitable shoes to go with it and Abigail's hair.

'Leave it as it is,' urged Mrs Macklin. 'It suits you, it's pretty.'

'Pretty? It's mousy and straight.'

'Mice are pretty little creatures,' her patient pointed out, 'and they have straight hair.' She began to talk about the numerous dances she had been to in her youth and not once during the evening did they mention the professor, although Abigail thought about him a great deal.

She found just the material she wanted in the Bijenkorf—rose pink chiffon and a matching silk to line it, both at sale price too, although even then their purchase made a great hole in her purse. But she was feeling reckless by now; drunk with the prospect of spending an evening in the same company as the professor, she purchased some silver slippers and a handbag and walked back happily clutching her purchases, and after getting the lunch for her patient and herself and settling her for a nap, went to see Juffrouw Blik.

Juffrouw Blik's house was really a flat, for she lived on the ground floor; the floor above was rented to a retired schoolteacher. Her sitting room was the same size as Mrs Macklin's but seemed even smaller, if that were possible, because of the number of half-finished garments hanging around its walls and over the chairs, and the old-fashioned treadle sewing machine taking up all the space under the window.

Abigail, eyeing Juffrouw Blik's dumpy, unfashionable person, felt a little dubious about handing over her precious material to the dowdy little woman, then took heart when she remembered that Mrs Macklin had recommended her very highly. In her difficult, halting Dutch she explained what she wanted, showed the pattern she had bought, made a date for a fitting and, with an eye to the urgency of the matter, allowed herself to be measured.

The dress was a success. Abigail, trying it on the day before the dance, had to admit that the professor's demand for rose pink had been completely justified, for the soft colour of the gossamer fine material gave her face a glow and Juffrouw Blik had cut it with panache so that it fitted where it should and the wide, wide skirt swirled around her as she turned and twisted before the mirror. And to complete the outfit, her patient had produced a Russian sable coat, its Edwardian cut exactly right for the dress, and when Abigail protested that she couldn't possibly borrow so valuable a fur she had declared, 'Nonsense, child—I wear it once, perhaps twice a year—it needs an airing. You will be the belle of the ball.'

At which remark Abigail had looked very doubtful, but since she had been invited to go, the least she could do was to look her best. She had seen very little of him during the past few days—true, he had spoken to her during his visits to his patient, but only upon matters which concerned that lady's welfare. Not once had he mentioned the dance, nor for that matter had he given her any sign that he had invited her to attend, which had such a damping effect on her spirits that by the day of the dance she felt no excitement at all, only a secret fear that he had forgotten all about it, and she would dress and then sit and wait in Mrs Macklin's little sitting room, watching the clock ticking through the hours, and he would never come.

It was the morning of the dance, after he had paid his visit to Mrs Macklin, professed himself pleased with her condition, reiterated that the daily help would come in three days' time and reminding her that she was no longer a young woman, that he turned to Abigail, standing like a silent, well-trained shadow beside him.

'You will be called for at nine o'clock,' his voice was pleasant and completely disinterested. 'The dance will not end until the small hours; if you become tired or wish to return here you have only to say so.'

As though she were an old lady or a cripple like poor Juffrouw Blik! thought Abigail, bursting with indignation. Perhaps he was hoping that once having done his duty in inviting her, she would choose to leave early, leaving him unencumbered to dance with the countless lovelies who would most certainly be there. She said coolly, 'I shall be ready, Professor,' and went with him to the door and showed him out with a convincing and utterly false calm.

She was ready by a quarter to nine that evening; she had cleared away the supper, made everything ready for her patient's night and then gone upstairs to the little room of which she had become so fond, to dress. The result was gratifying; she was no beauty, nor would she ever be, but there was no doubt at all that pretty clothes did a lot for a girl. She had taken Mrs Macklin's advice too, and put her hair up in its usual simple style and used the very last of the Blue Grass perfume she had been hoarding for just such an occasion as this one. Wrapped in her borrowed sables, she stood in front of the mirror and promised her reflection that she would enjoy herself and what was more, stay until the very last dance, despite the professor's offer to send her home early. Anyone would think that I was ninety! she told her face in the mirror. You go and enjoy yourself, my girl.

When the doorbell rang at exactly nine o'clock she flounced downstairs rather defiantly. That would be Jan, she supposed, or a taxi. She flung open the sitting room door, exclaiming: 'Will I do?' and stopped short at the sight of the professor, very grand in his white tie and tails, warming himself before the stove. He inclined his head by way of greeting and said nothing at all, which she found so disconcerting that her defiant mood ebbed away and she looked appealingly at Mrs Macklin, who said satisfyingly:

'Abigail, you'll have a lovely evening, no doubt of it. You look delightful.'

A sentiment hardly echoed by the professor, judging by the expression of his face, for he was glaring down his long nose at her and just for a moment she was tempted to turn round and go upstairs again and tear off her finery and not go at all, but common sense prevailed—there was no reason why she shouldn't have a good time once she got there. She glared at him, disappointment raging under the pink chiffon, to lose all other feelings but one of delight as he told her:

'You take my breath away.' He sounded his usual austere self, but at least he was paying her a compliment. 'I hardly recognised you,' which rather spoilt the compliment, but he actually smiled and she smiled warmly back, her eyes shining. 'Abigail pink and pretty,' he murmured surprisingly, and spoilt that too by adding, 'My registrar will be in the seventh heaven!'

The dance had already started, by the time they had arrived the dance floor was crowded and everyone, in Abigail's feverish imagination, knew everyone else, except her. The professor waited for her while she disposed of the sables and then danced with her. He danced very well, but with a remoteness which was decidedly chilling, so that after one or two attempts at conversation, successfully squashed by his gravely polite replies, she took refuge in silence and was relieved when the dance finished and she was introduced to the junior registrar—a young man of a most friendly disposition even if he was a little on the short side and inclined to be fat. He in his turn introduced her to friends of his own so that presently she began to enjoy herself despite the lack of interest shown by the professor. It was all the more surprising, therefore, when he sought her out and asked her to go in to supper with him. She had already been asked by Henk, the registrar, and was on the point of saying so, for the professor didn't look over-enthusiastic at the prospect of partnering her anyway, when Henk said, 'That's OK by me, Abigail—Professor van Wijkelen has first pick, since he brought you. We'll dance again after supper.'

The professor led her away towards the supper room, chose a small table for two, and only when he had seated her and fetched two plates of food did he speak. 'That was a little unfair of me, I'm afraid,' he observed coolly, 'but I haven't seen you for some time.'

'I've been here all the evening,' stated Abigail flatly, 'and it was very unfair.'

'Meaning that you prefer Henk's company to mine? I can well believe it, Miss Trent—he's still a young man and good fun, I should imagine, do you not agree?'

Abigail bit into a small sausage on a stick. 'Quite nice,' she answered. 'Why do you pretend to be Methuselah? I've no intention of pitying you.' She watched his eyebrows lift and went on recklessly, 'You really had no need to bring me in to supper, you know—I didn't expect it.'

His voice was all silk. 'The reason I did so was because I have something to say to you and this seems a good opportunity to say it.'

Abigail finished the sausage and started on a minute vol-au-vent. Surely he wasn't going to tell her she looked nice, or was being a success or something of that sort? Hardly twice in one evening. She took another bite and asked, 'Yes, sir?' She added the sir from sheer naughtiness because he looked so remote, just as though they were on a ward, discussing a patient and she in uniform. If he preferred her in her cap then she would wear it, metaphorically speaking.

'You leave Mrs Macklin in three days' time,' it was a statement, not a question. 'Unless you are committed to returning to England, you would oblige me greatly by remaining for a further week or so and working in the hospital. There is an outbreak of salmonella on the children's ward, both nurses and patients, I am afraid. We are short of nursing staff as a consequence just when they are most needed. I have a number of beds on the ward and we—that is, I and my colleagues agreed that it would be a good idea if you would be kind enough to help fill the gap while the emergency lasts. You will be paid your usual fee. As to where you will live, I am of the opinion that Mrs Macklin would be delighted if you were to remain with her as a paying guest—and it would be excellent for her to have an interest in life after her long illness.'

How like him, thought Abigail, everything worked out beforehand. She wondered what he would say if she refused. She chose a cheese straw and nibbled at it while she studied him across the table. He looked as impassive as ever, although he was staring at her in a rather disconcerting way. He said suddenly, 'Please, Abigail,' and she gave him a reassuring, almost motherly smile because she sensed anxiety behind the blandness of his face and she loved him far too much to allow him to be worried or anxious even when he was annoying her so excessively.

'Of course I'll come. I like children—besides, it will do me good to do some work for a change. Do you want me to come straight from Mrs Macklin's?'

'Thank you, Abigail. Yes, if you could manage it—I don't know about your days off.'

She shrugged. 'I have plenty of free time and I shall get two days each week in hospital, shan't I? If you will tell me the name of the ward to go to and what time.'

'The Beatrix ward, it's in the oldest part of the hospital, on the top floor. Could you manage ten o'clock? I'll see Zuster Ritsma—you will do staff nurse's duties, of course.' And when she nodded briefly, he went on:

'Can I get you anything else to eat?'

She shook her head; he had got what he wanted—he hadn't eaten anything himself, probably he was waiting to take one of the pretty girls she had seen him dancing with down to supper—it had been an excuse to get her alone and pin her down. 'When did the epidemic start?' she asked him.

He looked faintly surprised. 'Six days ago.'

The day before he had invited her to the dance. She managed a smile as she got up and her voice was a little high. 'Well, I think I'll go and find Henk—he'll be looking for me. . .' Which wasn't quite true but saved her pride a little, only to have it trampled upon a moment later by the professor.

'You look charming, that dress is most becoming.' He smiled a little as he spoke and she was conscious of a stab of humiliation. As they went back to the dance floor she said a little unsteadily, 'You didn't have to say that—I would have come to the hospital without any—any softening up.'

It wasn't until that moment the idea took shape that the whole thing had been a softening-up process—the invitation to the dance and the interest in what she would wear, being fetched by him and danced with and supped with. She went a little white and said in a voice that was almost shrill:

'Oh, there's Henk—I daresay I shall see you later.' She smiled with forced gaiety, ignoring the fact that the professor was about to say something, and lost herself in the crowd.

She danced for the rest of the evening and once more with the professor, with whom she kept up such a steady flow of chatter that he was hard put to it to get in a yes or no. He did indeed manage to say:

'There is something I should make clear. . .' before she interrupted him with: 'Oh, please need we talk shop—I'm having such fun.' She spoke to his shirt front in a brittle voice and avoided his eye, fearful that he was going to pay her another insincere compliment or launch into her hospital duties, neither of which she felt she could bear at that moment.

She had spent some time with Professor de Wit, sitting in a good deal of state, surrounded by friends and admirers and watching the dancing with a good deal of amusement. He welcomed Abigail with a delighted smile and urged her to sit with him. 'You look delightful my dear,' he said happily. 'What a pretty girl you are, to be sure—that pink dress is just your colour,' and he spoke with such sincerity that she very nearly believed him. 'You have danced with Dominic?' he asked, and she said yes, she had, and wasn't it a fab dance and how was he feeling. They talked cosily together until several elderly gentlemen, heavily bespectacled and delightfully mannered, presented themselves with the wish to spend a little time with their old friend, but on no account must the young lady feel called upon to desert them. Which she rightly interpreted as a flowery way of hinting that she should go. Which she did, leaving them prosing gently over Professor de Wit's book, oblivious of the gay scene around them. She was dancing the last dance with Henk when he remarked:

'We shall be seeing you in a day or two, so the Prof tells me. He's got beds in the other wards as well, but Children's is his pet. Very soft-hearted is our Prof, though you wouldn't think it sometimes—got a tongue like a razor and a voice like a deep freeze most of the time.' He glanced at her and added, 'He's a fine man, though. I wouldn't like to work for anyone else.'

Abigail nodded understandingly. 'I'm sure you wouldn't. I've seen some of his kindness.'

There wasn't much kindness evident in the professor's face when they met presently, however. She was wrapped once more in the sables, her plain little face radiant with the pleasures of the evening and her modest success. She saw him waiting by the entrance and exclaimed as she reached his side,

'Oh, it was fun. Thank you very much for inviting me.'

'You thank me when you believe that I did it merely to—what was the expression? Soften you up? How generous of you, Miss Trent!'

He led the way to the car and she got in silently and sat, still silent, while he drove through the quiet streets of the city to the Begijnsteeg. They didn't speak as they got out of the car either. They were half way across the square when at length he broke the silence, at the same time coming to a halt in the dim light of the street lamps.

'I wished to say something to you, to explain, while we were dancing, but I was unable to get a word in edgeways for your ceaseless chatter. I shall do so now, at the risk of us both catching a chill, but as the cold will doubtless preclude you from either interrupting me or answering me back, I feel the risk is worth taking.'

Abigail, from the depths of the sables, eyed him with her mouth open. She had become used, in the last few weeks, to the professor's deliberate way of expressing himself, and indeed, could not imagine him doing anything else, but she hadn't liked that bit about the ceaseless chatter, although she was fair enough to own that it was perfectly true. 'Yes, sir?' she prompted him encouragingly.

'Stop calling me sir,' said the professor nastily. 'You do not need to throw my age at me every time you open your mouth.'

Abigail, perhaps because it was darkish and his face was in shadow so that she couldn't see its usual harsh expression, said boldly:

'Don't talk rubbish! You're far too sensitive about your age—you're in your prime and extremely handsome and you must know that women adore men who are a little bit older.' She stopped, appalled at her own words, and hastened to rectify her mistake by adding belatedly, 'Well, most women.'

'Are you toadying to me?' he asked her in a dangerously quiet voice.

'Toadying?' She was breathless with rage now. 'Why should I toady to you? You—you. . .' the rage went as suddenly as it had come. 'I was trying to help you,' she said sadly, 'but I see I've made a mess of it.' She moved away a few steps, towards Mrs Macklin's house. 'I'll say good night.'

'No, you won't, not until I've done. You were wrong this evening. I wasn't—er—softening you up, I wouldn't stoop to such a trick. I meant what I said too—you do look pretty in that pink gown, it becomes you and you are charming. You're charming in whatever you wear.'

She couldn't see his face properly, but it didn't matter. She could hear the sincerity in his deep voice and her heart sang, she wanted to throw her arms around his neck and hug him, but all she said was: 'Thank you, Professor' in a voice devoid of all expression. 'I'm glad I was wrong.'

They walked on and at the door he took the key and opened it for her, then with it still in his hand stood looking down at her.

'Thank you for coming,' he said, and now his voice wasn't cold or austere but warm. 'I told you, did I not, that you had almost restored my faith in women. You have done more than that; you have restored my faith in human nature.'

He bent his head and kissed her on her mouth, a little awkwardly as though he hadn't had much practice at it lately. She longed to return his kiss, but didn't; with a murmured good night she slipped inside.

She had a great deal to think about, she decided, as she crept up to her room—the professor's contradictory behaviour for a start. Why was it that at times he looked at her as though he disliked her—no, it wasn't dislike, it was disquiet, as though he expected her to do something which would upset him, and on the other hand, at times he was charming and more than that. She paused on the top step of the precipitous staircase and remembered his kiss. Out of gratitude perhaps, her common sense urged her, and indeed, when she got to her room and viewed herself in the mirror she had to admit that common sense was right; the sables were magnificent, but her face was still unremarkable and her hair had become loose. She lacked glamour or whatever it was that made a man kiss a girl. It had of course been almost dark—she smiled a little bitterly; in daylight she would have stood no chance at all.

CHAPTER FIVE

THREE days later she reported for duty at the hospital. Mrs Macklin had received her news with glee and an instant offer of her room. 'Because, my dear,' she explained, 'it would be so very pleasant to have you living here. I know I'm perfectly able to manage for myself now, but I do so enjoy your company.' She added that Abigail was to consider the house as her own home and if she wanted to ask Bolly round at any time, she was to do so, and anyone else she liked to invite.

'I don't know anyone else,' Abigail pointed out.

'That nice surgeon you were telling me about?' enquired Mrs Macklin, 'or perhaps one of the nurses—or Dominic.'

Abigail had made some sort of a reply, trying to imagine herself inviting the professor round for tea. He had paid his usual visits during the three days, of course, and he had been pleasant enough, though a little distant, and she had caught him eyeing her warily; probably wondering to himself what on earth had possessed him to kiss her; wondering too how she would react to it. Well, she had no intention of reacting at all, she resolutely buried the memory of it under the activities relative to her removal to hospital, and if her thoughts were wistful, she took care that they didn't show.

She had paid a visit to Bolly, of course, carefully choosing a day when she knew the professor to be operating and therefore away from home. She and Bolly, in company with Annie and Colossus, had tea in the little sitting room and discussed the turn of events.

'Things are looking up,' declared Bollinger, well content. 'I must say I like this city, Miss Abby, and you look pretty bobbish yourself. I hope you stay a week or two at the hospital.'

A sentiment to which Abigail heartily subscribed!

The sister of the children's ward was glad to see her; her staff had been severely depleted by salmonella, and worse, several of the small patients were ill with it too. The ward was closed to outsiders; a great effort was being made to find the source of the infection, but as Zuster Ritsma explained, it wasn't so easy, for this wasn't the salmonella due to infected food, which would have been comparatively easy to trace, but an insidious type so that a nurse would be working on the ward, unaware that she was already infected.

'I hope,' she continued in her excellent English, 'that you are a strong girl, Nurse Trent.' She eyed Abigail's small, nicely plump frame with some uncertainty, and Abigail made haste to assure her that she was as strong as a horse and very healthy. Zuster Ritsma took her word for it. 'At least I am grateful to have another nurse on the ward,' she observed with relief, and proceeded to delve into the report, carefully explaining each case as she went. It took some time, and when she had finished, Abigail followed her round the ward and in and out of the glass-partitioned cubicles.

The ward was full, with the infected children away from the rest at the end of the ward—six of them, in various stages of illness, three with drips up and the other three, Zuster Ritsma said, getting better. There were four more suspects in the next two cubicles, and in the last large cubicle there were four babies, each isolated and each very ill. They were post-operative and all were infected. They lay making no sound, dangerously lethargic. Zuster Ritsma adjusted a drip and said, 'We shall save them all, but it will be much hard work.'

She smiled at Abigail as she spoke, and Abigail, who liked her and sensed her anxiety, agreed bracingly. 'What do you want me to do?' she asked.

'These babies. There are four, you see. It will be a heavy task, but if you would stay here, in these cubicles, then the other nurses can stay in the ward.' She picked up a chart and they bent over it together while she explained what had to be done. 'If you need help, I will come—there is a bell and an intercom—also a red light. The night nurse comes on duty at ten o'clock—we work in three shifts.' She hesitated. 'Would you work until then, do you think? Just for today—I have no nurse until tomorrow, and the professor insists that there are *gediplomeerd* nurses.'

'Yes, of course I will, and if this doesn't go on for too long surely two of us could manage between us—I'm quite willing if the night nurse is.'

Zuster Ritsma brightened. 'Oh, that would be excellent. But I do not know if Professor van Wijkelen will allow it.'

'Does he have to know?' asked Abigail. 'As long as there's a nurse here—we can have the time made up to us later. After all, we shall each get twelve hours off and the sick nurses will be coming back in a few days, won't they?'

'It is, how do you say? emergency,' mused Zuster Ritsma. 'You do not dislike?'

'No, I don't dislike,' Abigail agreed quietly, 'and I don't suppose he'll notice.'

But her companion shook her head at this rash statement. 'The professor notices everything.' She was very positive about it.

He came half an hour later, looking thunderous, but not, Abigail guessed, because he was annoyed, rather because he was deeply worried about the infection on the ward, especially the babies, each of whom he had operated upon for pyloric stenosis and who should have by now been on the way to recovery. He ground to a halt beside Abigail and wished her a good morning in a voice which implied that as far as he was concerned there was no such thing, and then, with Zuster Ritsma by his side, examined the babies one by one with meticulous care, throwing suggestions and orders at Henk as he did so. Abigail stood silently by, wishing that she could understand even a quarter of what he said; and in the end she had worried unnecessarily, for he repeated everything he had said to the other two in clear and concise English as he dealt with each baby.

When he had finished he came and stood beside her, looming large in his gown and mask. 'You're quite happy to be doing this work?' he wanted to know, and he sounded so irritable that she wouldn't have dared to say anything but yes, though that was the truth anyway.

'You're off duty,' he snapped at her. 'There is a grave shortage of nurses for a few days, but I have asked for extra staff. You will take your usual time off, Nurse.'

Abigail said, 'Yes, sir,' before Zuster Ritsma, who was looking guilty, could speak; if there were extra nurses, well and good, otherwise they would carry on as she had suggested and he would be none the wiser. This thought allowed a look of complacency to cross her grave face and he was quick to see it. 'Why do you look like that?' he demanded, 'as though you had been clever about something.'

Abigail gave him an innocent look. 'Me?' she asked. 'What have I to be clever about?'

He grunted, nodded briefly and went away, followed by Henk, who winked cheerfully at her as he passed. She was left on her own then, busy with the babies—their drips, their charts, their tiny, feeble pulses, their unhappy vomiting and the continuous cleaning up and comforting. When Zuster Ritsma did appear again she looked as agitated as someone so calm could look.

'The nurses—the professor asked for them, you know? Two of them have the first symptoms. . .the other one has gone home at a moment's notice because her mother is ill.'

'That's OK—we'll carry on as we said we would, shall we, Zuster? Provided the night nurse doesn't mind, I certainly don't.'

The professor came again in the afternoon, looking preoccupied, but beyond studying the babies' charts and altering his instructions accordingly, had nothing to say to her. And early in the evening Henk came and stayed for ten minutes or so and, unlike the professor, asked her if she was managing and was there anything she needed. She was feeling a little tired by now and longing to get out of her enveloping gown and mask; she hadn't had them off since she had been relieved for her dinner; tea had been brought to her on a tray and she had had it while she wrote up the charts.

It was a quarter to ten when the professor came again. Only his eyes showed above the mask, staring at her coldly, although he had nothing to say until he had examined the babies at some length. But presently he straightened himself, professed satisfaction that they were at least holding their own, and then in a voice of withering chill demanded to know when she had been off duty.

'Well,' said Abigail carefully, 'you see, it's like this—I haven't. It seemed a good idea.'

'You disregarded my instructions, Nurse Trent?' His eyes narrowed. 'No, don't interrupt me. I am not in the habit of having my wishes ignored.' He went on disagreeably but without heat, 'I asked you to come to this ward to help out temporarily, nothing more. When I need advice from you concerning its management, I shall no doubt ask you. Until then, be good enough to refrain from interfering.'

Abigail adjusted a drip to a nicety and said kindly, as though she were reasoning with a bad-tempered child, 'There's no need for you to get into a nasty temper, Professor. You know very well that everyone here falls over their own feet to satisfy your every whim, and don't pretend you don't. Zuster Ritsma carried out your orders to the letter, but she couldn't prevent two of the nurses due on duty from sickening with salmonella, nor could she stop the third one from going home to look after her ill mother. She was so worried that I suggested that the night nurse and I should do a twelve-hour stint each until there are more nurses. That's all—nothing to lose your cool over.'

She stopped abruptly; she had said much more than she had intended, and none of it very polite. He was, after all, a consultant in the hospital and a well-known surgeon. She met the stare from his blue eyes and tried not to feel nervous.

'I have not—er—lost my cool, Miss Trent—it is not in my nature to give way to my feelings, although I am bound to plead guilty to a bad temper.' His eyes gleamed above the mask and she wondered if he was laughing, but decided that it was most unlikely. 'I am indebted to you for your help and I apologise for jumping to conclusions. I will see that your off-duty is made up to you as soon as it can be arranged.' He turned and walked away as silently as he had come, leaving her feeling bewildered. She had expected a good telling off at the very least; instead he had been—what had he been? It was difficult to know, but she suspected that he had been amused at her outburst.

The night nurse came and they spent the next twenty minutes poring over charts and studying the babies together, until finally Abigail was free to leave the ward. She tore off her gown and mask, threw them in the bin and hurried to the changing room where she took off her uniform and cap and tugged on a skirt and sweater without much attention as to how she looked, bundled her hair up under the woolly beret, flung on her coat and made her way to the front entrance of the hospital. It was very dark outside and the wind seemed, if anything, more bitter than a month ago when she had first arrived in Amsterdam.

The winter was lasting a long time; she tucked her chin into her scarf and started down the steps.

The Rolls was at the bottom of them and the professor was at the wheel. He got out when he saw her and she made to pass him with a cheerful good night, but he put out a hand and stopped her. 'Get in,' he said.

There was nothing she would have liked more than to have sunk into the comfort of its leather-covered interior, but perversely she replied, 'The walk will do me good, thank you, sir. I need the exercise.'

Wasted breath. He urged her gently towards the open door. 'This is hardly the time of day to go walking around,' he said testily. 'As for exercise, we shall consider that presently.'

She saw that she had no chance against him. She got in and sat silent, fuming at his arrogance and wondering what he had meant about exercise. The journey was a short one. He turned the car silently into the Begijnsteeg and stopped and ushered her out, to fall into step beside her. 'I also need exercise,' he stated, and took her arm to lead her across the silent square. Abigail thought at first that he would stop at Mrs Macklin's door, but he didn't pause, striding briskly along, and she, perforce, keeping pace with his large well-shod feet. He didn't speak for a few minutes and nor did she; for one thing she had been surprised into speechlessness by his action and for another she was far too busy with her thoughts. She had been rude to him in the ward, so probably he was going to give her a telling-off. She sighed without knowing it and braced her tired shoulders.

He spoke at length. 'Have you the door key?' and when she said that yes, she had, he fell silent again. It must have been five minutes later before he asked her, 'How much terramycin are we giving Jantje Blom?'

Jantje was the smallest and the frailest baby. She told him the amount and they went on walking briskly over the cobbles, the wind creeping meanly through her coat so that she shivered.

The professor stopped and peered down at her in the dim light. 'I haven't done this for a long time,' he remarked thoughtfully, and she, thinking that he was talking to himself, said soothingly: 'No, I don't suppose many people do,' and was amazed when he burst into a bellow of laughter so that she said: 'Oh, hush, you'll wake all the old ladies!'

She shouldn't have spoken like that, she supposed, she stood still, waiting for him to snarl something nasty about young women being pert, but all he said was: 'That isn't what I meant, but you don't understand, it doesn't matter at the moment. I'm sorry I was ill-tempered this evening.'

'You had every right to be,' said Abigail fairly. 'I was abominably rude.'

'Yes. I didn't mind—at least you're honest.' His voice sounded bitter and she made haste to say, 'I expect it's worrying for you,' and he laughed again softly; she wondered why, shivering with cold, and he said at once,

'God, I'm thoughtless—you're cold.'

'Yes, but I enjoyed it.'

'Not if you catch a chill.'

She shook her head in the dark. 'I'm very tough.'

He walked her briskly to Mrs Macklin's house. 'Your spirit's tough,' he corrected her.

The house was in darkness. They stood very close in the hall while she found the light switch and then led the way to the kitchen, where, to her surprise, he said, 'I'll get the tea,' and sat her down by the table against the wall. Presently, with the teapot between them, sitting opposite her in one of the narrow wooden chairs, he began to discuss her small patients, and although she was very tired by now, she listened intelligently and even ventured one or two opinions of her own as to their treatment. It was a surprise to her when the Friese clock on the wall chimed midnight, and it surprised the professor as well. He got to his feet with the remark that he should be shot for keeping her from her bed, and although she protested, he washed the cups and saucers and tidied everything away before putting on his topcoat and going to the door. Abigail got up too, because she would have to lock it after him, and followed him out into the hall, but when she put out a hand to switch on the light his large one came down on hers and prevented it. 'No need,' he said very quietly, then caught her close and kissed her, and this time, she thought confusedly, he must have been putting in some practice. He was through the door and down the steps with a muttered good night before she could utter a word.

She went on duty the next morning with her thoughts in confusion—she had been too tired to do more than tumble into bed and fall asleep the night before, and there had been no time to think in the morning for Mrs Macklin had been full of questions about her work as they sat at breakfast together. Only at the end of Abigail's recital of the day's happenings had she said with something like complacency, 'I heard you come in last night, my dear, but Dominic was with you, wasn't he, so I knew you would look after yourselves and there was no need for me to come down.'

'Professor van Wijkelen was kind enough to bring me home,' said Abigail, with a composure she didn't feel. 'He came in for a cup of tea. It was very cold yesterday, wasn't it?'

Her companion ignored this red herring. 'He works too hard,' she observed, 'and I daresay he's worried about this infection—whatever it is. I hope you won't catch it, Abigail.'

Abigail assured her that she wouldn't, cleared the table, washed up, wished Mrs Macklin goodbye and set off for hospital. She went the long way round so that she could have a quiet think as she went, but somehow only one thing occupied her thoughts and that was the professor's kiss. As she went through the hospital gates she wondered how it would be when they met.

It needed only one look at his face as he came towards her in the ward to see that they were back to square one. He looked withdrawn and tired; she wasn't sure how old he was, but today there were lines she had never noticed before. He bade her good morning with the austere good manners which so daunted her, and went at once to work on the four babies.

They were a little better, she reported, her disappointment well hidden behind a professional manner not to be faulted. She gave chapter and verse of their progress during the night and since she had been on duty, adding that Jantje was not responding quite as well as the other three. His mother, she informed the professor, was waiting in the visitors' room on the landing and hoped for a word with him. He nodded without looking at her, got out his stethoscope and when he spoke again it was only to give her further instructions, and presently when Henk joined them, the two men talked together in their own language and it was Henk who turned to her at last and detailed the new treatment the professor had decided upon for Jantje. They went away together, with a cheerful wink and smile from Henk and the briefest of nods from the professor.

It wasn't until after the list that the professor came and then it was almost six o'clock, and although they discussed Jantje together he had little else to say. After he had gone she wondered sorrowfully what it was she had done to cause him to change so towards her. She had actually believed that at last he was beginning to like her, or at least to tolerate her, but she had been wrong. She tended the babies carefully and tried not to think about him.

Off duty at last, she changed rapidly, a little uneasy about the walk back to the Begijnhof; there was no bus going near enough to make it worth while to take one; it was only ten minutes' walk, but it was dark outside and looking out of the window she could see sleet beating upon it. She would get wet. She hurried through the hospital, her mind busy trying to remember some other way home which would save her going through the narrow dark lanes.

Long before she had reached the front hall she had

given up the idea; the day had been long and she was tired and the effort was too great. She went through the door and down the steps and the sleet bit into her face like miniature knives and forced her to close her eyes. When she opened them a few seconds later, the Rolls was within a few feet of her and Jan was already getting out and holding the door open for her to get in. He said cheerfully, 'Good evening, miss, I am to bring you to Mrs Macklin's house.'

'Oh, Jan, how lovely! But who. . .? Did Professor van Wijkelen tell you. . .?'

'Yes, miss.'

His tone was fatherly and final, and indeed Abigail was too tired to argue. She sat back in her seat beside him, wondering why the professor should take care of someone he could barely greet civilly; perhaps he was afraid that if she was out in the rain and caught cold, she would be of no further use to him—but that hadn't bothered him the previous night. Because she was tired and rather unhappy the memory of it brought tears to her eyes, and when the car stopped she thanked him in a quiet, normal voice and would have got out, but he got out too and started to walk with her across the cobbles. When she protested, he said merely, 'The professor told me to, miss,' and waited while she went up the steps before he wished her good night and walked away, back to the car.

She hadn't expected Mrs Macklin to be up, but that lady popped her head out of the sitting room as she went into the house and without appearing to notice her woebegone expression, said cheerfully, 'There you are, dear—I didn't feel like going to bed, so I've made a jug of cocoa for us both. You're tired—come in by the stove and be warm and comfortable for half an hour.'

She turned her back and went and sat down again, leaving Abigail to take off her outdoor things and brush away the tears. When she was sitting opposite Mrs Macklin in the comfortable warmth of the little room, her companion asked, 'A bad day?'

'No, not really,' Abigail admitted. 'Three of the

babies are much better and the fourth will do, I think, and there aren't any fresh cases today and none of the contacts are proved positive—I should think the worst's over. Henk seemed to think so—they've found the source—one of the porters.'

'Did you see Dominic?'

'Yes, he came to see the babies.'

'I heard the car—he didn't come in this evening.'

'No, Jan brought me home, actually. I hadn't expected. . .he was waiting for me. . .the professor had sent him.' Abigail drew a determined breath. 'Mrs Macklin, why is he so—so considerate of me, and yet he doesn't like me at all?' She sighed, took a sip of cocoa and looked enquiringly at the older woman.

'I've been hoping you would ask me that,' said Mrs Macklin surprisingly. 'I didn't feel I could tell you, but now that you've asked—' she nodded her grey head in satisfaction. 'One can't gossip about one's friends, but there comes a time. . . The reason Dominic dislikes women is because he mistrusts them—young women, that is.' She waited expectantly for Abigail to say something.

Abigail poured more cocoa for them both; all she said was: 'You're sure you want to tell me?'

'Oh, yes, I'm going to tell you, my dear—he's far too nice a man to be misjudged, especially by you, Abigail.'

Abigail let that pass. Mrs Macklin went on: 'He's—let me see turned forty now. When he was a young man, in his early twenties, he married—a lovely girl, tall and dark, I remember she was most arresting. I don't think that for one moment he loved her—infatuated perhaps, and that passes for love for a little while, doesn't it? She was the kind of girl men fall for, and because Dominic was young and handsome and knew everyone, as well as being a wealthy man—you knew that, Abigail?—she married him. Within a few weeks he discovered that she was having affairs; before six months were out she was killed in a car crash with her current boy-friend. Dominic changed from that day—oh, he wasn't brokenhearted, he had long since lost all feeling for her, but his pride was hurt. He was still charming to the girls of his acquaintance, but it was as though he had resolved to live his life without them. He had—still has—his work. It absorbs him, doesn't it, and always will. Mind you, he keeps his true feelings well hidden,' she paused, 'at least I always thought so, but now I'm not so sure—he goes out a great deal, because he has many friends and he's well liked. He's still a very good-looking man, of course, he has almost everything; looks, brains, an excellent position in life, more money than he knows what to do with—but no love.'

Abigail's hands were clasped so tightly round her cup that the knuckles showed white. She said in a tight little voice, 'Yes,' and went on inconsequently, 'He loves little children, and he's good to his patients; they trust him. It's very sad that he has no one to love and won't allow anyone to love him.'

Mrs Macklin gave her a long thoughtful stare. 'Very,' she agreed, 'especially as every female under forty who can get within striking distance of him has done her best to remedy that fact.'

Abigail, who seldom blushed, went becomingly pink. 'Oh, is that why he?—surely he would never think that I—he gets irritated with me, all the time—well, almost all the time,' she amended truthfully. 'I didn't know—I'll try and keep out of his way as much as possible. Perhaps he'll meet some girl who can make him happy. I hope so.'

She got up and went to the kitchen with the cups on a tray. 'You could make him happy,' her heart urged her silently, 'because you love him.' She drowned the lunatic thought with a gush of water from the tap and washed the cups and saucers with a deliberately empty mind, and when she went back to the sitting room, beyond thanking Mrs Macklin for her confidence, made no reference to their conversation. Instead she enquired how her companion felt and listened sympathetically to Mrs Macklin's small grumbles about her health. They went to bed soon after that, and Abigail lay trying not to think about the future, because it would be without Dominic and she couldn't imagine it without him, even though, because he had been let down once, so long ago, he wouldn't even allow himself to like her. After all, she told herself wryly, she had got used to his irritable manner and cold voice by now; they made no difference to her feelings, and now that she knew their reason, she wouldn't mind any more—well, not very much.

The days, with their strict routine and small crises, came and went. The weather became steadily worse, with little flurries of wet snow and leaden skies. Abigail's boots leaked and she didn't dare to buy another pair, since she had, as yet, had no money for her first week's work at the hospital and paying Mrs Macklin had made a hole in what she had. Possibly she would be paid when she had finished working for them, and borrowing from Bolly was out of the question, anyway. She didn't intend seeing him until the salmonella scare was over. The situation was improving fast now, although there were still a number of nurses off duty, but there had been no fresh infection for some days. The babies were out of danger too, although they still had a long way to go and needed a great deal of care. She had become very fond of them and delighted in their progress; even little Jantje was improving at last.

It was in the middle of the second week of her job at the hospital that the professor arrived alone one afternoon. He examined the babies, studied their charts and path lab reports, expressed his satisfaction and then asked her: 'When do you intend to revert to your normal working hours, Nurse Trent?'

She kept her voice coolly friendly. 'Tomorrow, sir. Zuster Ritsma may have told you that there are two more nurses returning to duty, and another one at the end of the week. Is it true that the ward is to come out of isolation in a day or two?'

'Yes. Which duty will you be taking?'

She knew that too, but she wasn't going to tell him. 'I'm not sure—Zuster Ritsma has it all arranged.'

'Your days off?' he persisted.

'I'm to have those as soon as possible. Zuster Ritsma has kindly said that I may choose.'

'Have you any plans for them? Do you wish to go away, or spend some time with Bollinger? He can be spared.'

'That's very kind of you. I hadn't begun to think about it. I think I should like to take him out for the afternoon—he loves the cinema.'

He looked at her unsmilingly, his eyes thoughtful, and she was hopeful that he had remembered that she was owed a week's salary, but all he said was, 'I see,' and stalked away.

She was to do an early shift; half past seven until four each day, and as the professor invariably came before noon and after five, it meant she would see him only once a day, and not at all on operating days. Which, she told herself, was all for the best. It would leave her evenings free to keep Mrs Macklin company too and she could call and see Bolly on her way off duty. An excellent arrangement for all concerned, she reiterated, and began to wonder how much longer they would need her in the hospital.

She had mentioned it tentatively to Zuster Ritsma over coffee and had been told kindly that the professor had arranged that she should work there and would doubtless tell her when he no longer needed her. 'Although,' Zuster Ritsma had added, 'I hope it won't be just yet, for we shall be short-staffed for another week or so yet.' Abigail hugged that fact to her as she went about her work.

It had surprised her that Jan came to fetch her each evening; she had thanked the professor on the day following the first occasion and he had looked down his nose at her and remarked rather testily that as there were so many nurses off sick, it behoved him to take care of those who weren't. So she hadn't mentioned it again, but it was nice to find Jan waiting for her in the cold dark and she was secretly glad that she didn't need to walk alone through the dim, deserted lanes around the hospital.

She was a little tired on the morning of her new shift; it had meant getting up at six o'clock to get her breakfast and take Mrs Macklin a cup of tea before she left the house, and she had been late off duty the evening before, but she cheered up as she walked along the familiar little back ways in the semi-dark, replying to the milkmen and postmen and paper boys' cheerful *Goeden Morgen*, as she hurried by. The night nurse was cheerful too, for the night had been without worries. The babies were asleep, so Abigail helped with the older children's breakfasts, laughing a good deal with them because half the time she couldn't understand what they were saying and when she spoke herself they found her accent so comical. Jantje woke up presently and she went to give him his bottle. He was very slow still; she sat on the low chair by his cot, cuddling him close and encouraging him while he blinked up at her with eyes still lacklustre from his illness. 'Beautiful boy,' she urged him, 'drink up like a good lad.' She kissed the top of his small bald head. 'I wish you were mine.'

'You like babies—children?' The professor's voice sounded harshly from behind her and the bottle jerked in her hand so that Jantje, sucking half-heartedly, stopped altogether.

'Yes,' said Abigail, and hoped that he couldn't hear the uneven thud of her heart, and then to Jantje, 'Come along, my lovely boy, it's good for you.'

'No,' said Henk from the doorway, 'it's Guinness that's good for you, is that not so?' It sounded funny in his strongly accented English and she gave a chortle of laughter and laughed again when he said, 'Since he seems to understand English, can you not also say, "Time, gentlemen, please?"'

'That's an idea, he's such a slowcoach.' They were both standing by her now and she looked up and smiled, to meet Henk's cheerful face and the professor's bleak stare, which she ignored, saying cheerfully, 'He's better, isn't he, sir?'

'Yes, Nurse Trent.' He turned away to examine the other babies as Zuster Ritsma joined them and they all talked babies for a few minutes while Abigail coaxed the last of Jantje's feed into him and popped him back into his cot. She was about to pick up the next baby when Zuster Ritsma said, 'Nurse Trent, there are nurses returning, is it not good? Today at one o'clock there will be two, one will work here tomorrow and you will take a day off. There are three days due to you, is it not, but the others you shall have when you wish. The professor wishes it so.'

Abigail looked at the professor who was frowning at nothing in particular. When he looked at her the frown turned into a scowl. 'We are still not fully staffed,' his voice was stiff. 'I do not wish you to be overtired, otherwise you will be of no use here. Also it is convenient.'

'Charming!' Abigail's voice rang with annoyance. 'Such thoughtfulness does you credit, I must say.' Her usually soft voice had an edge of sarcasm. 'It's nice to know I'm useful, even if only as a cog in your machine.'

She would have liked him to have looked uncomfortable or even ashamed—had she not, only the day before, told him that she was to choose her days off?—and now they were being thrust upon her without a by-your-leave. He appeared to be neither; there was a gleam in his blue eyes which might have suppressed temper, but his expression remained bland; beyond a faint lift of the eyebrows he might not have heard her. She turned her back, picked up the baby she was going to feed and bore it away to change its nappy. She hated him! The hate lasted a good five minutes and was then wiped out by a flood of love which made nonsense of her own bad temper and his own disregard of her as a person. She fed the baby and thought of all the good reasons why he should be so horrible, then forgave him for all of them.

He didn't come again that day. The two nurses, Zuster Vinke and Zuster Snel, came on at noon; the three of them worked together until it was time for Abigail to go off duty.

It was still cold and it didn't seem to have got light all day and now that was fading, making the lighted shops she passed seem very cheerful. Almost home, she stopped at a *banketbakkerij* and bought some crisp little biscuits, which would be nice for tea, for she had no doubt that Mrs Macklin would be waiting for her. She couldn't afford the biscuits, her store of money was now so low that even that small luxury was an extravagance, but she was feeling reckless and a little defiant. She turned into the square with the windows of its little houses shining a welcome, her head full of plans for the next day. She wouldn't be able to do much—visit Bolly, naturally, and perhaps take Mrs Macklin to see Professor de Wit. He didn't live very far away; she wondered uneasily if it was too far for the old lady, or would she have to have a taxi? She decided to break into her fare which she still had saved; after all, she would be paid soon, especially as she made up her mind, there and then, to ask about it at the hospital the moment she returned.

She opened the little house door and shut it thankfully upon the dark outside, calling, 'It's me, Mrs Macklin,' as she cast her outdoor things on to the banister of the little staircase. 'I'll get the...' she began as she went into the sitting room, and stopped, because the professor was standing before the stove.

His 'Good evening, Miss Trent,' was very stiff. 'I am just about to go—I am already late. I called to see how Mrs Macklin does and find her very well, so well, in fact, that she is going on a small outing tomorrow. There is a concert of Viennese music tomorrow evening in the Concertgebouw which she is anxious not to miss. Perhaps you would care to accompany her?' he added carelessly. 'I don't suppose you are interested.'

'Why should you suppose that?' enquired Abigail, falling neatly and unwittingly into his trap. 'I should enjoy it very much!'

'Yes?' If she had any doubts about accepting, the

one syllable would have decided her; it contained enough faint mocking disbelief to furnish a whole scathing sentence.

'Yes,' she reiterated, and realised too late why he had been so adamant about her day off—she would be company for Mrs Macklin who he would not wish to go alone. If it hadn't been that she liked her erstwhile patient far too much to disappoint her, she would have said a decided no. She gave the professor a smouldering look and saw that he knew exactly what she was thinking. She said hastily before her temper got the better of her, 'Shall I get the tea, Mrs Macklin? And does the professor intend to stay?'

It seemed that he didn't. She showed him to the door, wished him a chilly goodbye and went to put the kettle on.

They had almost finished tea, talking trivialities in which the professor had no part, when Mrs Macklin observed, 'Dear me, Abigail, I almost forgot. Dominic asked me to tell you that Jan would be here with the car at ten o'clock tomorrow morning and he will take you wherever you wish. Dominic will be away all day and if you would care to lunch with Bollinger at his house, he hopes that you will do so—he has already mentioned it to Bollinger, I believe.'

Which meant, thought Abigail, that Bollinger would be expecting her and she couldn't disappoint him. She might as well go straight there in the morning; it would be pleasant to have a long talk to him and having lunch there would solve the vexed question of her shortage of cash. Perhaps the professor was making amends, although he hadn't seemed particularly friendly just now. On the contrary; he had got his own way again. She said aloud, 'That will be very nice. I would have gone to see Bolly anyway, but I had thought that perhaps you and I could have gone round to see Professor de Wit in the afternoon.'

'A very kind thought, Abigail, but as it happens, he will be at the concert with us, so we shall be able to have a good chat there. I'm greatly looking forward to it. What will you wear?'

'Oh, lord,' exclaimed Abigail, dismayed, 'I haven't got anything—at least only a very plain velvet dress—it's brown and I've never liked it. I only packed it at the last minute because I thought it might be useful—it's that sort of a dress. Will it do, you think?'

'I'm sure it will. You're not a girl to need frills and flounces. Look how well that pink dress becomes you, and that's simple enough.'

Abigail agreed reluctantly and wished wholeheartedly for a new dress, although no one would see her at the concert and her two patients were much too kind to criticise her appearance. 'What will you wear?' she asked in her turn. The two ladies spent a delightful evening discussing clothes.

By the time Jan came she had breakfasted, taken Mrs Macklin hers on a tray, tidied her own room and dressed herself ready to go out. The weather showed no signs of improving, but in the comfort of the big car, it didn't matter. She spent the short journey practising her Dutch upon Jan, who obligingly corrected her many mistakes and helped out when she lacked a word. She thanked him nicely, as she always did, when they arrived at the professor's house and got out, to be admitted by a delighted Bollinger.

It was only a week or so since she had seen him, but it seemed much longer than that. He led her into the small sitting room and poked up the bright fire in the grate, then went away to return a few minutes later with a tray of coffee and with Colossus and Annie at his heels. They made much of her and then planted themselves side by side before the fire.

'Regular little charmer, is our Annie,' observed Bollinger, 'makes rings round the boss, she does, sits on his lap the instant he takes a chair. Lucky Colossus don't mind—fair spoils the little beast does that dog.'

'I'm glad. She's quite a beauty now she's plump and well fed. And now tell me, Bolly, how are you getting on?'

She listened patiently to the recital of his days. Not exciting, but she could see that he had enjoyed every minute of them, and when he had finished she explained carefully about not getting her pay and why she couldn't give him any money. As she had known he would, he offered to lend her all he had, but she refused gently and with gratitude, telling him that she would certainly be paid at the end of the week. And that awkward fact negotiated, she went on to give him a lighthearted account of her own week, making it out to have been much easier than it was.

Bolly, who was no fool, shook his elderly head and said, 'It can't have been much fun, Miss Abby—the boss told me each evening how you was getting on—real hard work, he said it was, and you not saying a word of complaint.'

'Well,' Abigail replied reasonably, 'I really didn't have much to complain about, you know,' at the same time swallowing surprise because the professor should have said that.

There was a great deal to talk about. Somehow sitting there in the comfortable room, life seemed suddenly secure and pleasant, with the dog and kitten between them and the cheerful firelight turning the silver coffee service to gold; for all the world as though it were home, thought Abigail wistfully.

Presently Bolly went away to return with Mevrouw Boot, both carrying loaded trays, the contents of which they proceeded to arrange on the small rent table under the window, and when, after a short chat, the housekeeper went away, Bolly said diffidently: 'Miss Abby, here's your lunch. The boss said you was to have it here. I usually eat with Mevrouw Boot, but the boss, he suggested you might like me to stay with you.'

'Well, of course I should love you to stay,' Abigail went round the table to give the old man a hug. 'You're my friend, Bolly, I don't know what I'd do without you.'

He beamed at her. 'That's the very words the boss used,' he commented, and pulled out a chair for her to sit down.

'Oh?' she tried not to sound interested. 'Did he?'

Bollinger placed a pipkin of soup before her and removed its lid, and its fragrance caused her small nose to twitch in anticipation of it.

'That's right,' he agreed. 'He's a fine gentleman, is the boss, once you get to know him.'

And that was something in which Bolly had been more successful than she—for she didn't know him at all and it didn't seem likely that she ever would. She sighed, dismissed the unhappy thought and applied herself to her soup.

They went for a walk when they had finished lunch, taking Colossus with them and leaving Annie curled up before the fire, and although it was cold and windy, Abigail enjoyed it, just as she enjoyed the tea they found waiting for them when they got back, for it was like the teas she remembered when she was a child—hot buttered muffuns in a silver dish, tiny sandwiches and a sponge cake as light as a feather.

'What a marvellous cook Mevrouw Boot is,' she commented, licking a jammy finger.

'You're right there, Miss Abby—made the muffins, she did. The boss said you was to have a good English tea—muffins, he says, and an English cake, and see there's plenty of milk in the jug. We done our best.'

'It's marvellous,' Abigail praised him, much struck by the professor's attention to detail—for instance, knowing that there was never enough, if any, milk served with tea in Holland. 'I must go to the kitchen and thank Mevrouw Boot.'

Which she did before setting out for the Begijnhof once more, after promising that she would meet Bolly for coffee in a day or two's time.

She found Mrs Macklin in her bedroom, doing things to her hair.

'Heavens, am I late?—it's not till eight o'clock, is it?—there's still supper. . .!'

'Yes, dear,' said Mrs Macklin, 'there's plenty of time. I thought I'd get all ready except for my dress; I can put that on after supper. *Erwten* soup—it's been on all the afternoon—and yoghurt for afters.'

'Very nice.' Abigail, who wasn't fond of pea soup, remembered her splendid lunch, went downstairs again to lay the supper table.

She dressed after supper when everything had been tidied away and she had laid her breakfast ready for the morning, but first she fastened Mrs Macklin into the handsome black dress, laid the table wrap ready and then went to her own room. Twenty minutes later she was standing before her mirror, eyeing her reflection with distaste, intent on her face and quite failing to see that the brown dress matched her eyes exactly and showed off her pretty figure to advantage. She had made up her face with care and had done her hair with even more attention to detail; now she put on her tweed coat over the despised brown velvet and went downstairs. She found Mrs Macklin already there, looking very *grande dame*, even though, as she pointed out to Abigail, she had lost so much weight that the dress was loose-fitting.

'And mine's a little too tight,' said Abigail, 'which is far worse.' She looked down at her person rather anxiously. 'I hope the seams don't pop. How lucky there won't be anyone there to see, though I expect you'll be bound to meet someone.'

'Certainly,' said Mrs Macklin, and her dark eyes snapped with amusement, but Abigail, with her head twisted over one shoulder trying to see if she looked all right from the back, missed that.

They were to be fetched by Jan, who would collect Professor de Wit first, Mrs Macklin told her and at ten to eight, Jan rang the door bell and escorted the older lady to the car, while Abigail made a few last-minute arrangements for Jude's comfort, she hurried after them and got into the seat beside Jan, leaving the two older members of the party to greet each other on the back seat and then talk non-stop throughout the entire short journey.

Jan seemed to know exactly where they were to go. He gave Mrs Macklin an arm up the stairs in the Concertgebouw, and Abigail, her arm tucked protectively in Professor de Wit's, followed him happily.

They had a box and once the party was seated Abigail looked around her with a good deal of interest.

The auditorium was full and, from what she could see of the audience, it was smartly dressed. It was all much more splendid than she had anticipated and she thanked heaven silently that the brown dress, although not exciting, was at least passable, but she forgot that presently when the music started. She was sitting beside Mrs Macklin with an empty chair beside her, but she forgot her companions too, leaning forward, her elbows on the red plush of the box, her chin in her hands, staring down at the orchestra. It was the faintest of sounds which caused her to turn her head. Dominic van Wijkelen was sitting beside her in the chair which had been empty; he nodded briefly into her surprised face and became at once absorbed in the music, and most unreasonably the thought that she might just as well not be there for all the notice he had taken of her crossed her mind, then she stifled a laugh, because she herself had been completely absorbed not a minute since, and anyway, what was there about her to rival the music? She focused her attention once more and found that although the magic was still there it was tempered by the presence of the professor, sitting so close and so withdrawn.

The music came to an end and the lights went up and in the general buzz of clapping and talk the professor got up and went to bend over Mrs Macklin's chair; he didn't take his seat again until the lights were lowered and he hadn't spoken one word to Abigail. She sat like a statue, wondering if she hadn't been meant to come with Mrs Macklin—whether she had misunderstood, and this, mixed with a rising hatred of the miserable brown dress, caused her calm face to assume an expression of extreme disquiet, which was perhaps the reason for the professor to place a hand quietly over her own, clasped in her lap. The expression on her face turned to one of great surprise; she turned her head slowly to look at him, her mouth a little open, her eyes saucer-round, and met a look to melt her bones, a look she had only seen on his face when he had been bending over a patient—kind and gentle and faintly smiling, and when she attempted to pull her hand away, he merely held it in a firmer grip, and the smile widened. There was nothing to do but leave it where it was, tear her gaze away from his and stare at the orchestra below.

He gave her her hand back when the lights went up and asked, still smiling: 'You are enjoying your day off, Abigail?'

She found her voice, a little high and squeaky. 'Yes, thank you. It was lovely to see Bolly—thank you for letting me spend the day at your house and giving me lunch and tea.'

'A pleasure which I was unfortunately prevented from sharing,' he replied. 'What do you think of our Annie?'

They talked about commonplace things and soon her heart stopped its absurd racing, and she was able to tell herself that probably the music had made him feel romantic and she was the nearest woman—a tale which held no water at all when presently the lights went out and he possessed himself of her hand again.

The evening was like a dream—a dream from which she had no desire to waken, but the concert came to an end and Abigail put on the serviceable winter coat once more, took Professor de Wit's old arm and walked slowly in the wake of the others, down to the car. Jan wasn't there this time. The professor stowed his passengers comfortably and got behind the wheel himself, disentangled the Rolls with remarkable patience from the multitude of cars around them and drove without haste through the city. They had stopped before his house before Abigail had even begun to wonder where they were going, and she found herself, in company with the two older members of the party, being ushered into the welcoming warmth of the hall, where Bolly, who had opened the door to them, took their coats and invited them to enter the drawing room—a room Abigail had not yet seen. She smiled at Bolly and paused a moment to have a word with him before following the others inside, and became aware that the professor was beside her, but beyond giving her a quick glance he didn't speak to her but to his guests in general.

'It seemed a good idea if we had a drink and a sandwich before we part,' he said pleasantly, and piloted them to the chairs scattered around the great fireplace, and as though she had been given her cue Mevrouw Boot came in with a trolley and Bollinger behind her.

Abigail, eating tiny hot sausages, *bitterballen* and vol-au-vents and drinking the Cinzano she had asked for, made conversation with Professor de Wit and contrived at the same time to look around her. The room was large and lofty with an ornate plaster ceiling and panelled walls painted white, divided by gilded columns. The floor was completely covered by a fine carpet of a delicate, almost faded pink, and the chairs, of which there were a considerable number, were upholstered in a variety of shades in that colour, as well as muted blues and greens. There was a chandelier hanging from the ceiling's centre, reflecting light into every corner, and a number of matching wall chandeliers. The curtains were of the same dull pink as the carpet, and the only dark colours in the room came from the paintings on the walls, family portraits and landscapes for the most part. It was a delightful room, restful as well as beautiful; it made her feel dowdy, and the knowledge that her host's eyes were upon her did little to make her feel anything else; she and her brown dress stuck out like a sore thumb in the beautiful pastel-tinted room. She turned her shoulder to the professor and listened attentively to the old man's dissertation on the music they had been listening to.

They stayed an hour before the professor drove them home, Professor de Wit first, to be handed over carefully to the ministrations of Juffrouw Valk and then on to Mrs Macklin's house. The professor accepted Mrs Macklin's offer of a cup of coffee with the air of a man who had had no refreshment for a considerable time, and sat down to talk to her while Abigail went to the kitchen to make it. But Mrs Macklin took only a few sips, declaring that she was now too tired to enjoy it and would go to bed at once, but despite this she refused Abigail's help, merely allowing her to help her off with her dress when she got to her room and then sending her downstairs again. Abigail had expected the professor to be on his feet, coated and ready to go home, but he was still sitting where she had left him, and now as she entered he got to his feet and fetched the coffee pot from the top of the stove and refilled their cups. Abigail sipped in silence, while her thoughts, like mice on a wheel, spun round, trying to find a suitable topic of conversation.

There was no need. The professor put his cup down and said in the kind of voice he used when he was giving her details of a patient: 'You look very pretty, Abigail.'

He was of course either being kind or joking—she thought the former. She was not in the least pretty, certainly not in the brown velvet. Probably her nose was shining too. She said in a small voice:

'Thank you, I don't know why you said that because it's not true, but thank you all the same.'

She gasped when he answered her blandly, 'No, it's not true. You're not pretty, you're beautiful, because you're honest and kind. I told you, did I not, that you had restored my faith in women, and now I'm a little afraid.'

'Why?'

'Because it may not be true. . .'

She got to her feet and walked over to him. 'It's quite true,' she assured him, and smiled up into his face. She only just stopped herself in time from telling him how much she loved him. But perhaps he didn't want love—not from her—perhaps she was just a stepping stone to some other girl, a girl who really was pretty and led his kind of life. She kept the smile there, though, and he smiled slowly back, towering over her. For the third time he kissed her, and this time it was a kiss to keep her awake for a very long time after he had gone.

CHAPTER SIX

SHE was talking to Henk when the professor came on to the ward the next morning. They had been laughing about something or other together and she turned a still smiling face to him, and although her good morning was quiet, her eyes were warm; a warmth dispelled instantly by the austerity of his face and his own dry, 'Good morning, Miss Trent.' He looked as though he had been up all night, she thought, which might account for his withdrawn air. When he asked for the reports on the babies, she gave them in a brisk friendly voice, not smiling at all. Perhaps when Henk went. . . Henk didn't go; he suggested it, for he was wanted on another ward, but the professor told him rather sharply to remain where he was, so that it was impossible to say anything, even if Abigail had known what to say. Which she didn't.

After a night of thinking, sometimes very muddled because she had dozed off from time to time and the thoughts became dreamlike and quite unmanageable, she had come to the conclusion that in some way she had been the means of making him realise that not all women were like the girl he had so disastrously married. She doubted if he had any feeling for her—gratitude perhaps, a slow dawning friendship which was destined to come to a premature end once she was back in England, and right at the back of her mind, hardly to be thought of, was the possibility that he had, much against his will, fallen a little in love with her.

She watched him stalk away from the ward after

a blandly polite goodbye and admitted that the possibility of him entertaining any feelings for her was so slight as to be non-existent. She picked up Jantje and put him on the scales. He was beginning to gain weight now and looked like a baby once more. He smiled windily at her and she said aloud:

'He's going to send me away, dear boy. I'll bet you my month's money on it, for either he has set his sights on some blonde lovely and wants me out of the way, or I embarrass him.'

She was right, of course. She didn't see him the next day and the following afternoon, just before she was due off duty, he turned up, with Henk and Zuster Ritsma. The babies were examined, a fairly short business now, and then he turned round to address Abigail.

'We seem to be over our emergency, Nurse. I must thank you for your help, we are all deeply appreciative of it. Shall we say that you can go at midday tomorrow?'

She had expected it, and now it had happened it wasn't as bad as she had thought it would be. She said matter-of-factly, 'That suits me very well, thank you.' She glanced at him and managed to smile briefly, then found his eyes upon her in a thoughtful stare. But when he spoke it was abruptly. 'I'll say goodbye, Nurse.' He offered his hand and she took it and remembered vividly how he had held it at the concert and how, later, he had kissed her. She smiled again, too brightly, quite unable to speak.

Mrs Macklin, when she was told, was so astonished that she could think of nothing to say for several seconds. 'I thought you would be here for weeks—months even,' she managed at last. 'I knew you wouldn't be at the hospital for ever, but Dominic always has so many private patients and he has often told me how difficult it is to get a nurse for those who want to stay at home. You're not mistaken, my dear?'

'No, I expected it—at least for the last two days I've been expecting it.'

'Since we went to the concert,' commented Mrs Macklin sharply.

'Well, more or less.' Abigail got up from her chair, 'If I'm to leave at midday I'll go back to England by the night boat, if I can get a ticket.'

It would be better that way, for she would be able to sleep on board and when she got to London she could go straight to the agency and get another job. She went up to her room and started to pack in a halfhearted fashion. She would have liked a good weep, but there was really no time; she had to see Bolly before she went and got her ticket and say goodbye to Professor de Wit, and what was the use of crying anyway? She screwed up the brown velvet dress into an untidy bundle and rammed it into her case. She didn't care if she never wore it again, but the pink dress she folded carefully in tissue paper and tucked it away, out of sight, under her spare uniform. It was a pity, she told herself, that she couldn't tuck her dreams away as easily.

She left the hospital the next day, handing over to the nurse who was to relieve her before going to say goodbye to Zuster Ritsma, who shook her fervently by the hand, wished her well and told her that any papers concerning her work would be posted on and what was her address.

Abigail gave the name of the agency, and when Zuster Ritsma, not quite understanding, persisted that she wanted Abigail's home address, explained that just for the time being she had no home. Zuster Ritsma, the eldest of a large family to whose welcoming bosom she retired on her days off, gave her a deeply pitying look, and Abigail, to forestall the sympathy she could see in the sister's eye, asked for her money.

Her companion looked blank. She knew nothing about it, she said. She had understood that the professor would be paying her as he had engaged her in the first place.

'I think you had better ask him, Nurse Trent—if

you would like to go to the consultants' room and see if he is there?'

Abigail liked no such thing; to ask him meekly for her salary after he had so thankfully wished her goodbye was more than enough. She had just sufficient money to get to London and a pound or two besides; she would manage until he sent it on to her. In any case, she consoled herself, Mrs Morgan's money would have arrived at the agency by now. There remained only Bolly to worry about; she was glad now that they had already discussed her return to England, leaving him behind for a little while. She made her way to the house on the *gracht*, doing hopeful, inaccurate sums in her head.

Bolly was surprised and disconcerted at her news. 'A bit quick,' he observed. 'I don't like the idea, Miss Abby—you on your own.'

'But, Bolly,' she made her voice reasonable and cheerful too, 'we did agree that it was the best thing, remember? I shall be quite all right, with any luck I'll get a job straight away and then I can start looking for a flat. I shall be much happier knowing that you're here while I'm doing it.'

And seeing Dominic each day, she added silently. Still determinedly cheerful, she went on: 'I must go now, Bolly dear. I'll write to you the minute I get fixed up, I promise.' She gave him an affectionate hug, bade farewell to Annie and Colossus and went round to Professor de Wit's house, where she told him her news and wished him goodbye. Unlike Bollinger, the old man didn't seem in the least surprised to hear that she was leaving.

'A natural sequence of events,' he called it, and when she enquired what he meant he told her she would have to wait and see, but she could mark his words. Abigail smiled and murmured and decided he didn't mean anything at all; he was old and so clever as to be a little eccentric at times. She kissed him goodbye with real affection.

She had plenty of time when she got back to Mrs Macklin's. The boat train didn't leave until the late evening. She ate a simple supper with Mrs Macklin, who was frankly tearful at the prospect of her leaving and only cheered up when Abigail pointed out that she would most certainly return one day, 'For if I can come once I can come again,' she pointed out, knowing that she never would, because then she might meet the professor again and she wouldn't be able to bear it. A clean break, she told herself silently, was by far the best.

She cleared the supper things away and made coffee, then sat by the stove, chatting with false gaiety until it was time for her to put on her outdoor things and fetch her case. She had refused Bolly's offer to take her to the station; he was an old man and she didn't like the idea of him being out in the cold darkness. She would go to the Spui and find a taxi. She told Mrs Macklin what she was going to do as she went to the door. It opened as she got to it and the professor, looking more irritable than ever, came in. He said without preamble, 'I intended to take you to the boat, but I'm expected in theatre in an hour. I'll take you to the station.'

Abigail frowned. How like him to be so awkward; they had said goodbye—not a very pleasant one, but still goodbye, and here he was again, just as she had schooled herself to be sensible about the whole wretched business.

'Please don't bother,' she told him, a little stiffly, and noticed as she said it how tired he looked. 'I was just on my way to get a taxi.'

He couldn't have been listening, for he took her by the arm and walked her back to where their mutual friend was sitting, calmly knitting as though she had the house to herself. The professor greeted her briefly and said smoothly, 'I was just telling Abigail that we must leave in five minutes.'

'Clever,' thought Abigail. 'Now he's got her on his side', but aloud she said, 'I'm most grateful, sir,' in the kind of voice she used on the wards when she addressed consultants. She saw him wince, which quite pleased her, and brightened still more when the idea that he might be going to pay her crossed her mind. She bade Mrs Macklin goodbye and followed him out on to the cobbles to the waiting car. The drive would take five minutes, perhaps a little longer, so there would be no need to talk—a view, apparently, not shared by her companion, however, for once he was behind the wheel he began testily:

'I find it impossible to talk to you, but there is something I must make clear. I have been deeply appreciative of your work for me—you are an excellent nurse, I can think of no one I would rather have to care for anyone I—loved. I should like you to remember that, Abigail.' He halted the car at the traffic lights. 'There is another thing I must say. My behaviour may have taken you by surprise—indeed, I am surprised at myself. I haven't been—sentimental for years. I intend to forget it and I hope that you will too.'

They had arrived at the Centrale Station. Before he could do anything, Abigail got out of the car, beckoned a porter, opened the car's door, hauled out her case, gave it to the man and then thrust her head through the window. She spoke in a voice thick with tears, and a little wildly.

'What a lot of fuss you make about nothing—nothing, do you understand?' and marched away without looking at him once.

London looked bleak and grey when she arrived the following morning. She got up early and went along to the restaurant and made an early breakfast; she wasn't hungry, but it was cheaper than having it on the train.

She took a bus from Liverpool Street to the agency and sat down thankfully in the waiting room. There weren't many other people there—the two girls who went in ahead of her came out looking so cheerful that she took it as a good omen when her own turn came. The stern woman hadn't changed in the least, unless it was to look rather more stern. She gave Abigail a sharp glance, said 'Good morning, Miss

Trent,' and handed her a bill. 'I understand that after the case you accepted from us you worked independently in Amsterdam.'

Abigail, a little overcome by so much efficiency, said a polite good morning and that yes, she had, and took a look at the bill. It wasn't much, Mrs Morgan had only lasted three weeks, but seven pounds and fifty pence would just about take all the money she had. With commendable calm she asked, 'Is there a letter for me? Mrs Morgan—my patient—said she would forward my fare. . .but she forgot.'

The severe woman smiled thinly. 'Yes, I have a letter for you here.' She opened a drawer and handed Abigail an envelope and waited while she opened it. The cheque was inside. 'Perhaps you would like us to put it through the bank for you?' she enquired.

'Oh, please,' said Abigail thankfully. All at once the woman looked quite human. She paid the commission at once and stuffed what was over into her purse; it was amazing how much better she felt. She still had only enough to live on for a week, but a lot could happen in that time.

'Have you a case for me straight away?' she asked.

The woman shook her head. 'I'm not sure, but I think not,' she got up and thumbed through the filing cabinet. 'There are several nurses wanted urgently for mental—you're not trained for that?'

'No, only general.'

'A pity. It's most unusual for us not to have a number of cases waiting.' She resumed her seat and picked up her pen. 'Come in again tomorrow morning, Miss Trent,' she advised, 'there will probably be something.' Her gaze swept over Abigail. 'You don't mind where you go?'

Abigail thought of Bolly. 'London or somewhere not too far away,' she said slowly, and added a polite good morning as she went out.

She went to the Golden Egg again because her case was heavy, and ordered a cup of coffee. She could of course apply for a job in hospital—her own training school would take her back, she supposed, but then what about Bolly? It was impossible, after seeing his happiness in Amsterdam, to condemn him to some back room again; besides, if she went back into hospital she wouldn't be paid for a month and how was she to manage in the meantime? She brooded over her coffee and then went out into the street once more. She had to find somewhere to sleep for the night—one night, she told herself bravely, there would be a job for her in the morning. She found a small hotel not too far away and left her case in her room, then spent the rest of the day looking in shop windows and eating as economically as she could at Woolworth's cafeteria.

She was early the next morning and the first to go in. She could hardly believe her luck when she was asked if she would go to Virginia Water as a companion nurse to a widowed lady who was, most regrettably, suffering from delirium tremens. It would involve some night work, but there was daily help for the rough; the pay was twelve pounds a week, all found. It sounded ghastly, and Abigail had her mouth open to say an emphatic no when the woman behind the desk got in first with the news that there was nothing else at present and she was under the impression that Abigail wanted work as soon as possible. 'You can always give it up after two weeks,' she told Abigail. 'If you leave before that time, I'm afraid we take you off our books.'

Abigail thought rapidly. It would certainly be an awful job, and very underpaid, but it would be a roof over her head. On the other hand, something much better might turn up in a day or two and she would miss it.

The woman at the desk tapped her fingers impatiently on the desk. She asked sharply: 'Well?'

Abigail started to get up. She ignored the other woman's frown and began 'I. . .' but was interrupted by the telephone.

She stood patiently while her companion lifted the receiver and stated who she was. After a minute she took the receiver from her ear. Her voice was frigid.

'This call is for you, Miss Trent. Most irregular, I cannot think what made you give this number.'

'But I haven't! I don't know who would want to...' Bolly? the professor? Hardly. She took the receiver and said worriedly, 'Hullo.'

The professor—and speaking as though they were on the ward, together by a patient's bed while she listened to his instructions. 'Abigail? How fortunate that you should be there. You have no case yet?'

She shook her head, just as though he were there to see, and then said faintly: 'No.'

'Good. I want you for someone special—my niece, in Spain with her parents.'

'Your niece?'

'My niece—kindly don't interrupt me. Two weeks ago she swallowed three coins, pesetas. She was X-rayed and my sister was assured that nature would take its course. Unfortunately this has proved to have been too hopeful a view. She is now vomiting and dehydrated, and an operation is necessary. My sister refuses to have anyone touch Nina but myself. I intend going to Spain and bringing her back with me to hospital here. I should like you to come with me. You would be expected to remain in hospital with her until she is fit enough for her father to come and fetch her back. You will be paid expenses and your usual fees.'

The silence between them was profound until Abigail heard him explode with: 'My God, I haven't paid you!'

She said, 'No,' and waited, listening to the rush of her heartbeats; she was so happy at that moment that she would gladly have agreed to work for nothing.

His voice again; unhurried, concise. 'Abigail, you will go to Coutts' Bank,' he gave her the address, 'and ask for Mr Cross. Take your passport with you. He will pay your expenses for the journey and the salary which I owe you. It is Wednesday—there is a Swedish Lloyd ship sailing for Bilbao at six o'clock this evening from Southampton, you will have plenty of time to catch it. I will arrange to have your ticket ready for you. I will meet you when you dock in Spain. Is there anything else you wish to know?'

There was a great deal; she remembered that she hadn't agreed to go. Of course she would, but it would have been nice if he hadn't taken it for granted that she would come running.

'Abigail?'

'Yes, Professor.'

'Will you do this for me? Nina is very dear to me—she must have only the best—you remember what I said?'

High praise indeed and, she supposed, better than nothing.

'You have no other case?' he asked again.

'No—that is, I was just going to accept one, but I hadn't actually said that I would.' She looked across at the severe woman, silently fuming behind her desk, and watched her close the folder containing the widow with delirium tremens. She said, 'I'll be glad to help,' and heard him sigh.

His voice sounded very clearly. 'Abigail? I'm sorry—about your salary. I should have remembered—I was worried. Why didn't you ask me?'

She didn't answer but asked instead, 'Would you do something for me, please?' She heard his grunt and took it for yes. 'Tell Bollinger.'

'I have already done so—it was he who furnished me with the address of the agency. I will see you on Friday morning about seven o'clock.'

He rang off with a brief goodbye which she had no time to answer and she looked across at the severe woman, who looked positively grim. 'The idea,' said that lady, 'you have been on that telephone for more than five minutes! Heaven knows how many calls. . .'

'I'm sorry,' said Abigail, finding it impossible to feel anything else for the poor creature, condemned no doubt to spend the rest of her days at a dreary desk instead of going off to Spain to meet the only person in the world who really mattered. 'They'll ring again,' said Abigil kindly.

'I take it that you have accepted a post not connected with this agency?'

'Yes—I worked for a Professor van Wijkelen in Amsterdam—there is a case in Spain which he has asked me to take.'

The older woman stared at her. 'At least you're a sensible girl,' she offered. She meant plain, both she and Abigail knew it, but there was no point in being rude.

Abigail smiled, not minding in the least, and bade the woman good morning, then skipped out of the agency, still smiling. She went back to the hotel, told the desk clerk that she wouldn't want her room for another night and went upstairs to review her wardrobe. She had left her trunk at Bolly's lodgings, so presumably it was still there. She repacked her case; she would go and forage through her clothes, leave the pink dress in the trunk and then go to the bank. During the bus ride she occupied herself trying to guess what the professor would have done if she hadn't been at the agency when he had telephoned. Presumably he would have gone on telephoning at intervals throughout the day. She wondered, too, how long it would take him to go to wherever it was they were to meet in Spain. Bilbao was in the north, she knew that, he would drive through France and return that way. She hoped the little girl wasn't too ill, and became engrossed in trying to remember the treatment for such cases. As far as she knew they could be serious but not fatal; once the coins were removed the child should recover rapidly. She wondered why the mother didn't take the child to Amsterdam herself—after all, the professor was a busy man and it was quite a journey. She got off the bus pondering, and rang the bell of the shabby little house where Bollinger had lived.

Her trunk had been stored in a cupboard-like room, too small to take a bed. She sorted out what she wanted to take with her, packed the pink dress away in the trunk, gave the brown velvet to the daughter of the house, and left again. It was ten past twelve when she reached the bank, by now beset with the fear that no one there would know anything about her and what on earth was she to do if they didn't?

She was wrong—she had only to mention her name to the imposing messenger at the door to be whisked into an enormous room, occupied by a small, bewhiskered man who leaped to his feet as she was ushered in and offered her a chair.

He gave only a cursory glance at her passport and embarked at once upon the matter in hand. 'Professor van Wijkelen is an old and valued client of ours,' he said by way of opening, 'we are only too glad to oblige him in any way.' He rang a bell and a clerk slid in, laid a folder before him and slid out again.

'We have arranged for you to collect your ticket at the Southampton Docks office,' he began. 'Take a taxi from the station, Miss Trent, the driver will know where to take you. Here is your train ticket from Waterloo, and I have been asked by Professor van Wijkelen to remind you to take tea on the journey. Here also are the expenses for your journey and the salary due to you. If you would be so kind as to check the amount?'

Abigail, a little overawed by such smooth, effortless efficiency, did as he asked. There seemed to be much too much money. She said so and the bewhiskered gentleman smiled kindly at her. 'No, no, dear young lady—your salary, money in lieu of days off and spending money for your journey. There are bound to be a few comforts you will require on the journey.'

Champagne with my early morning tea, for instance, thought Abigail, feeling lightheaded. The professor must have extravagant girl-friends if that was the amount he found necessary for a two-day journey. She frowned, uneasy about the girl-friends. She put the money carefully into her handbag, promising herself to keep strict account of what she spent and to return the surplus when she met the professor, wished her new-found friend goodbye and was ushered out with grave courtesy.

She spent the next two hours shopping. Over a slightly extravagant lunch she made a list of things she needed and then made a beeline for Marks and Spencers. She had prudently left her case at Waterloo Station; now she wandered uncluttered from one counter to the next, making her choice. She settled finally for a pleated tweed skirt in a warm brown and oatmeal with a matching brown sweater and a gay little neck scarf. She bought a plain wool dress too, a soft blue, nicely cut and easily packed, as well as some undies. Lastly she bought an overnight bag with a wide zippered mouth so that she would be able to get at things easily while they travelled. She went back to Waterloo then, had a cup of tea, fetched her case and joined the queue for the train. It wasn't until she was handing her ticket to the collector at the barrier that she noticed it was for the first class.

It was pleasant to travel in such comfort and when the steward came along and asked her if she would like tea, mindful of the professor's instructions, she said yes. She had barely finished it when the train was at Southampton. It was in the taxi that she realised that she knew very little about the journey and still less about her destination. The professor hadn't bothered to tell her where they were going or how long they would stay, nor indeed, if her memory served her right, had he told her anything other than the bare bones of the case. But at the ticket office she found that she had underestimated him, for with her ticket was a long envelope addressed to herself. Abigail put it into her handbag and once inside her cabin, sat down on the bed to read it.

It was, naturally enough, typed and signed by Mr Cross and obviously made up from the professor's instructions. She was not to stint money upon her enjoyment during the short sea journey, it was stated. She would be met at Santurce at half past seven on Friday morning and she would be good enough to leave the ship at this hour, go through the Customs and contact the professor, who would be waiting for her. If by any chance he was not there, she was to go to the waiting room and remain there until he was. Their destination was his sister's house, situated some kilometres from Baquio, a small seaside resort half an hour's run from Bilbao. Probably they would stay the night there, but it might be necessary to leave before this; it depended on the child's condition. The return journey would take two days, if all went well. She was wished a pleasant journey.

She read the message through twice, then folded it neatly and returned it to her handbag. Presently, when she had unpacked, she would find a map and find out exactly where she was going. In the meantime she explored her cabin, a large and airy one on the promenade deck with its own tiny shower, and most adequately furnished. Even if she had been a fussy girl, which she was not, she would have had a job to find any fault in it. She put away her few things and went along to find out about table reservations, then wandered about the ship. It seemed half empty, which in mid-February was to be expected, but the restaurant, when she went along for dinner, seemed comfortably full. She shared a table with a young married couple and a man of about her own age, on his way out to Guernica where, he informed her, he had something to do with the tourist trade. And when she mentioned, almost apologetically, that she had never heard of that city, he spent the rest of the meal describing it to her, and a host of other, smaller towns besides, and when they adjourned to the bar for their coffee he obligingly found a map and explained exactly where she was going. It seemed natural enough to dance for a little while after that and they parted on excellent terms, with an agreement to meet before breakfast and walk the decks. All the same, it was of the professor Abigail thought as she got ready for bed.

The sun was shining the next morning and although the sea looked cold and the ship was rolling a little, the idea of exercise was inviting. Her companion of the evening before was waiting for her, and they walked briskly, arm-in-arm, pausing every now and then to view the vast, empty sea around them before going down to breakfast. They spent the rest of the morning lounging about on the comfortable promenade deck, reading and talking and playing the fruit machines. Abigail wasn't quite sure if she wasn't wasting the professor's money on them, although he had told her to have anything she wanted; when she won a minor jackpot, her relief was profound.

They went to the cinema after lunch and Abigail watched the film without seeing it because the professor's handsome, remote, ill-tempered face was printed indelibly beneath her eyelids. And the evening, although pleasant, went on for ever. She retired to her cabin as early as she decently could and hardly slept for excitement.

There were quite a number of people at breakfast, for some of the passengers were to spend the day ashore. She ate little, one eye on the clock, and presently, accompanied by the young man in the tourist trade, she walked along the deck for the last time, bade her companion goodbye and went down the gangway, paused briefly in the Customs shed and walked out of the door at its end, the porter with her cases hard on her heels. The professor appeared with such suddenness that she was strongly put in mind of a genie in a bottle. He said briefly, 'Good morning, Abigail,' tipped the porter, took her case, whisked her into the Rolls and got in beside her. 'You had a good journey, I hope?' His voice was cool and its chill swallowed up the warmth of her excitement at seeing him again.

She said pleasantly: 'Yes, thank you—I met some people. . .'

'I saw him as you left the ship,' his voice was dry. 'You must have been disappointed that the voyage didn't last longer.'

He was in a bad mood; probably he had been driving all night, or had slept badly, so she took care to make her voice sound reasonable.

'I don't wish that at all. He was a nice young man. He's going to marry a Spanish girl in a few weeks, he told me all about her. I expect,' she went on in a matter-of-fact voice, 'it's my lack of looks that makes people confide in me—people always pick plain confidantes, you know.'

She was rewarded by a faint twitch of the corner of his mouth. 'Have you been driving all night?' she wanted to know.

'No, since about four o'clock this morning. We'll go if you're ready.'

An unfair remark. She had been sitting, composed and unfidgeting, for the length of their conversation. She stole a look at his profile; it looked stern and a little bad-tempered and although he was freshly shaved and as immaculate as he always was, his face was grey with fatigue. He had driven himself too hard. If he had a wife. . .she snapped off the thought before she became too immersed in it, and waited until they had left the quayside behind them and were on the road to Bilbao before she suggested that they should stop for coffee. 'It's twenty odd miles to Baquio, isn't it? Have we time to stop for a little while so that you could tell me a little more about your niece?'

He might have been tired, but he was driving superbly. The road was narrow and the traffic, even so early in the day, was dense. Abigail, gazing out of the window, could see that they were running through shipyards and a muddled mass of factories, modern flats and tumbledown little houses. She was disappointed, but probably it would get better later on. The professor hadn't answered her. Only after he had negotiated a crossing jammed with traffic and sent the Rolls purring ahead once more did he remark, 'A good idea. We'll stop, there's a place in Bilbao which may be open.'

It was hard to see where Bilbao started and the shipyards and factories ceased, but presently the blocks of flats grew larger and more affluent-looking and the shops, although small, looked more interesting. They passed a modern hospital and then a much older one and at last reached the centre of the city.

The main streets were broad and tree-lined with imposing buildings on either side and a good deal of traffic. The professor, who seemed to know his way about, turned the car into a side street and nodded ahead. 'Behind that store,' he said briefly. It looked like Selfridges on a small scale, with gaily dressed windows which she would dearly have loved to look at, but he drove round the block and parked the car at the back and led her to a row of shops on the opposite side. The café they entered was empty, indeed, only just open, but they were greeted with smiles and an unintelligible flow of words which the professor answered without apparent effort.

The coffee, when it came, was dark and rich and a little bitter, and Abigail was intrigued to find that the milk came in the form of a powder in decorative little sachets. She looked up, her face alight with interest and caught him looking at her with an expression which, although she couldn't decide what it meant, caused her to say quickly:

'About your niece, Professor. . .'

He went on staring at her. 'You understand why I asked you to come?' He spoke quickly, as though the subject was distasteful and he wanted to get it over with. 'I am sorry if I have interfered in any way with your plans, but I cannot take chances with Nina and I can trust you as a nurse.'

'And not as a woman?' Abigail hadn't meant to say that, and she was appalled at the frozen expression on his face.

'That is hardly a relevant question.' His tone implied rebuke. 'Nina is high-spirited and three years old. My sister is awaiting the birth of their second child, that is why I have made this journey; it was quite out of the question that she should travel that distance at such a time. Her husband is attached to the Netherlands Consulate in Bilbao. They have lived there for more than a year now, but Odilia remains very Dutch in her outlook. The idea of allowing Nina to go into any hospital other than the one in which I work is quite abhorrent to her, absurd though this may seem. I have no choice other than to come for Nina myself and bring a nurse with me.' He paused, his voice was suddenly curt. 'That is my only reason for asking you to return, Abigail.'

She said sensibly, 'Yes, of course, Professor, what other reason could there be?' and was pleased to hear that her voice sounded exactly as it always did, which was surprising, because she was engulfed in a wave of disappointment all the more bitter because she had been buoyed up by the false hope that there might be another reason. Despite his abrupt greeting when they had met, she had taken heart from his evident annoyance at seeing her with the tourist agent, but now it was apparent that his annoyance hadn't been for that reason at all, much more likely that he had considered she had been wasting precious minutes of his time while she said goodbye.

She drank the rest of her coffee in silence and said rather defiantly that she was going to powder her nose. She had gone some steps from the table when she realised that she had no idea what to look for. She paused, trying to remember the Spanish for Ladies, but perhaps they didn't. . . She glanced over her shoulder at the professor, who said gently:

'You should look for flowers on the door, Abigail.'

She returned some five minutes later and he said at once, 'I see that you are big with information of some sort—am I to be told?'

'Well—there's no one else to tell,' began Abigail, 'but I'm not sure if it's quite. . .'

'My dear good girl, in this day and age? And you forget that I have a sister—a most outspoken woman, I might add. Further, I am completely unshockable.'

'Oh, it's nothing shocking,' said Abigail with endearing forthrightness. 'It's just that it was all so grand—like being on one of those Hollywood film sets.' She watched the corners of his mouth twitch. 'Powder blue velvet walls and little upholstered chairs and gilt wall lamps, and a carpet I got lost in, and I washed my hands in a gilded shell. I don't feel I shall ever get over it!'

The twitch came and went again. 'It sounds incredible and a little vulgar,' said the professor. He added gravely, 'I expect they do a roaring trade during the tourist season.'

Abigail laughed, her ordinary little face transformed, so that it wasn't ordinary at all, but very attractive. Then she became grave again. 'I'm sorry, I'm holding you up, Professor.'

They drove uphill out of Bilbao, and because it was now a bright, cloudless morning, she was able to see the mountains around them, with little green fields, each with its red-tiled house, shutters closed and rather shabby but delightfully picturesque with red peppers drying in colourful strings from the windows, and occasionally a man working in the fields and once a pair of oxen drawing a plough. She exclaimed at each new sight until she remembered that he had seen it all before and apologised for being tiresome. She turned in her seat and smiled at him, but he didn't reply, nor did he smile. It was as though he wished she weren't there beside him—but she was and, she reminded herself, at his invitation. Perhaps it was the Spanish air or the strength of the coffee which emboldened her to ask:

'Why do you sometimes call me Miss Trent and sometimes Abigail?'

They were approaching a town and he slowed the car's rush. 'I forget.'

She stared around her while she pondered this brief answer. It made no sense, for what had he to forget—but he gave her little time to think about it; they were approaching Munguia, he told her, where there was an interesting church of the Gothic period and the old tower of the Palacio de Abajo, and she obediently gazed in the directions to which he pointed as they passed through the small place, and then, because the silence was so heavy between them, she asked, 'Are we nearly there?'

'Yes. We go to Plenzia next and then take the coast road to Baquio. My sister lives a mile or so beyond the village.'

She sat quietly, not speaking until they reached Plenzia, and although she had promised herself that she wouldn't annoy him with any more comments, she exclaimed with delight as they entered the little town and turned on to the coast road, cut into the towering hills which ran down to the sea.

The road followed the hills bulging into the sea and began to descend. Baquio lay beyond and below them, and even the blocks of new flats along its sandy bay couldn't spoil its beauty. The Rolls tiptoed round a hairpin bend and tore happily down the hill into the village, along its shore and then up the hill on its other side. The road curved presently so that the houses were hidden behind them and only the sweep of the rugged coast was before them. They slowed momentarily while an old man in the flat cap of the Basque country, and carrying a rolled umbrella, trudged past them, urging along a donkey almost hidden under a load of wood.

'He doesn't look strong enough,' said Abigail.

'They live long lives here—hard work and a good climate—they walk a great deal too.'

'I meant the donkey. I'm sorry for it, it should be free in one of those fields.' She sighed. 'I've heard that they aren't very kind. . .they eat horses and they like bullfights.'

'Are you showing me yet another side to your many-sided nature, Miss Trent? kind Miss Trent, gentle Miss Trent—the rescuer of kittens from gutters and old men from attics, the nurse who tends old ladies and grizzling babies.' He sounded so savage that she was struck to dumbness, and when she forced herself to look at him she could see that his mouth was curved in a sneer. He had made her sound a prig, a do-gooder, and she wasn't, just an ordinary girl, with her living to earn and doing a job she liked. She concentrated on hating him, but that didn't seem to help much, so she tried despising him instead, but her companion snapped, 'Up here,' and turned the car, with inches to spare, through an open gate on to a narrow, well surfaced road, leading, as far as

Abigail's apprehensive eyes could see, straight up the side of the mountain, to lose itself in the trees which crowned its summit. She had decided that even the Rolls wouldn't be able to manage it when the professor swung the car round a right-angled bend and continued uphill, but now less steeply, but now she could see the sea again, only to lose it as they turned once more, this time into the trees, to emerge on to a wide sweep of tarmac before a modern and very large bungalow. They had arrived.

The front door stood open and even before they were out of the car a girl was coming towards them—the professor's sister, quite obviously, for she had his good looks, softened into beauty. She flung herself at him and he suffered her rather tearful embrace for a few moments with commendable calm and then spoke to her in Dutch, and she laughed a little as she turned to Abigail.

'Nurse Trent,' said the professor, 'my sister, Mevrouw de Graaff,' he turned back to her. 'Odilia, you do not need to worry any more, we will take Nina back with us and you will have no need to cry about her.' He patted her shoulder in a brotherly fashion and turned to greet a thickset, fair-haired man coming out of the house towards them.

'Dirk—I didn't expect to see you.' The two men shook hands and the professor went on, 'Nurse Trent, this is my brother-in-law, Dirk de Graaff.'

Abigail shook hands and stood quietly while the professor enquired after his niece. 'Nina? She's here? No worse?'

'She's in bed,' it was his sister who answered him. 'The nursemaid's with her for a minute or two, but she doesn't want anyone else but Dirk or me—it makes it difficult.' She glanced at Abigail. 'I hope she will like you, Nurse.'

Abigail murmured that she hoped so too and smiled reassuringly at Nina's mother because she looked so worried, as they followed her into the bungalow.

It was a roomy dwelling and most elegantly furnished. They crossed the wide hall and entered a room at one side of the bungalow with a wide window overlooking the sea and with a magnificent view of the coastline stretching away into the distance. The nursery, and a very nice one too, thought Abigail. There was a small white bed in one corner and the girl sitting beside it got up as they went in. She said something in Spanish and went away and the small creature in the bed cried 'Mama!' in a whining voice and began to grizzle. Her mother went to sit on the bed and spoke softly to the child, and presently said:

'She would like to know your name. She understands a little English—she speaks Dutch, of course, and Spanish too.'

Abigail looked with something like awe at this three-year-old who had already mastered more than her mother tongue and smiled at the pinched white face on the pillow. The child was ill, that was obvious, and despite her peevish greeting Abigail thought that when she was well again she would be a delightful small girl. She was blonde like her father, with enormous blue eyes. She had a distinct likeness to her uncle too; Abigail loved her on sight because of that.

'I only speak English, I'm afraid, and about a dozen words of Dutch. My name's Abigail.'

She smiled and Nina smiled faintly in return. 'Why?' she demanded.

Abigail thought it wise to ignore this question. Foreseeing language difficulties ahead, she said instead, 'I'm going to look after you for a day or two.'

The small mouth turned down ominously. 'Oom Dominic. . .'

'He'll be with us.' Abigail had the satisfaction of seeing the mouth right itself and marvelled anew that the child could understand her.

'Speak Dutch,' demanded the moppet, and added please because her mother told her to.

'Oom Dominic. . .' began Abigail slowly, not in the least sure what she was going to say.

'Is right behind you,' said the professor from the doorway, and passed her as he spoke to swoop down on his niece. It was obvious that they were devoted to each other, for the small face lighted up as Nina gabbled away to him, her two arms clutching him tightly round his neck.

Presently he disentangled himself and sat down on the side of her bed, still talking—explaining, Abigail thought, why he had come. When he had finished he listened patiently while Nina argued shrilly, and then said:

'Nina wants to leave now—this minute. I've told her we must wait until I have seen the doctor and studied the X-rays—it will give us the chance to pump some fluids into her before we go. Today, I think, from the look of her.'

He went on to give instructions and Abigail said, 'Yes, sir,' then he got up off the bed and went away, presumably to telephone the doctor. When the door had closed behind him, his sister asked, 'Do you always call Dominic sir?'

'Not always. Sometimes I call him Professor, although I suppose while Nina is with us I had better address him as Oom Dominic.'

Odilia smiled. 'And I suppose he calls you Nurse. I'm going to call you Abigail, if I may, and will you call me Odilia? What a pity you can't stay longer, but Dominic says he wants to get Nina to hospital as soon as he can, and he's bound to be right, he always is.' She sighed. 'I've been a dreadful nuisance, haven't I, but the baby will be here in another week and I simply will not let Nina go into a hospital here. Oh, they're very good, but I'm a dyed-in-the-wool Dutchwoman and if she's got to have something done then Dominic is the only one who must do it, and there was no other way; Dirk would have taken Nina to Amsterdam, but who could have gone with him to look after her? The nursemaid's a good girl, but she's not trained and she gets excited, and I'm no use either, I get so upset each time Nina's sick.'

The word had an unfortunate effect upon her small daughter. Abigail caught up a bowl and reached her just in time. She was sponging Nina's face and hands when the professor put his head round the door to speak to his sister and then in English, 'Oh, lord, at it again? No pesetas, I suppose?'

He strolled over to the bed and pulled a hideous face at his niece, who giggled weakly, but when he spoke to Abigail it was in his usual austere fashion. 'Glucose and water, Nurse—as much as you can get into her—getting a bit dehydrated, isn't she?'

He looked at Odilia enquiringly. 'Her things are packed? She had better travel in her nightie and dressing gown—we'll wrap her in blankets and she can sit on Nurse Trent's lap. We'll want several things with us,' he began to list them and Odilia interrupted him to say, 'I've got most of them. Abigail's going to sit with you?'

'Yes.' He stared across the room to where Abigail was sitting with her small patient, coaxing her to drink.

'I'll send Rosa in,' began Odilia, but he interrupted her. 'Nurse Trent will, I know, be glad to stay here and get to know Nina.' He took his sister's arm. 'Let's find those odds and ends and you can tell me how life's treating you—I must say you look prettier than ever.'

His sister smiled, she looked much happier now he had come. Abigail guessed that she had been in the habit of leaning on him whenever she wanted help.

They went out of the room together and Odilia said as she went:

'We'll have lunch together presently, all of us.'

'Thank you, that would be nice.' Abigail was still busy with the glucose drink and smarting under the professor's manner towards her. She would, she promised herself, say as little as possible to him on the journey back, and that would be of a professional nature.

The doctor came, held a consultation with Dominic and went again. Abigail had been present, because as it was pointed out to her, it would save time if she was told the results of their talk as they went along, so she sat between the two men, listening to the professor speaking Spanish with almost as much ease as he spoke English; it made her feel inferior until he said in English:

'How fortunate that you can't understand Spanish, for mine is so shockingly bad, I wonder Doctor Diaz can understand a word of it and I should be ashamed to speak it before you.'

She thought it was rather nice of him, but the idea of him being ashamed of anything he did was so amusing that she smiled and then straightened her face to gravity because she had discovered that whenever she smiled he seemed to dislike her more.

They were to leave at three o'clock, the professor informed her after Doctor Diaz had gone. They would spend the first night some two hundred and twenty miles away, midway between Biarritz and Limoges, and they would leave early on the following morning again, provided that Nina was well enough, and get as far as possible; if necessary he would drive on to Amsterdam, a matter of seven hundred miles, but only if it was advisable because of Nina. As it was he considered that they should be able to do the journey in two days. 'Indeed,' he went on, 'we must, for I have a number of engagements I cannot miss. I rely upon you, Nurse Trent, to take such good care of Nina that I shall be free to devote my attention entirely to driving, nor do I want any display of nerves, as I intend to drive fast when it is safe to do so.'

'I'm not given to nerves.' Abigail's voice was tart even while she wondered just how fast a Rolls-Royce went when pushed.

She lunched with Odilia and her husband and, of course, the professor, who when he did speak to her at all, engaged in the detached conversation of someone who had met her for the first time and didn't much care if he never saw her again. But Odilia was nice, Abigail liked her and she believed the liking was reciprocated. Abigail went back to her small charge after that and prepared her for the journey, and at the last minute Nina burst into loud sobs, shrieking her intention of staying with her mama in the three languages at her command. It was her uncle who picked her up out of her bed, whispering something or other as he did so, causing the shrieks to turn to an occasional snivel. Her mother, almost in tears herself, demanded, half laughing:

'Dominic, what are you saying—what are you promising, something wildly extravagant?'

'A bicycle—a Dutch bicycle, and I'll come down in the summer and watch her ride it.' He smiled very kindly at her. 'Don't worry, *lieveling*, everything will be all right, she will be safe with us. Abigail is a splendid nurse—I trust her, so can you. I didn't bring her all this way without good reason, you know. I'll telephone you this evening and again tomorrow and as soon as she's well enough I'll have her home with me and Dirk can come up to Amsterdam and fetch her back.'

Odilia smiled then and kissed him, then went over to where Abigail was standing, holding blankets and thermos flasks and all the impedimenta of a long journey. 'I'm so glad it's you,' she said, and kissed Abigail too. 'We shall see each other again. Have a good trip.'

'We will, I'm sure, and I'll take care of Nina for you. Good luck with the baby.'

The two girls smiled at each other and Abigail said goodbye to Dirk, got into the car, and the professor arranged his niece on her lap. When he had tucked the child around with a variety of wraps, he asked:

'Anything else?'

'The bowl and that packet of Kleenex tissues,' Abigail begged him, still practical even though he was so close that his cheek brushed hers. She wasn't sure what the journey was going to be like; perhaps Nina would get worse, perhaps the professor would be bad-tempered for the whole way, she didn't really mind; a thousand miles, or nearly that, her heart sang, as he got in beside her, even if he didn't speak more than a dozen words in those two days, he would be there, beside her. She smiled out of the window at Odilia and held Nina close as the professor waved too, then began a headlong dive down the road towards the gate and the road back.

CHAPTER SEVEN

ABIGAIL'S vague fears about the road were justified; it looked a great deal worse too by reason of the angry black clouds racing towards them from the sea. It was barely three o'clock, but the day was already darkening, the road reeled from one bend to the next and the professor drove along it as though it were a motorway with no traffic in sight. Presently the road turned inland, following the river, with its wide, peaceful mouth ringed by a picturesque village before it changed to a turbulent stream tumbling between the rocks below them. 'Guernica,' said the professor briefly. 'We cross the bridge in the centre of the town and turn back to the coast.' A piece of news Abigail took with resignation; probably, she consoled herself, the coast road wasn't half as bad as the roads through the mountains crowding in on them as they approached the town—if there were any roads. They hadn't gone very far when the rain started, a fierce, heavy downpour which washed away any views there might have been. They passed through several villages, dismal in the wetness and with not a soul to be seen in their single streets, and streaked up towards the mountains Abigail sensed were in front of them.

'Lovely scenery here on a fine day,' observed her companion laconically. 'Is Nina all right?'

'Dozing,' said Abigail, 'worn out with excitement, I fancy. You know this road, Professor?'

'Yes—it's a good one—rather a lot of bends, but we're not likely to meet much traffic in this weather.'

He sent the Rolls swooping round a curve at the top of a small ravine running down to the sea on their left. 'We reach Lequeito shortly. There is a thirteenth-century basilica there—it is also famous for the tuna fishing championships each summer.'

He offered her these titbits of information rather impatiently, as though he found it a nuisance to say anything at all and her answer was a little cool in consequence.

'You have no need to talk if you don't wish to. I can read it up in a guide book when I get back,' and was disconcerted by his low laugh. He didn't bother to answer her, though.

He was driving very fast and, she suspected, in an ill-humour despite the laugh when, in response to Nina's urgent and plaintive whisper, Abigail asked him to stop. He shot her a baleful glance and she met it firmly.

'It is awkward, isn't it? but Nina's the one to consider, I imagine. Perhaps there's somewhere where we could pull in. . .?'

She said it with more hope than certainty, for it wasn't that sort of a road; it snaked in breathtaking curves, mountains on one side, plunging ravines tumbling down to the sea on the other. Nevertheless the professor slid to a stop between one bend and the next. He got out, saying, 'Make it as quick as you can,' as he made for the side of the road in the pouring rain, adding as an afterthought, 'Do you need any help?'

'No, thank you. Give us three minutes.' She was already busy unwrapping Nina.

He gave them five, which, in view of the weather, was generous of him.

'You're very wet.' Abigail's soft voice sounded almost motherly as he got in beside her again. She went pink under the ferocity of his look.

'A singularly apt remark,' he commented. His voice had a bite in it, but as his glance fell upon Nina his face softened and Abigail felt a pang of envy that he would never look at her like that.

'She's all right?'

'Yes, she was a little sick as well, but she's had a drink. I'll cuddle her up and perhaps she'll go to sleep again.'

'Yes—you're all right until we can find somewhere where we can get tea?'

'Yes, thanks.' She spoke cheerfully and smiled at him, but all she got was a frowning glance as he started the car.

They came to an hotel on the side of the road, perched rather uneasily on the side of the cliffs above the sea, and although it looked deserted there was a light burning dimly from somewhere inside, despite its closed shutters.

'This will do,' said the professor, and drew up before its door. 'I'll carry Nina inside, you follow me in.'

She did so, pausing to catch a glimpse of the bay directly below them, fringed with rocks and the grey sea boiling past them to reach the sand. Inside she found herself in a small dark room, half café, half bar, rather smoky and smelling of the day's meal. But it was pleasant enough, with little tables scattered around, covered with red and white checked cloths. She sat down and took Nina into her arms while the professor went over to the bar. He came back after a minute.

'There's only coffee—do you mind?'

'Not a bit,' she answered readily, and longed for tea.

'What about Nina?'

'I've got milk and water for her. I brought the thermos with me.'

'Sensible girl!'

They drank their coffee in almost total silence; it was warm in the room and after a little while one didn't notice the smell of food.

Refreshed and warmed, they set off again; the road seemed even worse than before; now and again the clouds would lift just long enough for Abigail to glimpse the spectacular scenery on either side of them, but the rain still fell steadily, forcing the professor to slow his pace. He slowed even more as they went through Deva's narrow streets, with its harbour full of fishing boats and the sea breaking against the grim, grey cliffs. The road climbed out of the little town and wound its way towards San Sebastian, the sea still in view and the foothills of the Pyrenees ahead of them. Only in Zarauz did they leave the sea briefly as they passed through the town's main street, lined with a mixture of picturesque old houses, ornate villas and modern hotels. The professor hadn't spoken for a long time, and although Nina was awake she was content to lie quietly in Abigail's arms. She looked pale and listless, and Abigail, thinking of the long journey ahead of them, hoped that she would get no worse. She offered the child a drink, speaking in her clumsy Dutch, and Nina rewarded her with a weak giggle. 'Do you want me to stop?' The professor spoke without taking his eyes off the road, and when she answered that no, she thought she could manage, he didn't speak again, not until they reached San Sebastian, where, he told her, he would stop for a few minutes. 'For I don't intend to stop again until we reach Marmande,' he advised her, 'and that's just over a hundred miles away.'

It was a bare ten minutes before they were on their way again. As Abigail settled herself in the car once more and put out her arms to take Nina, the professor gave her a long searching glance, as though he had expected her to say something, and when she didn't he turned away and got into his own seat. As he started the car he said, 'There's chocolate in the pocket beside you—I imagine you must be getting hungry.'

'I'm perfectly all right, thank you, and so will Nina be until we reach Marmande,' her eyes searched around her and she nodded to herself, 'and if she's not, we've everything we need within reach. I rather think she'll go to sleep for a while, sir.'

He muttered a reply which she scarcely heard, but she did hear him when he said suddenly: 'Be good enough not to address me as sir at every other breath, Abigail,' and she spent the next five minutes or so wondering what she should call him. All in all, Oom Dominic seemed both suitable and blameless.

They crossed into France with hardly a pause, and Abigail, who had been considering that they had been travelling quite fast, discovered how wrong she was. The road was a good one, and the Rolls, as though aware that speed was essential, tore, silent and powerful, along it, with the professor, just as silent, at the wheel. And when Nina piped up that she felt sick Abigail said at once, 'Don't slacken speed, we're perfectly able to manage.' And manage she did.

They reached Marmande just after seven o'clock, to Abigail's relief, for Nina had been awake for the last hour of the journey, lying silent—too silent for a moppet of three. The professor had barely opened his lips and she, for her part, was heartily sick of her own thoughts, for they had been far from happy. From the comfort of the big car she had looked ahead into a future which, in its very uncertainty, was unsatisfactory. It was a good thing they had arrived, she told herself bracingly, for now she would have something to do other than think.

The hotel wasn't a large one; it looked old and very clean, though, and the foyer was comfortably furnished. Abigail sat down once more and took Nina from the professor and listened to him talking to the reception clerk. Her French was quite good; the boarding school had taken care of that. It amused her to hear the professor, in glacial, perfect French, refusing a double room and explaining that she was the nurse, that the child was his niece and that it was necessary for them to have two rooms, each with a bathroom. The clerk smiled and shrugged and beckoned the porter, apologising as he did so. On their way upstairs, Abigail, just behind the professor with Nina in his arms, said soberly, 'It would have been better if I had worn uniform, you know—I never thought. . .'

'You have a knowledge of French?'

'Quite a good one, as it happens.' She heard the tartness of her voice and was disconcerted by his chuckle.

The room she was shown into was well furnished

and warm and the bathroom was more than adequate. She got Nina ready for bed, gave her a drink she didn't want, took her temperature, which was quite high, and tucked her up for the night. A few minutes later the professor tapped on the door to spend ten minutes with his small niece, studying her carefully as he laughed and joked with her. Presently, he asked Abigail: 'You're comfortable?'

'Yes, thank you. Perhaps I might have something here on a tray. . .'

'Certainly not. I have arranged for the chambermaid, a sensible woman, to sit with Nina while we have dinner. You will have it with me downstairs.'

'An invitation or an order?' she wanted to know quietly, and saw his unwilling smile.

'An invitation.'

'On the assumption that any company is better than none?'

The smile had gone; perhaps she had imagined it. 'If you wish, Nurse Trent.' He turned away. 'I'll be back to see Nina in half an hour, I will bring the maid with me.'

He was as good as his word. He walked in with a middle-aged woman with a kind, sensible face, and such was the strength of his niece's affection for him that she closed her eyes and promised to go to sleep at once when he bade her to do so.

They dined in an empty restaurant, which on a summer's evening must have been a very pleasant place. Abigail was hungry. She chose the soup, which the waiter assured her had been made in the hotel's kitchen—the asparagus tips and herbs, thickened with tapioca and piping hot, followed by cutlets with an orange sauce, and while the professor contented himself with cheese she allowed herself to be tempted by the little something the chef had whipped up for her; a delicious concoction of Chantilly cream, fruit, nuts and liqueur brandy, which, combined with the dry white wine the professor had chosen, had the effect of combining with the table lamps to give everything around her a rosy hue. Not that the professor made much effort to entertain her; he talked, it was true, at great length and with great attention to detail, of the local customs, and when he had exhausted those, he embarked on the customs of the Basque country. Abigail, listening politely, was strongly put in mind of her student days, when with rows of other nurses she had sat listening to lectures delivered by the various honoraries of the hospital. The professor's manner was exactly similar.

They had their coffee at the table and when they had finished she suggested that she should return upstairs and went scarlet in the face when he asked, 'Dear me, was I so dull?'

'Of course not,' she said hastily, 'I enjoyed it very much, but I don't like to leave Nina too long.' She frowned. 'She's. . .it will be a good thing when she's safely in hospital.'

His smile was mocking, and the scarlet, which had just faded, flamed anew. 'I didn't mean—that is. . .' She paused and added carefully, 'She's in safe hands with you, but we're an awful long way from home.'

'You think that she will get worse?'

'I don't know—it's just an idea, a feeling. . .' She looked at him helplessly. How could she explain the premonitions all nurses had from time to time? As it turned out there was no need for her to explain, for the waiter came hurrying over to their table to ask if they would go upstairs immediately.

Nina was being sick again. The maid had coped without worrying overmuch to begin with, but the child seemed unable to stop. The professor thanked her calmly, tipped her with discretion and sent her away, then went over to the bed where Abigail was doing all the necessary things which had to be done with a complete absence of fuss, and even though the child couldn't have understood the half of what she was saying, her gentle, placid talk and unhurried movements, which nevertheless got things done, calmed the child, so that she stopped crying and listened to what her uncle was telling her. He made it sound amusing; he fetched his case from his room, took off his jacket, and made preparations for putting up a saline infusion. He did it without haste, talking all the time, so that presently Nina laughed a little and laughed a little more when Abigail, swathed in a towel to protect her blue dress, joined in the conversation in her own halting Dutch, not minding at all when the little girl giggled at her comic way of pronouncing the words. The drip was up and running with a minimum of fuss, for the professor had shamelessly used all his powers of persuasion upon his small niece as well as promising her a bell to go on the bicycle and a little gold chain with a pearl on the end of it for her birthday, as well as ice-cream every day as soon as she could eat again. 'And heaven alone knows what your mother will say to me when she's told,' he observed in English.

'She won't care a fig,' Abigail assured him as she cleared away his mess and tidied things away in his case. 'She'll be so glad to have Nina well and home again.' She shut the case on an unconscious sigh. 'How fast is this to run in? There's to be a second vacolitre, isn't there?'

He nodded. 'If she has a good night's sleep, I think we had better press on tomorrow.' He handed her a bottle. 'Largactil syrup. Give her a dose, will you?'

Abigail did as she was bid, tidied the room, pulled up a chair to the side of the bed and was on the point of sitting in it when his hand hauled her to her feet again.

'No,' he said firmly, 'go and have your bath and get into bed—use my room. I'll call you about three, have a bath myself and an hour or two's sleep; that way we'll both be rested. I'll get them to send breakfast up here at eight o'clock and if everything's all right we'll get away soon after. It rather depends on Nina.'

'But you've got to drive—I shall be quite comfortable here, truly—I can always doze in the car tomorrow.'

'Why do women argue?' he wanted to know

pleasantly. 'Do as you're told, Nurse Trent.' He smiled suddenly. 'Please.'

There was no further use in argument. She collected her night things and went away to the bathroom, then to his room and got into bed; she was asleep immediately.

She wakened at once to the touch of his hand on her shoulder, and sat up instantly. 'Nina's all right?' she wanted to know.

'Hasn't stirred,' was his reassuring answer. 'I've just changed the drip—it should be through by seven. Take it down if I'm not about.'

He went away leaving her to scramble into her dressing gown and slippers and pad back to her own room. A minute later he had wished her good night and disappeared.

The rest of the night passed uneventfully. Nina hardly moved, even when the drip had run through and Abigail took the needle out of the small thin arm and covered the tiny puncture with strapping, and when she opened her eyes, frowning a little, Abigail said:

'It's all right, darling, you're much better, aren't you?' and the moppet nodded and, obedient to Abigail's suggestion that she should go to sleep again, closed her eyes.

The professor came in a few minutes later, with his hair ruffled and an unshaven chin, but his eyes were as calm and untroubled as a child who had slept the night long. He nodded his satisfaction, patted Abigail on the shoulder, said 'Good girl' and then: 'How about some tea—I'm dying of thirst.'

Abigail rang the bell and waited to see what would happen. The maid who had looked after Nina came in answer to it, smiled a good morning and promised tea within five minutes.

The child slept peacefully while they drank it, sitting side by side on the other bed with the tray between them. Abigail poured second cups and enquired of the professor if he had slept well. 'You must have been tired,' she added.

His blue eyes swept lazily over her and she became aware that her hair was hanging in a mousy curtain around her shoulders, and her dressing gown, warm as it was, was hardly glamorous. To cover her discomfiture she asked, 'Do you intend to leave directly after breakfast, Professor?'

'Yes, as things are I think perhaps we should try and reach Amsterdam as quickly as possible. It's roughly six hundred and seventy miles.'

She thought. 'About fourteen hours' driving.'

He laughed. 'Less, with luck. There are some splendid stretches of road where I can give the car her head.'

'A hundred miles an hour?'

She wasn't looking at him, so she missed the engaging twinkle in his eyes.

'Probably more—are you nervous?'

'Not in the least.'

'Am I to take that as a compliment?'

'As you wish,' she forced her voice to casualness. 'Which of us shall dress first?'

'Would you like to? I imagine there isn't much to do for Nina, but if you will, perhaps you can do whatever needs doing before breakfast. She might have some tea—no milk.'

When Abigail got back to the bedroom, very neat as to hair and dress, and with her face nicely made up, it was to find the professor stretched out on the second bed with his eyes closed. She stood looking down at him, studying every line of his handsome face. He looked more approachable with a bristly chin, she considered, and lonely. He opened his eyes with a suddenness which took her completely by surprise and asked:

'Why do you look at me like that?'

'Like what?' She took a step backwards, and he got off the bed and stretched hugely, but all he said was: 'You have a very expressive face, Abigail, did you know?'

At least the rain had stopped. They got off to a good start soon after eight o'clock with a wide-awake

Nina on Abigail's lap. For the time being at least she seemed a great deal better, a fact amply demonstrated by her chatter, which for the first hour at least was ceaseless. They stopped briefly at Limoges, having covered over a hundred and thirty miles in two hours. Refreshed by coffee and a glucose drink for Nina, they took to the road again, at first running through high country. But this didn't last long. Once more on level ground, the professor urged the Rolls forward, and they reached Châteauroux in time for a hasty lunch, more glucose for Nina, who had by now become silent and rather sleepy, and tore on towards Orleans and Paris.

South of Paris the professor broke the long silence to say, 'We'll stop for tea, and get through Paris before dark. What do you think about going straight on?'

She was surprised that he should ask her. He had seemed remote the entire morning; when he had spoken, he had been civil and that was all.

'It depends entirely on how tired you are. There's a great distance to go, isn't there? More than three hundred miles, and you've already driven more than that.'

'I'm thinking of Nina,' he reminded her coldly, and she saw that he wanted—probably intended—to drive through the night. She looked at the child on her lap, awake once more and looking decidedly sickly. 'Let's go on—you intended to anyway, didn't you?'

'Discerning of you—but you are the child's nurse—I needed your opinion.'

They stopped shortly after that at a roadside hotel and Abigail tried not to look as if she had understood when the waiter referred to her as the professor's wife, but her faint astonishment at his not denying it betrayed her. He said shortly: 'If you have no objection, I'm sure that I have not—it is a waste of time to correct such a ridiculous mistake.'

Several telling replies to this piece of arrogance bubbled upon Abigail's lips. She longed to utter them, but suppressed her feelings, outraged though they were, sternly; now was not the time nor the place to have words with the professor.

It took some time to get through Paris even though the professor knew the way. It was obvious to her that her companion was concentrating on his driving to the exclusion of all else. She thanked heaven that Nina was still quiet; the child was running a temperature again; she could feel the heat of the little body through the blankets and Nina's small face had become even paler. They still had three hundred miles to drive, a long way still, but there was a motorway into Belgium; presumably the professor would make good time once he got on to it. She was perfectly right. He hadn't looked at Nina for some time and she had said nothing to him, but he seemed to sense that she was uneasy about her, for he sent the car tearing along at a great speed, and yet, thought Abigail, looking at him stealthily, he seemed quite relaxed; his hands rested lightly on the wheel; he wasn't frowning. Without looking at her, he said, 'Not long now, Abigail.'

An hour and a half later, going through Bapaume, he asked her how Nina was.

'Dozing, but her pulse is up. She's got a temp. too.'

'Roughly two hundred miles to go—I'm going via Antwerp and on to Tilberg and Utrecht.'

A name which sounded reassuringly Dutch in Abigail's ears, it made home seem very near.

They had travelled quite some distance before he spoke again. 'Can you last out until we reach Amsterdam?'

'Easily.' Her voice was steady; even at the speed they were travelling at, the journey seemed endless and she was worried about Nina. Her relief when later, he said briefly, 'Holland,' was so great she could have cried.

'How is she?' he wanted to know.

'Asleep. I think when she wakes she'll probably be sick again.'

To her surprise he laughed, a normal, relaxed sound with no sound of tiredness in it. 'My dear Abigail, what a sensible girl you are! I should like to have you with me in a tight corner—although this one's tight enough—I can't think of any girl of my acquaintance who wouldn't have been in tears or hysterics long ago. Aren't you tired?'

'Yes,' said Abigail, smarting under his good opinion. Who wanted to be called sensible? That was twice in twenty-four hours! 'Aren't you?'

'Yes, but it's worth it.'

They lapsed into silence again until it was broken by the professor's forceful opinion of the rain which began to beat against the windscreen. After a little while he asked, 'Are you prepared for Nina; in case she's sick?'

'Yes.' Her answer was brief because she sensed that he didn't want to talk. They were through Utrecht, on the motorway and only a few miles from Amsterdam, when Nina woke up and did exactly as they had expected, and in the ensuing minutes which followed, Abigail had no time to feel relief as they slid through Amsterdam's lighted streets and at last stopped before the hospital entrance. It was almost midnight.

The professor wasted no time but carried his small niece into the hospital and Abigail, left on her own, got out too, much more slowly because she was cramped and stiff, and now that they had arrived, deathly tired.

The entrance hall was empty, although she could see the night porter in his small office, but he had his back to her, telephoning; she decided to wait. She had no idea where she should be or what the professor wanted of her. Nina would go to the children's ward, but there would be a nurse on duty there.

It was quiet in the hall, the night sounds of hospital reached her ears faintly, but she was so familiar with them that she hardly heeded the far-off rustles and thumps and door shuttings and clanging of metal as some nurse cleared a trolley. Presently she peered through the porter's lodge window again; he had disappeared altogether now—there was a small inner room, so probably he had retired to eat his meal. She felt shy about disturbing him; besides, her tired brain felt unable to cope with asking questions in Dutch. The professor wouldn't be very long; he would have to go home and go to bed, he needed rest before he operated upon Nina, and the child needed a night's sleep in a proper bed, too. Somewhere close by a clock chimed twelve and she went to the door and stood looking at the Rolls, still majestic despite its deplorably dusty condition. It was a pity her case was in the boot and that the boot was locked, otherwise she could have taken it and been in bed by now, although that wouldn't have been very polite, she supposed.

She shivered and went back inside and walked round once more. 'If ever I'm rich,' she said to herself as she walked, 'I shall give a bench—two benches, to this place. There must be a waiting room.' But she couldn't see one, only corridors, disappearing into gloom on either side. She hadn't been in this part of the hospital before, only to pass through it on her way in or out when she had been working there. She yawned widely and sat down on the floor, her back to the wall. It was a dark corner and she was almost hidden. She closed her eyes.

And opened them again almost immediately, because the professor was bellowing her name in a furious voice, which to her mind was far too loud for that time of night in a hospital, even though he was an important surgeon. She called hastily. 'I'm here, in this corner,' and before she could get up he was towering over her.

'Good God, girl, what in the hell are you lying there for?'

He was in a bad temper; he wasn't his usual cool, bland self at all, his voice was almost a snarl. He bent down and plucked her to her feet, keeping his hands on her shoulders, and she had a strong feeling that he would have liked to have shaken her. Before he could do so she spoke, her voice low and reasonable.

'I wasn't sure what you wanted me to do and I'm

tired. If I could have my case I'll go over to the Home. How's Nina?'

The hands lost their ferocious grip and became gentle. 'Nina's asleep. Henk's with her, I'm too tired to be of much use. My poor girl, what a thoughtless brute you must think me!'

She looked up into his grey weary face. He looked every day of his age and a year or two besides, but she loved him a little more because of it. She would have liked to have told him what she did think of him, but that was something she would have to keep a secret, probably for ever and ever.

'No,' she said gently, 'I don't think anything of the sort. It's Nina who matters, and I'm perfectly all right. If I could just have my case—you could get home to bed.'

'Didn't I tell you? You're coming back to my house for the night. I shall want you on duty tomorrow morning at eight—you can move into the Home during the day.'

'But I can't—it's past midnight. . .'

'Don't tell me the conventions worry you,' he paused, 'although I daresay they do; you're that kind of girl.'

'No,' she snapped, very ruffled, 'I'm not in the least worried. Why should I be—even if you expected it? I was thinking of someone having to get a bed ready at this hour of night.'

'My dear good girl, Bollinger and Mevrouw Boot will have prepared a room. I told them I expected to be back at some ungodly hour.'

There seemed nothing more to say, he took her arm and they went out to the car again, and in five minutes had arrived outside his house on the *gracht*. Bollinger and Mevrouw Boot were still up. Bolly had the door open before the professor could get his key out and Abigail, quite forgetting him, flung herself at the old man.

'Oh, Bolly dear, how lovely to see you!' she cried, and hugged him fiercely before saying good evening to the housekeeper, who smiled and nodded and said a great deal, none of which made any sense to Abigail at all.

'A bath and bed, and Mevrouw Boot will bring up your supper,' ordered the professor, and when she would have protested, said:

'Please do as I say, Abigail. I want you on your toes tomorrow morning. We leave the house at a quarter to eight.'

Bolly had gone to get their cases, Mevrouw Boot was on the stairs, on her way to run a bath. Abigail said meekly: 'Very well. Good night. I hope you sleep well, you must be very tired.'

'Not so tired that I cannot find the time to thank you for your share in this whole business.' He stared at her from under frowning brows. 'You didn't complain once; you must have wanted to.'

A dimple appeared in her cheek. 'Oh, a dozen times.' She turned away as Bollinger reappeared with the cases, and started up the stairs after him. As her foot was on the first tread the professor said: 'Abigail,' and she turned round again. Bolly turned round too and watched from the top of the stairs. The professor had followed her across the hall; she turned round into his arms, and they held her with a gentleness she had never imagined as he bent to kiss her.

Abigail ran upstairs without a word or a backward glance and tried not to see Bollinger's delighted smirk. She refused to think about it while she undressed and had her bath and got her uniform ready for the morning, and then, warm in the little canopied bed, ate the delicious supper Mevrouw Boot brought her. She looked about her room as she ate. Not very large, but furnished with excellent taste with dainty Regency furniture as well as an ultra-comfortable easy chair and a soft carpet underfoot, it was exactly the kind of room she would have chosen for herself. She pushed the bedtable away and lay back on the pillows, drowsily contemplating the flower painting over the fireplace. The housekeeper would be back for the tray presently and she must stay awake and thank her. She closed her eyes and went to sleep even as she thought it.

She was called at seven and told that breakfast would be in exactly half an hour, and with five minutes to spare she went down the staircase, very trim and crisp in her uniform, her starched cap perched on her bun of hair, her packed case in her hand. Half way down the stairs she remembered that she had no idea where to go. There were several doors—she knew where the little sitting room was and she knew the great drawing room too, but there were other doors, all shut. One of these was flung open as she stood hesitating, and the professor said, 'In here, Nurse Trent. Good morning.'

He had already been at table, with papers, letters and an open notebook before him. There was some coffee, half drunk, and a slice of toast half eaten. She sat down opposite him and gave him a wary greeting, and he lifted his eyes to hers briefly and asked her how she had slept.

He looked rested himself, she saw that at once, and as bland and cool as ever he had been. Abigail sighed and he said at once, 'Oh, would you rather have tea—I'll ring. . .'

'I like coffee, thank you.' She poured herself a cup and took a slice of toast. 'I see that you have slept well too, Professor,' and some small imp of mischief prompted her to add, 'Things that happened yesterday seem so different after a good night's rest, don't they?'

He put down the letter he was reading and stared at her with faint suspicion. 'And just what does that mean?' he wanted to know.

'Why, nothing—would you pass me the sugar? I expect you're one of those people who prefer not to talk at breakfast, I don't mind in the least if you want to go on with your letters.' She smiled kindly at him and helped herself to toast and marmalade, and although she knew that he was staring at her, she didn't look up; after a moment he picked up his letters again.

In the car, driving to the hospital, he told her:

'I telephoned Odilia last night—she asked me to thank you for taking such care of Nina. She sent her love too and hopes that she will see you again. She hopes too that you will find time to write to her.'

'Of course I will. She'll want to hear about Nina—all the little things, you know,' she explained, 'that mothers worry about.'

Nina was awake and quiet after a restful night—she had a little room to herself for the time being, but later, when she had recovered from the operation she was to have in an hour's time, she would be able to go into the ward with the other children. She kissed her uncle with childish fervour and kissed Abigail too, and presently the professor went away and Abigail busied herself getting the little girl ready for the theatre. She was to go with her, she had been told, and afterwards nurse her on day duty until she was fit to leave hospital. Zuster Ritsma had told her too that there was a room ready for her in the Nurses' Home, and would she mind taking her off-day each afternoon so that the day shift could cover her. Abigail, still thinking about the professor, said that she didn't mind in the least, and went off to X-ray with her little patient, so that her uncle could have a last-minute check of the three pesetas.

The operation was a complete success. The professor, with no difficulty at all, removed the coins through the smallest of incisions which would leave only the faintest of scars, and when the wound had been clipped, peered down his little niece's gullet with his gastroscope to make sure that nothing had been left behind, a state of affairs confirmed by the portable X-ray machine, trundled into the theatre before Nina was lifted on to the trolley ready to take her back to her bed. Abigail had stood by the anaesthetist during the operation, doing what was asked of her quickly and competently, her mind deliberately closed to any thought other than those connected with the job on hand, and back in the small hospital room once more, with Nina in bed, there was plenty for her to do and no time to think of her own affairs.

She had regulated the drip, taken Nina's pulse and charted it, inspected the tiny wound and written up the chart by the time the professor came in. He had Henk with him, and that young man, who had had no chance to speak to her that morning, said, 'Hullo, Abigail, nice to see you again. We must get together. . .' and Abigail murmured something, conscious of the professor's eyes upon her and wishing Henk wasn't quite so pleased to see her. But when the two men had gone she brightened a little, cheered by the thought that a little competition was supposed to be a good thing, and then chided herself for being a fanciful fool; the professor didn't care anything at all for her; she was a useful nurse, probably he knew how she felt about him and took advantage of it. It had been stupid of her to come running the moment he called. . .and as for his kisses, there were a dozen good reasons why a man kissed a girl, and none of them necessarily because he loved her.

She was kept busy for the rest of the morning, for Nina, once she was conscious, was rather cross and inclined to cry as well. Abigail, watching her drop off to sleep after she had given her an injection, was glad to go off duty for a few hours.

She had the same room in the Home as she had had previously. She unpacked her case, changed rapidly into her outdoor clothes and hurried through the well-remembered streets to Mrs Macklin's house. It would be nice to see that lady again; they would have time for a chat and a cup of tea before she was due back on duty. She stopped at the baker's shop and bought some cakes before turning into the peace and quiet of the Begijnhof.

Mrs Macklin received her with rapturous surprise. 'My dear,' she exclaimed as Abigail took off her coat, 'I knew you would be back, but I didn't expect you as soon as this—what has happened?'

Abigail told her while they had tea, toasting themselves round the little stove and drinking cup after cup of the strong brew Mrs Macklin liked.

'Dear Dominic,' she declared when Abigail had finished her tale, 'how like him to go tearing off for hundreds of miles to help someone. He adores Nina, of course, you'll have seen that for yourself, my dear, and he's devoted to Odilia—she's fifteen years younger than he is, you know, and they've always been very close. He missed her very much when Dirk was appointed to Bilbao—Dirk's a good man too, did you meet him?'

'Yes—I liked him too, and I thought Odilia was charming.'

'You say Dirk's coming up to fetch Nina?'

'Yes, I think so, though I think it all depends on the baby—when it arrives. Nina won't take long to get over this.'

'No. I suppose Dominic will take her back with him to his house when she can be moved, until her father can come for her. He'll need someone to look after her, though.' She gave Abigail a shrewd look and Abigail, aware of what her companion was thinking, said nothing. It wasn't very likely that the professor would ask her to go back to his house with Nina; a couple of weeks and she would be on her way back to England.

Nina was still sleeping when she got back and there was little to do but sit by the bed getting up from time to time to do the small tasks necessary for the little girl's treatment. The professor had come in again just after she had got back and gone again, well satisfied with his small relative's progress. He had hardly spoken to Abigail beyond leaving her fresh instructions and asking her to tell the night nurse that he would come again about ten o'clock. He scarcely looked at her as he bade her a quiet good night.

Nina recovered rapidly; long before she was able to eat them, she was demanding impossible and unsuitable meals of sausages and chips, pea soup and *poffertjes*, delicious, indigestible fried dough balls. Abigail, plying her with suitably milky foods, heaved a sigh of relief when ice-cream, often demanded, was allowed.

Nina was getting up each day now, sitting in a chair, swathed in blankets and wearing the new dressing-gown her uncle had bought her. It was pale pink and frilly and quilted and there were slippers to match. She was a pretty child and as beguiling as most small girls of that age, it was no wonder that he was fond of her. In a few more days she would be able to play with the children in the ward; the only reason she didn't do so now was because she might be tempted to eat the sweets and cakes their mothers brought in for them. And during these days, the professor came and went, saying little to Abigail that wasn't to do with her work until one evening when he walked in just before the children's bedtime, to find Abigail, with Nina and several other children from the ward.

Nina was curled up on Abigail's lap, the other children lay about her feet, rolled up or stretched out according to their several whims, each of them had a bulging cheek as they sucked on a bedtime sweet. Abigail was singing to them; she had a voice like a little girl's, rather high and breathy and sometimes off key. She was singing them nursery rhymes and children's songs which she had almost forgotten so that she had to sing da-de-da from time to time, but as none of them understood a word she was singing anyway, it really didn't matter. She was half way through 'Cry Baby Bunting' for the second time when Nina lifted her head from her shoulder and cried: 'Oom Dominic!'

Abigail stopped singing, as though the thread of her voice had been cut by the professor's scissors. He advanced into the centre of the small room, while the children, quite prepared to accept him as their uncle too, all began to talk at once. It was strange, thought Abigail, watching him, how they saw through his austere look and took no notice of his frown at all; he waved to them now and pulled a hideous face so that they roared with laughter as he came to a halt before her and bent to kiss his niece.

'I liked the one about the king in his counting house,' he remarked.

She had sung that one quite five minutes previously. 'Have you been here all that while?' she wanted to know. 'I would have stopped. . .'

'Yes, I thought you would have done.'

She said miserably, 'I wish you hadn't—I can't sing.'

'No, but it sounded charming, all the same.'

He picked Nina up and enquired of her how she was and left Abigail to meditate on sounding charming even when one sang habitually out of tune. Just then Zuster Ritsma came in and he went away with her to look at a sick child, leaving Abigail to shoo the children back into the ward and Nina into her bed.

It was two mornings later that he told Nina that she would be going home with him the next day. Abigail was making the bed, and Nina, sprawled on the floor, was playing with a doll, which she threw down to rush at her uncle and embrace his knees, shouting rapturously.

'Noisy little brat,' said her uncle fondly. 'You will accompany her, if you please, Abigail. Mevrouw Boot and Bollinger have enough to do without having this imp to look after—besides, they're a little elderly.'

Abigail folded a blanket with precise, neat movements. 'For how long, sir?'

'I can't tell you that. Why do you want to know? Have you another case?'

'No. I was just curious. Of course I'll come.'

'Odilia had a son last night, so as soon as she is up and about, Dirk will come and fetch Nina.'

Abigail smiled widely. 'Oh, I am glad, how lovely for them—Odilia is quite well?'

'Yes, she telephoned me an hour after he was born. Dirk is naturally delighted.'

'I can well imagine it. I suppose men want sons. . .' She could have bitten out her tongue when she saw the bleakness of his face. He turned away and when he spoke again his voice was without expression. 'I'll see the Directice about you leaving tomorrow, Nurse Trent—Zuster Ritsma will give you all the details.'

He walked away without another word.

She didn't pretend to herself that she hadn't hoped to go with Nina when the little girl left the hospital; she allowed herself to feel happy about it, but only in moderation, for the professor hadn't shown himself particularly pleased to have her. She supposed that she would stay ten days at the most, and then Nina would go back to Spain and she would be back in London again, looking for another case. Professor de Wit, when she had gone to see him one afternoon, had urged her to remain in Amsterdam. 'For,' he had said, 'Dominic must have any number of patients who require a nurse, you could be employed for months to come,' and she had taken heart from his words, hoping each time that she saw the professor that he might suggest this, but he never had done so. She packed her case with the few clothes she had with her and which she now heartily hated, and prepared to leave the hospital. There was another thing—she had received no salary, and because the professor had been so irritable when she had offered to pay back the surplus from her travelling expenses, she hesitated to say anything about it now. Perhaps he intended to pay her when she left Amsterdam. In the meantime, she was running low again, and Bolly had had nothing for some weeks.

They left after lunch the next day, with a jubilant Nina, her clips out, carried through the hospital in the professor's arms, and when he set her down in the entrance hall and she began to jig around with excitement, he exclaimed, laughing:

'No one would believe that I carved you open such a short time ago,' to which sally she screamed with laughter and asked to be told, for the hundredth time, how exactly he had done it.

He was called away on some urgent business or other soon after that, and they went home with Jan in a Mercedes she hadn't seen before, to be welcomed by Mevrouw Boot and Bollinger, but of the professor there was no sign for the rest of the afternoon.

CHAPTER EIGHT

SHE was taken to the room she had had before and Nina had the room next to it; a room as charming as Abigail's and thoughtfully provided with a miniature chair to accommodate Nina's smallness, and a table to go with it. It took most of the afternoon to arrange her toys and dolls in exactly the positions she wished and by the time she had had her tea she was tired. Abigail carried her off to her room with the promise of a bedtime story if she was a good girl, then undressed the small creature and bathed her with a good deal of giggling and chatter, for they understood each other very well by now, even though they mostly spoke different languages. She was in bed, with a bowl of bread and milk, nicely flavoured with sugar and cinnamon, by way of supper, and Abigail sitting on the bed beside her, telling her, in English of course, all about the old woman who lived in a shoe, by seven o'clock. The tale took a long time to tell, because almost every word had to be explained, which meant searching for it in Abigail's dictionary. They were hugging each other with merriment over Abigail's peculiar way of pronouncing even the simplest Dutch word, when the door opened and the professor came in.

He said pleasantly enough, 'Good evening, Nurse Trent, I see that you have settled in,' and went to bend over his niece, to be hugged and kissed and chatted to while Abigail got up and went to the pillow cupboard against one wall and busied herself putting away Nina's clothes.

It was to be a 'Nurse Trent' evening, she supposed a little sourly. Come to that, it would probably be no evening at all; she hadn't the least idea if she was to take her meals with him or have them served alone, or if she was to have them with Bolly and Mevrouw Boot. She decided not, remembering how annoyed he had been when she had used the tradesmen's entrance. She shut the cupboard door in time to hear him say:

'I dine at seven, Abigail. I hope you will keep me company.'

She said thank you in a polite voice which hid her pleasure, while she brooded over the difficulty of falling in with his moods. In the space of ten minutes she had been both Miss Trent and Abigail; she found it a little wearing on her nerves.

They were half way through their soup—hare soup and home-made, as Bollinger informed her as he served it, and they were alone in the elegant dining room. Bollinger had gone back to the kitchen to see about the next course, and the professor, making polite conversation, had fallen silent, and she, who had been turning over in her mind his insistence on calling her Miss Trent, found herself voicing her thoughts.

'I can't think why you will persist in calling me Miss Trent with one breath and Abigail with the next,' she remarked suddenly. She looked at him as she spoke and he was neither frowning nor smiling the faint sneering smile she so disliked.

He said simply, 'I told you once before. I forget.'

'Forget what?' she persisted.

'You may have restored my faith in women, Abigail, but it's been so long—I'm not quite used to it, perhaps I haven't quite learned to trust.' He paused and smiled at her across the table, and for fear that she would give herself away she said a little shortly, 'I haven't the least idea what you mean,' and wished that she had never started the conversation, while at the same time longing for him to go on. It was a pity that Bollinger came back just then with the *Boeuf Bourguignonne*, served, as it should be, in a brown glazed casserole; it smelled delicious and she was hungry, and so, she expected, was her host. Abigail ate with appetite and abandoned her questions for just sufficient polite conversation to make for good manners.

There was fruit tart next; an elaborate dish which not only contained fruit but cream and eggs and cream cheese. When the professor pressed her to a second helping, she hesitated. 'It was delicious...' she began.

'Then have some more—I don't think you've been eating enough, you've got thinner.'

He was right; she had been eating as sparingly as possible because she had had to pay for her meals in hospital and she was counting every cent now. She had told herself bracingly that it was a good thing, for she was far too plump, but she had sometimes been a little hungry. She passed her plate; in a week or two she would probably be on short commons again.

They had their coffee in the little room where she had had tea with Bollinger and when she had handed him the delicate Meissen cup and saucer he said blandly:

'We were talking about you.'

'No, not really.' She spoke too quickly, but it made no difference, for he went on just as though she hadn't spoken.

'You didn't understand what I meant, Abigail. Will it help if I call you Abigail all the time?'

'You mean you don't dislike me any more?'

She was unprepared for his explosive, 'Dislike you? My dear girl, I have never...'

She cut in ruthlessly, 'Oh yes, you have, from the very first time we met. I don't know why—perhaps you're one of those men who can't bear plain girls. I don't mind being plain—not any more, now I'm used to it, but you don't have to make it so obvious...'

He was looking at her gravely, his eyebrows arched, and she sensed that he was laughing silently, which irked her.

'Your eyes are lovely—you have a dimple, did you know? and the sweetest smile.'

'Which hardly adds up to good looks,' she answered him crisply. 'If you don't mind, we won't talk about me. How is your sister?'

He followed her lead without apparent regret and presently excused himself on the grounds of work to do. She sat on alone for another hour or two, staring into the fire, deep in thought. She had won his friendship; she was almost sure about that, and perhaps, just a little, his regard.

She saw him only briefly the following day; just long enough to be told his wishes concerning Nina. There was little enough nursing to do, for the little girl was almost well again and full of life and mischief—it was largely a question of keeping her amused and making sure that she didn't tire herself out. As he left the room, the professor said:

'I'll be away for a day or so, Abigail, so please feel free to go wherever you wish in my house. Bollinger will look after you. Nina will need more clothes, I imagine, take her to 't Kleuterhuis in P. C. Hooftstraat and get what you need and have the account sent to me—if she needs shoes, there's a good shop in the same street—Pennocks; they can send in their account too. Jan will take you if you wish it.'

They shopped two days later, with Jan driving them in the Mercedes, for the professor had taken the Rolls, spending the morning in the most agreeable fashion to them both, buying, without bothering too much about the prices, a new outfit for Nina and some red shoes which she had set her heart on. They went back to the house for lunch and afterwards Abigail tucked her small charge up for a nap, left Bollinger on guard, and went out for her hour or two's off-duty.

She went to Mrs Macklin's, and that lady was delighted to see her.

'Sit down,' she invited, 'and tell me all your news,' and Abigail took the chair opposite the old lady's in the small, overwarm room.

'Dominic told me that he intended asking you to remain with Nina until her father could come to fetch her, and I told him he was wise to do so, after all, what would he do with a three-year-old to look after and your Bollinger and Mevrouw Boot would spoil her hopelessly—besides,' she added dryly, 'his well-ordered household would have been chaos. He spends most of his days working, but that doesn't prevent him from expecting—and getting—a perfection of comfort which most of us only dream about. You like his house, my dear?'

'What I've seen of it—it's a great deal bigger than one would suppose from the outside, and the furnishings are beautiful.'

Mrs Macklin nodded agreement. 'It's been in the family for hundreds of years. Such a pity if Dominic doesn't marry again, because if he doesn't everything will go to a distant cousin of his, who farms his lands somewhere in Gelderland and dislikes city life, which means that the house here would be neglected, or worse, sold. No, Dominic needs a wife, Abigail, and children too.'

Abigail stirred in her chair, rocked by a brief, glorious daydream. She got up. 'I'll get tea, shall I?' she offered, anxious to have something to do, and as she went to the door: 'I expect he'll find a wife sooner or later. He has a lot of friends in Friesland, hasn't he?'

'Dozens. He's there now—I expect you know that.'

She hadn't known, and after all, there was no reason why he should have told her. She murmured something which meant nothing as she went through the door to the kitchen. Neither of them mentioned him again for the rest of her visit.

He came home that evening. Nina, tired out from trying on her new clothes, not once, but several times, had had her bath and was tucked up in bed, already half asleep. Abigail arranged the nightlight where the child could see it if she wakened, and prepared to go to her room. She left the door open as she always did so that she would hear if Nina called, and sat down in the easy chair by the window. She had meant to do her hair and her face and then count her money, something she had done several times in the last few days, as if by doing so she would increase the small sum left in her purse. Instead, she sat idle, thinking about the professor and wondering where he was and what he was doing.

He was on his way up his own staircase, having let himself into his house with surprising quietness, considering his size. She had heard nothing at all until he asked from the door, 'Is Nina asleep?' and then, when she turned round, 'Hullo, Abigail.'

He looked so pleased to see her that she forgot how untidy she was and that her face needed doing, and smiled warmly at him.

'Oh, nice to see you, Professor,' she spoke impulsively. 'Did you have a good time? Nina's been such a very good girl.'

He leaned against the wall, his hands in his pockets, smiling faintly.

'I'm glad to hear that. May I come in?'

'Of course—but don't you want to see her? She's not been in bed long, I daresay she's still awake. I put her to bed a little early because we went shopping this morning and she was excited and tired.'

He made himself comfortable on the side of the bed. 'What did you buy?'

'Oh, a zipper suit—a nylon one with ribbed cuffs and a high neck; she likes to play in the garden in the morning and she can't do that properly if she's wearing something she has to be careful of. And another dress—she only had two with her, you know, and a pair of red shoes and a little fur bonnet.' She paused, then added guiltily, 'I do hope I haven't been extravagant. . .you did say. . .'

He shrugged wide shoulders. 'I don't think we need worry about that. You're not out of pocket? You must let me know if you are.'

Here was a splendid opportunity to bring up the matter of her salary. She said, 'No. . .' but was interrupted by the entrance of Bollinger, who knocked on the open door and came in with a cheerful air. 'Nice to see you back, boss,' he remarked, 'I seen the car below and there's a Doctor Leesward on the phone for you. He says it's urgent.'

The professor, with a brief word of excuse, went out of the room and Bolly with him; Abigail was left to take off her cap and do her hair and her face, wondering the while if she would have the chance again that evening of bringing up the subject. No chance at all, as it turned out, for when she went downstairs for dinner, a few minutes early, it was to learn from Bollinger that the professor had gone to the hospital and was likely to be late home. She ate the meal as quickly as she could, trying not to feel lonely, then sat by the fire, knitting a pair of red mitts for Nina to match the new red shoes. She had been in bed for more than an hour when she heard the professor come in.

He had gone when she and Nina got down in the morning. They were eating their simple lunch together when he came in. He took his seat at the table to Nina's delight and after glancing at their plates, exclaimed:

'In heaven's name—fish, steamed fish and potato purée!' He looked so horrified that Abigail burst out laughing.

'It's very good,' she said, 'and it's good for Nina's tummy. Besides, there's ice-cream for afters.'

'Good God, who perpetrated this menu?'

'Me,' said Abigail, paying no attention to her grammar. 'It's nourishing and easy to digest.'

'Are you eating it too?'

'Of course—it would be the height of extravagance to have something different—besides, think of Mevrouw Boot.'

'Very commendable. I hope you don't expect me to join you.' He spoke a little absentmindedly and with a muttered word of excuse, pulled some papers out of a pocket and became engrossed in them; Abigail could see that he had other more important things on his mind than his companions at table, so she urged Nina to eat up like a good girl, and went back to her own lunch.

Bollinger came in presently, bearing a magnificent steak, which the professor ate with the same absentminded air, while Abigail, who didn't care for steamed fish at all, tried to keep her nose from twitching at the appetising aroma from his side of the table. She ate the rest of her fish as a good example to Nina, and went on to the ice-cream, while the professor, with every sign of enjoyment, ate hugely of the apple pie and cream Bollinger had brought for him. The cream he shared with his small relative, who had asked, with a good deal of vehemence, if she might have some, but when he offered the dish to Abigail she refused with such promptness that he asked her if she didn't care for it—a singularly annoying question, for they had shared enough meals together by now for him to have noticed that she had never refused it before.

He caught her smouldering gaze and said coolly, 'Ah—I think I understand. I'm breaking my own rules, aren't I? I must say you look very ill-tempered about it.'

A remark calculated to stoke her ill humour, so that she said sharply:

'Yes, you are. You told me exactly what Nina was to eat and I've kept strictly to your wishes. She's clever enough to remember this the next time I give her rice pudding or egg custard. And I don't like steamed fish.'

He shook with laughter. 'My poor dear girl, how tiresome I have been! Excuse me while I explain to my niece.' Which he did, amidst a good deal of giggling from Nina and a bellow of laughter from himself, so rare a sound that Abigail stared.

'It's all right, Abigail, we're not laughing at you. Well, I must go back, I suppose. Would you walk round to Professor de Wit's for me this afternoon? There's a book I particularly want him to have.'

He smiled at her and her heart beat a little faster, and after he had gone she wondered if he could possibly be the same irritable, cold-seeming man she had first met. Probably Nina's company, she thought; he was so fond of the child, and she was indeed a dear little creature. Abigail was fond of her too; she would miss her when she returned home to Spain, and that would be very soon now.

The professor joined her for dinner that evening, and because she could see that he was tired, Abigail, beyond answering his brief enquiries as to the afternoon, made no attempt at conversation. They were eating Mevrouw Boot's perfectly turned out chocolate soufflé when he said:

'Anyone else would have chattered—how did you know that I didn't want to talk?'

'Well,' said Abigail frankly, 'you looked a little forbidding, you know, and weary. I daresay you had something on your mind you wanted to think out quietly, and in that case you would hardly wish to make conversation, would you?'

'Do I usually make conversation with you, Abigail?'

She nodded her neat head at him. 'Oh, yes, but mostly you don't talk at all.' She smiled at him as she spoke, but he remained unsmiling, until:

'Do you find me a bad-tempered man, Abigail?'

She put down her fork and thought before she answered this. He was asking awkward questions again and if she gave the wrong answer he might change back into the same cold, irritable man she had always thought him. On the other hand it would be of no use to fib to him. She said finally:

'No, not bad-tempered—that is, not bad-tempered underneath, are you? otherwise the children would be afraid of you, and they're not, they're sold on you, aren't they? You have always been,' she hesitated, 'abrupt, as though. . .no, that's not quite right. I think you were annoyed at having to meet me; I had the strong impression that you disliked me, that you still do, but not always, and I can't understand that. Is it because I'm English? or perhaps because I'm nothing to look at, although you said it wasn't. . .'

'I'll say it again, if only to convince you. But you are right, I didn't want to meet you, I've had no interest in women—girls—for a long time, but after I had met you I found myself arranging for you to take over a case so that I could see you every day. Do you not find that strange?'

She shook her head, for it seemed no stranger than her own acceptance of his offer for the very same reason. She longed to tell him so, but something warned her not to say anything—not yet.

'Contradictory behaviour, was it not? And you know why?' His blue eyes searched hers, he looked suddenly grim. 'I was once married. It was a long time ago.' The bleakness of his voice hurt her.

'Yes, I know about that.'

He looked suddenly ferocious. 'Who told you? Not the servants—they know better.'

'No, it wasn't the servants, and it wasn't gossip either. It was the only way someone could answer a question I had asked.' She went on hurriedly, trying not to see the arrogantly arched brows, 'You see, I couldn't understand why you were sometimes. . .just as though you hated me. . .and others. . .' she became a trifle incoherent, remembering the other times. 'I got upset once or twice and—and angry, and to make me understand better, this—person told me about you—just that you had been married and had lost your wife. I didn't ask any questions, it wasn't my business.' She added with a little flare-up of feeling, 'It isn't my business now; you started telling me—I should never have dreamed of mentioning it.'

'It's something I don't talk about. I'm surprised that I'm talking about it now, but I wanted to tell you, Abigail—I had to tell you, before. . . ' He paused as Bollinger came into the room to enquire where they would have their coffee.

'Oh, here,' said the professor impatiently. 'We'll ring when we're ready for you to clear, thank you, Bollinger.'

Bollinger was back very quickly, and a good thing too from Abigail's point of view, for in the deep silence in which they sat her thoughts were racing round and round inside her head, thoughts she hardly dared to think. If she had been a cool, poised girl, she would have used those few minutes to good purpose instead of allowing her brain to seethe with nonsense.

She poured the coffee when it came and handed him his cup across the table and met his eyes as she did so, her own troubled and bewildered.

He said thoughtfully, 'It's strange, Abigail, but in all these years I have never wanted to tell anyone—and I must admit to several—er—friendships in that time—about my marriage, but I want to tell you, because you're different; you know what it is to be unhappy and you're honest too and I think that you would keep a confidence. But you see, my dear, I have grown wary of women, and I found it difficult.'

'You're sure you want to tell me? You're not going to feel awful about it in the morning?'

He laughed a little and shook his head, then passed his cup for more coffee and she busied herself filling it, then put the cup down, forgetting to give it back to him, her eyes upon his as he began to speak.

'I married when I was twenty-five—fifteen years ago. Did you know that I am almost forty-one, Abigail? She was very pretty and gay too, she loved clothes and jewels and furs and fast cars and she was the kind of girl men like to be seen about with—I counted myself very fortunate when she agreed to marry me. It took me just six weeks to discover that she didn't love me, and another six weeks for me to find out that I didn't love her. Perhaps if I had loved her I could have forgiven her the affairs she had. She was killed in a car crash, together with the current boy-friend, five months after we were married. I swore I would never love another woman again, for although I had no feeling for her, my pride suffered, and although, as I said just now, I became—involved, shall we say, from time to time, it meant nothing to me.' He put out his hand for his coffee cup. 'Now you know why I have never allowed anything—any woman, to interfere with my life.'

Abigail emptied the cooling coffee from his cup and poured fresh with a steady hand, which was surprising, for inside she was trembling. It seemed to her that she had been warned that, even though he liked her, he had no intention of allowing his feelings to take over from the life he had decided upon. What other reason could he have had for telling her something he admitted he had never discussed with anyone? The only good reason would be because he loved her, and he had had plenty of opportunity of saying so; it could be dismissed without a thought. He had felt the urge to talk; he was used to her by now and presumably, as she was a suitable recipient of his confidences, he felt himself able to talk to her. She summoned a smile.

'Thank you for telling me, Professor. It was a truly awful thing to happen to you and I can well imagine that it's made you wary of women. But it's a long time ago. I'm sure you will find someone who will change your views for you. Perhaps you don't get out enough to meet people; you work so hard, don't you? There are a great many nice girls in the world, you know.'

'You suggest that I should find one and marry her?'

'Yes, why not? Just because there's one rotten apple in the barrel doesn't mean that the whole barrelful is bad.' She made her voice as matter-of-fact as she could.

'But I enjoy working hard. If I took a wife she might try to change that.'

'But she wouldn't—not if she loved you, she would want to help you in every way she could.'

He looked amused. 'How?'

She was suddenly out of patience with him. 'How should I know? She's the one to answer that question.'

'I must remember to ask her when the time comes.' He spoke gravely, although there was a gleam in his eyes. 'And now, much as I have enjoyed this conversation, I have to go back to the hospital. There is a case. . .'

He told her about it and she listened with interest

and asked questions too; it was another ten minutes before he got to his feet.

And as for Abigail, she rang the bell for poor patient Bollinger and went to sit by the fire, and when he came into the room, said how sorry she was that they had been so desultory over their dinner.

'That's OK, Miss Abby,' said Bollinger, busy with the table, 'I was right glad to see you having such a nice chat. The boss don't often talk. He must like you.'

Abigail swallowed from a throat thick with the tears she would have liked to shed. 'I do believe he does, Bolly,' she agreed sadly.

The professor was at breakfast when she and Nina went down the following morning. He lifted his niece into her chair, tied her bib, urged her to eat up her porridge and then turned his attention to Abigail, who had sat down silently after a quiet good morning. Unlike her, he seemed in the best of spirits.

'I'm going to Friesland tomorrow; Bollinger will be going with me, for he has to see about bulbs for the garden there. I think it would be nice if Nina were to accompany us—you too, naturally, Abigail.' He gave her a bright glance. 'I feel that Nina has deserved a treat, do you not agree?'

'Yes, she's been as good as gold, but are you sure you want me to come?' She coloured faintly and added hastily, 'She doesn't really need a nurse now.'

'No? Bollinger and I love her dearly, but I believe we should both be mentally deranged by the end of the day if there wasn't someone to take her off our hands for at least part of the time. I have business to attend to and Bollinger takes his bulbs seriously.'

Abigail couldn't help smiling at him. She had never seen him look so relaxed. 'Then I'll come, I should like to. What time do you want us to be ready?'

'Could you manage eight o'clock? We could make it later if you like—it's barely a hundred miles.'

'I'm sure we can be ready by then. Nina wakes early, you know.'

'Does she? She keeps very quiet about it.'

'Well, she gets into my bed and I tell her a story.'

'In English?' He was laughing again.

'A little of both. She understands quite a lot, don't you, poppet?' She turned to look at the small girl beside her, tucking into a boiled egg and fingers of bread and butter with remarkable energy. 'Yes,' said the poppet from a full mouth, adding rapidly, 'No—Mary, Mary, quite con. . .con. . .' a frown marred the small features, to be replaced by a rapturous smile. 'Little Boy Blue. . .' she began.

'Lovely, darling,' said Abigail fondly, 'you're a clever girl, but eat up that nice egg and Oom Dominic will tell you something very exciting.'

The egg was forgotten. 'Oom Dominic,' she smiled eggily up at him, 'tell,' she commanded in an imperious pipe.

Her uncle told her and rather unfairly left a few minutes later, leaving Abigail to calm a very excited little girl. He didn't come back all day and Abigail ate her dinner alone, not sure whether to be relieved or not. She had spent a good part of the night and most of the day persuading herself that the only way possible to her was to forget most of what the professor had said and to remember that within a very short time she would be going away and would never see him again, and in the meantime to behave exactly as she always had done. Breakfast had been a test; she considered she had come out of it rather well. She talked to Bollinger as she ate, glad of the opportunity of explaining that she would be able to pay him some more money very soon—quite a lot of money, she pointed out; she hadn't been paid for three weeks, and there would be some money over, even after that, for she still had her fare intact. After her old friend had gone, she curled up by the fire. There would be enough left to buy some clothes; she occupied herself deciding what she would buy when she got back to London.

They were ready as she had promised by eight o'clock, with Nina in the fur bonnet and the red shoes to match the zipper suit. Abigail, standing beside her in the hall, wore the tweed coat, which she now loathed, her knitted beret and the scarf to match. She hated those almost as much; only the gloves Professor de Wit had given her gave her pleasure. Her boots still leaked, but Bolly, bless him, had cleaned them beautifully and no one knew about the leak. But she felt shabby beside her small charge and she had an uneasy feeling that the professor shared her feelings as he came into the hall, for the look he gave her was a leisurely and searching one, starting at the pompom of her beret, and going slowly down to her feet. The little smile he gave her did nothing to mollify her ruffled feelings.

There had been some late snow during the night, just sufficient to turn the roads to slush and powder the bare trees, but once out of the city, the flat country on either side of the motorway was blanketed in white; only the road ahead of them gleamed blackly. Abigail, sitting comfortably in the warmth of the big car, with Nina cuddled close to her and Colossus beside her, felt sorry for the drivers of the slow-moving farm carts drawn by plodding horses, but Nina, untroubled by this aspect of the winter's morning, wanted to know about the horses; she wanted to know about the cows and the canals and the windmills and bridges too; Abigail's Dutch was strained to breaking point and the professor, helping her out from time to time with the right words laughed a good deal, and Bollinger glanced at him several times, surprise all over his wrinkled face.

They went by way of the sea dyke, over the Ijsselmeer, and there was nothing to see because the snow blotted out the view on either side and the road ahead was straight, fading into an unseen horizon. Abigail scarcely noticed when they reached the mainland and the professor told her that they were in Friesland. They went down the coast of the great inland water and then turned inland to Bolsward and on to Sneek, both of which small towns Abigail had but the briefest glimpse of, but what she saw enchanted her, for despite the snow and the grey sky and the lack of people about the streets, they were picturesque.

They turned off the main road presently, and then again, this time into a much narrower road, running between fields with no villages to be seen. They could, thought Abigail, be in the middle of a snow-covered desert, and had her thought answered by the professor, who remarked easily:

'A little bleak today, I'm afraid, but when it is clear weather, the country is charming.'

The road gave way to a still narrower one, made of bricks and uneven, with a signpost pointing to Eernewoude, but before they reached there the professor swung the car into a side lane lined with bare trees, and almost at once through an open gateway. The lane ended abruptly in a wide sweep of cobblestones and before them was the house.

It was an old house, with a multitude of gables, and built of rose bricks, and while not large, appeared roomy enough. Its windows were small and arched and its panelled door studded with nails. The door swung open as they got out of the car, Nina was whisked up into her uncle's arms, and with an invitation to follow him, Abigail went inside, with Bollinger behind.

It was similar to the house in Amsterdam, with the same square hall with its black and white flagged floor and its lovely linenfold panelling, but this hall extended back a good deal further and the staircase rose out of its centre and divided from a little landing half way up it. It smelled of wax polish and potpourri and was pleasantly warm. Abigail's coat was taken from her and she was invited to go into one of the rooms on the right of the entrance, but not before the professor had introduced the old woman who had opened the door. Joke, he called her, and it was apparent that he and she had known each other for a long time.

The room they went into was quite large and a little dark by reason of the weather outside and the small windows, but the lamps in their wall brackets gave it a cheerful air, as did the fire burning briskly in the old-fashioned cast-iron fireplace. It was furnished in much the same style as the small sitting room in Amsterdam; a happy blend of comfort and antiques.

The professor offered Abigail an easy chair by the fire and Nina immediately perched on her lap. Bollinger had disappeared. 'To see to those bulbs of his,' explained the professor. 'My gardener, the man Bollinger has replaced so well, is convalescing here, they will no doubt have a most interesting talk over their coffee.'

'However can they talk?' Abigail wanted to know, 'unless your gardener knows any English.'

'He does. He was in England during the war. Besides, they both know the Latin names of everything that grows, which makes it easy.'

The idea of Bollinger being so clever hadn't entered Abigail's head. She said in astonishment, 'How extraordinary, Bolly speaking Latin.'

'He's a clever old man when it comes to gardens,' replied the professor, and went to take the coffee tray from Joke.

Over coffee he said, 'I shall be busy for an hour or two. Can you amuse yourselves, do you think? The garden is quite large. It's stopped snowing again. I daresay if Nina's sufficiently wrapped up, she might like to make a snowman—there's just about enough for that.'

Abigail, thinking uneasily of her leaking boots, agreed because Nina wanted to go outside so badly, and moreover, the professor had finished his coffee and she sensed that he wanted to be gone. There was a wide stretch of lawn behind the house and plenty of snow to make the promised snowman. Between them they made a magnificent specimen and then snowballed each other and Colossus until they were warm and Nina was tired.

'Time to go indoors,' said Abigail firmly, and scooped up the little girl and bore her inside. Even after they had tidied themselves in the cloakroom surprisingly hidden in the hall panelling, there was still an hour till lunch. They went back to sit by the fire, and Nina, on Abigail's lap, recited her jumble of nursery rhymes. She was giving her own version of Baa Baa, Black Sheep when the professor joined them. He listened gravely to his niece's efforts, congratulated her with suitable enthusiasm and offered Abigail a drink before stretching himself out in the chair on the opposite side of the hearth. It was pleasant sitting there in the warm, delightfully furnished room. Abigail sipped her sherry, on the edge of a daydream, and was brought back to reality by his voice.

'Nina's going home in two days' time, Abigail. Dirk telephoned me. We shall miss her, shan't we?'

'Yes, very much.' She contrived to make her voice normal. 'Will she go by car?'

'Yes, Dirk will be here tomorrow evening and will spend the night, and they will leave the next morning. You will wish to return to England as soon as possible?'

She could only say yes to that and add: 'Is Bollinger to come with me?'

'Not unless you want him to, but it's entirely up to you—and him—to decide.'

Abigail looked relieved without knowing it. 'Oh, well, if he could stay—you see I shall have to find another job and—and somewhere to live, and if it's a case where I have to live in, I must find a room for Bolly. It would be nice if I could have it all settled before he goes back to England.'

'It would be nicer still,' said the professor, not looking at her at all but into his glass, 'if you would stay on for a while and work in the hospital.'

Her heart rocketed into her throat, she swallowed it back, staring at his downbent head. 'Oh, yes, it would, but is there a job for me there?'

'My dear good girl, we are as short of nurses here as they are in England. I can think of half a dozen vacancies. . .you don't mind where you work?'

'No—at least, I know Zuster Ritsma already and

she speaks English, which makes it easier for me, and I prefer surgery.'

'Theatre?'

'Yes—I did six months.'

He nodded and put down his glass, half smiling. 'Good, that's settled then—how about having your room at Mrs Macklin's again?'

'Do you suppose she would let me? I should like that very much.'

'So will she.' He got up and lifted Nina into his arms. 'Shall we have lunch, and then while this young lady is having her nap, I'll show you round the house.'

Lunch was a gay meal and the food so good that Abigail felt constrained to mention it.

'Joke's daughter,' the professor told her. 'It's her husband who does the garden. Joke attends to the housekeeping although she has retired, but she's lived here all her life and it's home to her. She lives with Arie and her daughter in the little cottage behind the garage.'

They ate thick pea soup, followed by grilled sole and a salad; the sweet, as a concession to Nina's youthful appetite, was a pile of waffles and a great dish of whipped cream. They drank a dry white wine with it and the professor poured Nina's orangeade with the same care as he poured the wine. Abigail, watching the two of them, thought what a splendid father he would make, for he was surprisingly patient with children. Only with himself, she thought sadly, was he impatient.

When they had finished, he led the way upstairs to a small room on the first floor, where Joke was turning down the coverlet of a narrow bed with a carved headboard.

'Odilia used to sleep here when she was little,' the professor told Abigail. 'I've never changed it, it seemed so right for a little girl. It hasn't been used for a long time. . .' He frowned a little and Abigail busied herself with Nina because she could guess why he was frowning—there might have been a small daughter of his own in that room. Out on the landing after tucking Nina up under the pink eiderdown she asked, 'Have you really got the time to take me round? I shall be quite happy on my own if there's something else you want to do.'

'There's nothing else I want to do,' he spoke briskly. 'Let's go downstairs first, shall we?'

There were two other rooms besides the sitting room and the darkly splendid dining room; one a vast drawing room, hung with silk panels in a faded strawberry pink, with an Aubusson carpet on its floor and dark green curtains of velvet. Its walls were lined with cabinets displaying china and silver and glass and on either side of its vast fireplace were velvet-covered sofas flanked by rosewood sofa tables. Here too the chairs were a happy mixture of modern comfort and antiques and what paintings there were were light flower studies or pastoral scenes.

The other room was the library, its walls crowded with books, and from the look of it, frequently used. The furniture was heavy and smelled faintly of tobacco and leather, and Abigail wrinkled her nose. 'Nice,' she commented. 'What a marvellous collection of books. I suppose most of them are in Dutch.'

'Some—there are quite a number in English, though, and German and a few in French.' He gave her a sidelong glance and smiled. 'I have to keep up with my studies, you know.'

She agreed gravely, 'Yes, of course, but I expect you write too, don't you?'

'Only when I have something worthwhile to say.'

He led her back into the hall and up the staircase to the bedrooms, more numerous than she would have supposed, each with its narrow windows and each too, with its own colour scheme, pale vague blues and pinks and greens which acted as magnificent foils to the beautiful old furniture, and was echoed again in the thick carpeting.

Abigail sighed gently as they went downstairs again. 'It's a beautiful house, as beautiful as your house in Amsterdam—have your family lived here for a long time?'

They were back in the sitting room, facing each other across the fireplace with Colossus between them. The professor eased himself into his chair and answered her in a leisurely fashion.

'Yes, three hundred years or so. My family are Friesian, you know, with strong ties with Amsterdam. While I was married we came here very seldom. My—wife disliked it, it is so quiet, you see. Only the country around us and a handful of small houses, but I find it delightful.'

Abigail nodded. 'And Amsterdam—surely you love your house there?'

'Yes, equally, I suppose—but here I can escape, you see.'

She saw very well. Away from the bustle of the hospital and his eternal round of patients and still more patients, this old house would be like a quiet heaven. She said so and was rewarded by his smile. 'You see how you have changed me,' he said quietly. 'Before I came to know you I should have suspected you of saying that merely to please me.'

'Isn't that a little conceited of you?'

'Yes—but perhaps you don't know that for a number of years I have been regarded in the light of a good—what is the word?—catch, I believe. I have come to regard any girl who agreed too readily with me or said something obviously meant to attract my attention or win my approval as highly suspect.'

'So that's why you accused me of toadying. But they may have meant it—they might have been charming. . .'

'Just as my wife was charming?' He gave her a bitter little smile. 'Do you not say in your own language: Once bitten, twice shy? I am very shy, Abigail.'

She eyed him warily. He looked irritable again and all set to say something ill-tempered. Perhaps it would be a good idea to talk about something else.

'You have a lovely garden,' she told him brightly. 'Do roses do well here?'

The look of bitterness left his face; he looked as

though he was going to laugh. 'Excellently—there is a large bed in the centre of the lawn at the back of the house, and there's a rose walk besides, at one side.'

'I should have loved to have seen it,' said Abigail regretfully. 'We had a rose garden, when we lived in the country. Bolly was very good with them and my mother had great bowls of them around the house.'

He said deliberately, 'Tell me about your parents, Abigail.'

'I don't think I want to. . .'

'Yes, you do, only you have buried them deep down, haven't you? You shouldn't, you know. Happy times are for remembering. When did you move to London?'

She found herself telling him about her childhood and her parents, and Bolly and the pleasant house they had lived in, and he scarcely interrupted her, sitting in his chair, smoking a pipe and staring at the ceiling and not at her at all. When she had finished she felt as though she had talked all the sadness away for ever and left only happy memories. She sat up straight, aware that she had been talking for a long time. 'I'm sorry,' she said shyly, 'I didn't mean. . . I must have bored you. . .'

He got up and pulled her to her feet and stood in front of her, her hands still in his. 'No, never that. You deserve a happier future, Abigail.'

She reddened. 'I don't pity myself in the least; I'm very fortunate to have a job—and there's Bolly. . .'

'Don't you have other friends?'

She answered reluctantly. 'Yes—quite a number, but one doesn't burden friends, they have their own lives.' She fidgeted under his steady gaze. 'Shall I go and fetch Nina down?'

'By all means. I have to work for half an hour or so.'

He sounded aloof, even annoyed, perhaps because she had refused to talk about herself; indeed, thinking about it she thought that perhaps she had snubbed him although she hadn't meant to do so. She went slowly from the room and up the lovely staircase to where Nina was waiting impatiently to be got up.

They went back after tea, and Abigail, half hoping that the professor might suggest that she and Nina should sit beside him, was disappointed. The two men talked about gardens and gardening for the whole of the journey. Nina had dropped off to sleep, curled up like a kitten in her lap, Colossus slept too, and Abigail was left with her thoughts again, and they weren't very happy.

She dined alone, for the professor, Bollinger informed her, had gone out. 'Some big do or other,' he confided. 'All got up, he is, and very handsome too. Must give the ladies a treat. I hear you're to work in the hospital for a while, Miss Abby, and very nice too, if I may say so. You'll be living with that nice Mrs Macklin again?'

'Yes, Bolly, though I don't know for how long. I'm so glad for you—you're happy here, aren't you?'

'Not half! Lovely bit of garden in that house where we went today, and no one breathing down your neck—I missed me garden, Miss Abby.'

'Oh, Bolly dear, I know, and I'll never be able to repay you for giving it all up when Father died. What should we have done without you? You've been a real friend. I hope I stay for ages, just to make you happy.'

'Won't you be happy too, Miss Abby?' He sounded wistful and full of curiosity all at once.

'Yes, I shall, actually, Bolly.' She didn't look at him. 'I think I'll go to bed early, I'm almost as tired as Nina.' She gave him a sweet smile and presently wandered through the quiet house and up to her room.

She didn't hurry over her bath and it was an hour or more before she was ready for bed, and when she went into Nina's room as she always did at bedtime, it was to find the child awake. It took only a few minutes for her to discover that Nina wasn't ill, only excited. She had slept and wakened and remembered that she was to go home in a day's time and she wanted to talk about it. Abigail fetched her some warm milk from the kitchen and then curled up beside her on the bed while she sipped it, very slowly and with pauses for excited chatter. But presently she had said it all and the milk was nearly finished. She edged nearer Abigail. 'Not pretty,' she informed her, fingering Abigail's dressing gown, a serviceable one she had received from her aunt and uncle at Christmas. Nina was right, it wasn't in the least pretty; a dim red, thick and woolly, it made Abigail's plumpness assume enormous proportions and the colour merely emphasized the mediocrity of her features.

'Hideous,' she agreed, and Nina cheerfully echoed her. 'But it's warm,' Abigail went on, just as though Nina could understand every word she said, 'and it covers me up. I hate it.'

'What do you hate with such vehemence?' asked the professor from the door, and Abigail jumped and said crossly, 'Don't you know that you shouldn't creep up on people. It's most upsetting.'

He advanced into the room, looking twice his usual size in his tails. Definitely a reception, thought Abigail, eyeing his snowy waistcoat and white tie. He bowed his head in mock humility. 'My apologies, Abigail. I had no intention of frightening you, only to make sure that my niece was sleeping.'

He looked at her enquiringly as he spoke and she made haste to explain.

'She's had some milk, and now we've had a little talk, she'll go back to sleep. I'll stay with her until she does.'

He said nothing to this, merely bent to kiss Nina and be hugged before going to sit in a rocking chair in a corner of the room, blandly ignoring Abigail's look of enquiry in her turn.

'Baa, baa, black sheep,' demanded Nina sleepily, and Abigail obediently repeated the verses; she did so several times until she saw that the child was asleep again, and got up quietly to leave the room. On the way to the door she paused. 'Good night, Professor,' she whispered to the silent man sitting so still, and was shocked into a gasp, for he was beside her, going through the door almost before the words were out of her mouth.

The landing was dim and warm, through the half open door of her room she could see the cheerful glow of the bedside lamp. Somewhere downstairs Bollinger was tramping about, closing windows and shutting doors. For a moment she had the illusion that she lived in a safe, secure world which she shared with the professor, a world where she was cherished and loved and even, absurdly, admired. She tightened her mouth to prevent her lips quivering with the sudden horrid threat of tears, and with a nod in the general direction of the professor, who was behind her, started towards her room. But he wasn't behind her, he was beside her, in front of her. His arms were round her and all so quickly that she had no means of eluding him, and anyway, she didn't want to. He asked: 'What were you hating?'

The question was a surprise, all the same she answered it truthfully.

'My dressing gown—it's hideous.'

He held her away from him and surveyed her slowly. 'Indeed it is—not your own choosing, surely?'

'No.'

'Then go out and buy yourself the most glamorous garment you can find,' he advised her.

Perhaps not quite the right moment to mention her salary, but probably as good as any; at least they were alone and uninterrupted. She opened her mouth and began: 'I wonder...'

'Don't talk,' said the professor with a touch of his old imperious manner, and kissed her. He kissed her several times, and with a fine disregard for good sense, she kissed him back.

It was only when, five minutes later, she was in her room again, that she remembered that he had said nothing at all and she, to her chagrin, had. Not much, but enough. It had, at the time, seemed quite natural to address him as Dominic darling.

CHAPTER NINE

SHE went down to breakfast the next morning, with Nina holding her hand; she looked as calm as was her habit and her neat appearance gave no indication of the sleepless night she had passed. Most of it she had spent reassuring herself. The professor might not have heard her, she had told herself over and over again, and even if he had, it didn't really matter, but these brave thoughts were reduced to meaningless nonsense by the certain knowledge that although she hadn't spoken loudly, she had certainly repeated herself several times—there was nothing wrong with the professor's hearing either. Her pale cheeks reddened painfully as she entered the dining room with the gaily chattering Nina dancing beside her, a prey to a variety of expectations, all of them unthinkable.

None of them materialised. The professor was sitting on the side of the table, with a cup of coffee in one hand and the telephone in the other. He lifted his eyes from the thoughtful contemplation of his elegantly shod feet, met Abigail's look with a vague one of his own, said 'Morning,' and broke into a lengthy monologue in Dutch. When he had finished he listened for a moment, frowned, said something loud and rather violent, which she was glad she couldn't understand, gulped his coffee and said:

'I must go, Abigail—something's turned up. Tell Dirk to come to the hospital as soon as he arrives.'

He dropped a hand on to Nina's small head and ruffled her hair, nodded to Abigail and left the room, and very shortly afterwards, the house, banging the house door after him quite unnecessarily.

Abigail drank coffee while Nina munched her way through her breakfast. She felt a little let down, just as one would feel when, having screwed up courage to go to the dentist to have a tooth pulled, one was told that there was no need. The professor couldn't have heard her. Perhaps he was a little drunk; after all, he had been to a banquet or something similar. It was a pity that this comforting theory was quite shattered by her complete certainty that he wasn't the sort of man to get drunk, not even slightly. All that remained was that he had heard her, and—mortifying thought—had dismissed the incident as so trivial as to be beneath his notice.

Dirk arrived a couple of hours later, had coffee with them, an enraptured Nina on his knee, gave Abigail a brief account of his wife and son's health, and departed for the hospital. She saw neither him nor the professor until dinner that evening, when the conversation was of Spain, Odilia, the new baby and his journey back the following morning.

The professor had talked to her, from time to time, with his usual faint aloofness; he certainly hadn't bothered to look at her overmuch. She retired to her room early, pleading packing for Nina, wishing the two gentlemen a cool goodnight as she went.

She was getting ready for bed when she remembered that although she was to go to the hospital on the following day, no one had told her how or when she was to go and the professor would either be gone or on the point of going by the time she and Nina got down in the morning; she decided to pack her own case too, so that, if necessary, she could leave at a moment's notice—she went down the back stairs too, and explained to Bollinger. She then returned to her room, slightly out of temper, to sleep fitfully and be awakened much too early by a joyful Nina wanting to get up and dress and go with her papa on the instant.

They were early for breakfast, only to find that the professor had left the house at six o'clock that morning to undertake an emergency operation. There was still no sign of him by the time Dirk and his small daughter were ready to leave in the former's Mercedes-Benz 350 SL; they were making their final farewells when the telephone rang and Abigail answered it. The professor's voice sounded quietly in her ear. 'Abigail? Ask Dirk to come to the telephone, will you? And Nina.'

It was a short conversation; Nina gave Abigail a last hug, Dirk wrung her hand and they had gone. She went back into the house with Bollinger and Mevrouw Boot, wondering what she was supposed to do. At the end of an hour she decided to go to the hospital. She couldn't stay in the house without a patient and she had a job to go to anyway—besides, she still had to find out if Mrs Macklin would have her again. She put on her outdoor clothes, fetched her case downstairs, said a temporary goodbye to Bollinger and went to the front door. The professor opened it as she put her hand on its massive brass knob.

He said instantly, 'Running away?'

The unfairness of this remark stung her to snap, 'Don't be ridiculous! I'm on my way to the hospital. You asked me to work there, if you remember, and there's no reason for me to remain here any longer.'

He answered this logical remark by shutting the door firmly behind him and leading her by the arm across the hall to his study. He shut this door too before taking off his coat and tossing it untidily over a chair, then he caught hold of her arm again and propelled her across the room, so that she was standing by a window with the cold, unkind March light on her face.

'Did you sleep?' The question was unexpected and she was taken off her guard. She faltered: 'Well, not. . .' she looked up at him, aware that her face wasn't at its best in the harsh grey morning. He didn't look tired, nor did he look aloof, and the little irritable frown had gone completely, and his eyes, which had looked at her so coldly on so many occasions, were warm and twinkling. She began again: 'Not very. . .' to be interrupted:

'I heard you, dear Abigail, did you think that I did not?' He put a hand lightly on her shoulder. 'You and I, we have to talk, but not now. Zuster Ritsma wants you on duty at midday; it seemed quicker to come and fetch you than telephoning.' A smile touched the corners of his mouth. 'That's not true, I wanted to see you—that's why I came. I didn't know that you would be packed and ready, but as you are, we had better go. Will you come with me?'

Abigail smiled at him; she felt happy and excited and intensely curious as to what they would talk about. 'I'm quite ready,' she told him, in a voice which shook very slightly with these feelings. He took his hand from her shoulder and ushered her out into the hall. Bollinger was there, standing by her case. He carried it out to the car for her, his face alight with smiles. He shut the car door on her, wished her goodbye, admonished her not to work too hard and then stood on the steps to watch them go. Abigail turned to wave as they reached the corner of the *gracht*.

They were almost at the hospital when the professor spoke.

'I have a great deal of work which must be done,' he sighed, 'and this evening I have to go to Brussels for two days. When I return, there are things to tell you, Abigail, dear girl.'

She turned her head to look at him and for a fleeting moment his eyes met hers and he smiled. Two days seemed a very long time, but if that was what he wanted, she would wait. She said rather breathlessly, 'Very well, Professor,' and when he said on a laugh, 'Did you not call me Dominic?' she repeated obediently, 'Dominic.'

They parted in the front hall of the hospital and she didn't see him to speak to alone after that. True, he did a round in the children's ward where she had been sent to work, but beyond asking her one or two questions about the baby she was bottle-feeding, he said nothing. He hardly looked at her—indeed, she had the strong impression that he was deliberately avoiding her eye. Only as he came to a halt at the ward door did he turn round to look back at her, a look, brief though it was, to destroy the ridiculous doubts which had edged into her mind during the day.

The two days were endless, even though they had been busy ones on the ward, and her off-duty had been fully occupied settling in again with a delighted Mrs Macklin. She had visited Professor de Wit too, who seemed to take it for granted that she would remain permanently in Amsterdam and invited her for tea the following week. The day the professor was to return was a renewal of winter. Abigail walked to work through the bleak coldness of the city streets, sure that, despite the fact that it was the first week of March, it would snow before nightfall—not that she minded, for Dominic was coming. Within a few hours she would see him again, and the world, despite a regrettable shortage of money and her still leaking boots, seemed a lovely place.

She looked at the clock as she went to feed the first of the babies. Even now he might be getting on the plane although it was early enough—too early perhaps, but some time that day. . .beyond that delightful thought she was careful not to think; there was a good deal of work to get through, and she would need all her wits about her to get done. She dismissed the delights of the future and picked up an urgently crying baby.

It was a tiresome morning; Zuster Ritsma was off duty, the other two nurses spoke only the most basic of English, and it was a relief when Henk strolled on to the ward and after doing a round stopped for a chat. They were standing with their backs to the door and he was telling her in his inaccurate unidiomatic English about his latest girl-friend—a lady, it seemed, of many charms but a good deal older than he. He asked anxiously of Abigail: 'Too old, you think?'

Abigail laughed at him. 'Of course it's too old,' she spoke gaily. 'A gap of how many? fifteen years, isn't it? It's absurd—but of course it's not serious—just a passing fancy and a chance to have a good time.'

He rolled his eyes at her and said dramatically, 'My *lieveling*. . .' and Abigail, trying not to laugh at him said, 'No, no—your darling,' and laughed then because he looked so funny and she was so happy she could have laughed at anything. The slight sound behind her caused her to turn her head. The professor was standing behind them, in the doorway, only a foot or so away, staring at her; her smile faded before the iciness of his eyes.

He said with a cool blandness which hurt her, 'Good morning, Nurse Trent. Henk, I want you in the theatre in ten minutes.' As he turned away he added in a voice like a razor's edge, 'I'm sorry to interrupt your—er—conversation.'

He didn't wait for Henk, who, preparing to follow him, exclaimed, 'And what's he in a rage for? And he's back hours earlier than he said. Perhaps he missed his dollybird in Brussels.' He saw the stricken look on Abigail's face as he said it and added hurriedly, 'I joke, Abigail—he has no dollybird. *Dag*.'

He hurried away after his chief and Abigail, left alone, went to see why the baby in the first cubicle was crying. She had no idea what had come over the professor; he hadn't looked like that for a long time now and she had been quite unprepared for it. She tended the baby with gentle, competent hands, telling herself that something must have happened in Brussels to have upset him, trying to ignore the fact that he wasn't a man who was easily upset.

He did a round in the afternoon, surrounded by students, with his senior registrar and Henk flanking his every movement. He was delightful with the children and curt with everyone else. Abigail, trailing along behind Zuster Ritsma, felt sorry for the students, who, unless they came up with the right answers to the professor's barked questions, were subjected to a withering fire from his tongue and a look of such irritation that the most stouthearted of them were quailed. From the safety of Zuster Ritsma's rear, she watched him; not only did he look ill-tempered, he looked weary too. Perhaps when they were alone together he would tell her what the matter was. He glanced round and she caught his eye and gave him a small loving smile which stiffened on her face as he looked through her. She felt her cheeks pale and for the rest of the round didn't look at him at all. Only after he had gone, and it was time for her to go off duty, she made her way down to the porter's lodge and asked where he was and if she could see him. The porter looked surprised, but he went to the switchboard and after a few minutes he shook his head. 'Professor van Wijkelen is *weg*,' he told her.

She walked slowly back to the changing room. Why had he gone without leaving a message? She stopped in the middle of the corridor. Surely she hadn't imagined all that he had said to her—worse still, mistaken his meaning?

She had cheered up a little by the time she reached Mrs Macklin's house, having persuaded herself that Dominic would come that evening. She stayed in the little sitting room, her ears strained for his footsteps, and when Mrs Macklin wanted to know if he was back, explained in a colourless voice that yes, he was but that he seemed to be busy.

'Not too busy to see you,' stated Mrs Macklin decidedly, and when Abigail gave her an enquiring look, 'He's a different man since he met you, my dear. It's amazing what love will do.'

'Love?' faltered Abigail.

'You love him, don't you? He needs someone to love him and to love. He has become so embittered over the years that I was beginning to think that he would never allow himself to love another woman, but I think you have changed that. I wonder why he doesn't come.'

Abigail looked up from the contemplation of her nails. 'I don't know. When he went away, he said—he said there was no time to talk then, but when he came back. . .he came back this morning, but he's. . . something's happened. He's not coming.' She was sure of that now. 'Perhaps tomorrow.' She looked appealingly at her companion. 'I expect he's tired.'

The old lady eyed her thoughtfully. 'You're tired too, Abigail. Go to bed, my dear. Things are always better in the morning.'

Abigail did as she was told for the simple reason that she didn't much care what she did and bed was as good as anywhere else; contrary to her expectations, she slept all night.

She was off duty at four-thirty the next day too. The morning passed quickly enough; there were two cases for theatre and she went with both of them; tiny babies with pyloric stenosis and the professor operating. If he saw her in the theatre he gave no sign, but she hadn't expected him to. She stayed by the anaesthetist, performing the small duties he required of her throughout the two operations. When she got back from her dinner it was to discover from Zuster Ritsma that the professor had been to see his patients and since he would be operating for the rest of the afternoon, the chance of seeing him was slight. She went off duty a little late, spinning out the minutes in case he should come; she even went a long way round to the hospital entrance in the hope of seeing him, despising herself for doing so—she had never thought much of girls who chased men, and here she was doing just that. There was no sign of him, so she went back to the Begijnhof and after tea went for a long walk. Let him telephone and find her out, she told herself bracingly, it would serve him right if she wasn't there at his beck and call. Only he didn't telephone. She went to bed early and cried herself to sleep.

She was on at one o'clock the next day and would work until nine in the evening. Zuster Ritsma was on too and a couple of student nurses, and because the ward was full and some of the children and babies were very ill, they were kept busy. It was well after three o'clock when Abigail went to the office to pour the tea for Zuster Ritsma and herself. They had barely sat down to drink it when the professor walked in.

Zuster Ritsma looked at him with resignation. She had been on her feet for a long time and now here he was, wanting to do a round, she supposed. Before she could speak he said, 'No, no round.'

'A cup of tea?' she smiled her relief.

'Thank you, no.' He hadn't looked at Abigail, but he gave her the briefest of glances now, a look of cool enquiry which prompted her to ask:

'You would like me to go, sir?'

'Since it concerns you, Nurse Trent, I see no need for that.' He smiled thinly. 'We are now fully staffed, or nearly so; it only remains for me to thank you for the help you have given us and tell you that there is now no further need of your services. I am sure that we are all most grateful to you for the way in which you helped out, but I am sure you will be glad to be free to arrange your own future.'

Abigail listened to this speech with absolute amazement; she wasn't even sure if half of it were true to begin with, but she could hardly challenge him on that score. She was a freelance nurse, under no obligation to give or receive a month's notice, so presumably the hospital could terminate her job when they wished. She found her voice and filled the awkward pause with an over-hearty, 'Oh, splendid, I shall be able to go back...' Her voice petered away, because unless someone paid her, she couldn't go back to England; she hadn't got her fare any more, for she had paid Mrs Macklin for her room, and she had been paying for her meals in hospital too. She could borrow from Bolly, but that was something she wasn't prepared to do; she had leaned on Bolly enough in the last few years.

Neither Zuster Ritsma nor the professor appeared to notice her hesitancy.

'We shall miss you, Nurse Trent,' said Zuster Ritsma kindly. 'You are good with the children, is that not so, Professor?'

'Very good.' He spoke shortly and turned to go, his face blandly polite, no more. 'You will leave tonight, Nurse Trent.'

It was a command, no less, and she seethed, but she didn't bother to answer him, nor did she look up as he went. He could at least have wished her goodbye. She blinked back tears and said shakily, 'I'll make a fresh pot of tea, shall I? This lot's cold.'

And Zuster Ritsma, after one look at her face, sat down at her desk, instantly absorbed in the papers on it, so that Abigail had time to compose herself and subdue the searing misery and bewilderment and rage which worked so strongly beneath her starched apron.

It was a good thing that the rest of the day proved to be so busy she had no time to think at all, and when at length it was nine o'clock and she was free to go, she made her farewells as quickly as possible before hurrying through the hospital which had suddenly become alien ground. She couldn't get away faster, she told herself.

She had told Zuster Ritsma about her delayed pay and that kind soul had been sympathetic but quite unable to do much about it. She had sent Abigail down to the hospital office where they dealt with such things and she had been met with blank looks and shrugged shoulders. As far as she could understand from the clerk she wasn't on the hospital pay roll at all; Professor van Wijkelen had engaged her to work for him and had made himself responsible for her salary, and beyond suggesting that she should find him and ask for herself, the clerk had no advice to give.

She went past the porter's lodge without hearing the man on duty wishing her good night and plunged outside into the dark. The desultory snow had ceased again, the pavements were wet under her feet and she shivered as she ran across the forecourt. She was totally unprepared for Jan's voice calling, 'Miss, miss!' from the car which slid silently alongside her. He smiled and opened the door, saying in his heavily accented English, 'I am to take you home, so please to get in.'

Abigail shook her head. 'Thank you, Jan, but there must be some mistake—Does the professor know that you've come to fetch me? And anyway I don't want to.'

Jan looked at his most fatherly. 'I am just this minute told by the professor to take you home, miss,' he contrived to look worried. 'He will be angry if I return and say that you would not go with me.'

She got in beside him, answering his polite remarks absentmindedly while her mind ran on and on, trying to decide what she would do. To remain in Amsterdam was unthinkable, to go back to England was impossible for the moment. She would have to get a job until she had enough money. When they arrived at the Begijnhof she thanked Jan and asked if he would take a message for her. 'To Bollinger,' she explained. 'Just tell him that I've gone away for a few days and he's not to worry, Mrs Macklin will let him know more about it later.' It sounded harmless enough like that, by the time Bollinger got worried enough to ask Mrs Macklin, she would certainly have another job, and she could always think of something to tell him when the time came. It was all a little vague, but it would have to do. She wished Jan goodbye and reminded him not to tell anyone else but Bollinger what she had said, and he agreed cheerfully, wishing her *Tot ziens* as he went back to the car, a hopeful form of farewell to which she was unable to subscribe. She wished him goodbye and went soberly indoors.

Mrs Macklin was in the kitchen making their bedtime drinks. She turned and smiled as Abigail walked in, saying, 'There you are, child—how nice and early. You must have been walking fast.'

'Jan brought me in the car.'

'Dear Dominic, what care he takes of you.' Mrs Macklin spoke with a satisfied pride which sparked off Abigail's held-down feelings.

'He does nothing of the kind,' she declared hotly. 'He doesn't care a brass farthing for anyone but himself! He's cold and heartless and I detest him. He's given me the sack, today—this very afternoon—just like that—he said. . .' she choked. 'He owes me weeks of salary too. . .' She burst into tears.

The whole story came out; in fragments which didn't make sense at first, but Mrs Macklin had patience. Slowly she sorted out the facts from the fiery condemnation of the professor's character, the bewilderment as to why it had happened and determination, repeated many times, never, never to see him again. 'And I would rather die,' declared Abigail in far too loud a voice, 'than take a penny from the man!' She turned a tear-blotched face to her listener. 'I love him so,' she said miserably.

'There is, of course, a mistake somewhere,' said Mrs Macklin with kind firmness. 'Someone or something has caused him to behave like this.'

Abigail took a drink of cooling cocoa which she didn't want. 'But why didn't he at least tell me? I thought he trusted me, I even thought that he was beginning to love me a little—that's absurd, of course. Look at me, no one ever looks at me more than once—no man, that is.' Which wasn't quite true, but she was in the mood to exaggerate. 'And Dominic least of all.' She put down her cup. 'I'm going away, Mrs Macklin.'

'Yes, dear. Where to? England?'

'I can't—I haven't any money, at least, not enough.'

'I will gladly lend...'

'You're a dear, Mrs Macklin, but no, thank you, I won't borrow unless I'm quite desperate. If I could get a job somewhere away from Amsterdam, just long enough to save my fare. I must get away.'

'You're sure that's the right thing to do, Abigail?'

Abigail got up and took the cups and saucers over to the tray on the table. 'Yes, I'm sure. I couldn't stay, you see, I might see him. I haven't known him long, I should be able to forget him.'

Both ladies knew that this was a silly remark, but neither of them said so. Mrs Macklin nodded her head and offered:

'In that case, I believe I can help you. I have a friend, a Mevrouw Hagesma. She lives in Friesland, in a tiny village north of Leeuwarden. She's had a stroke and although she can get about, she finds it difficult on her own. Her daughter is going home to be with her, but not for a week or so. I think she would be delighted if you would go and stay with her and help her. The only thing is, she's very poor.'

Abigail said quickly, 'She need not pay me; as long as I could have a room and some food, it would give me a chance to decide what to do—there must be some work I can do, I don't care what. Even if it's only a few gulden a week—I don't need much to make up the money for my fare.'

'I still think you should borrow from me, my dear.'

Abigail crossed the little room and planted a kiss on the smooth, elderly cheek. 'What a kind person you are, Mrs Macklin, but I won't. I'll go to your friend if she'll have me, at least I'll be out of the way.' She gulped, determined to put a bright face on things. 'I'll go back to England just as soon as I can and get a job and then Bolly can come back.'

'He's very happy at Dominic's house,' Mrs Macklin reminded her.

'You think he'd like to stay? If—if Dominic would keep him and he'd be happy, then that would be wonderful. He deserves better than I can offer him.' She sighed. 'Could I write to your friend tomorrow and ask. . .?'

'She sits up till all hours,' Mrs Macklin interrupted her to say. 'I'll telephone her now.'

Ten minutes later Abigail said wonderingly, 'Well, I can hardly believe it—all fixed up so quickly. I'll pack tonight and leave on that early train—you're sure it runs?'

'Yes, my dear,' Mrs Macklin smiled at her. 'I shall miss you. What am I to say if—when Dominic calls?'

'He won't. He's—he's finished with me, I think. Perhaps he remembered his wife and thinks I should get like her—he must be mad,' Abigail's voice rose a little, 'if he thinks that. His wife was lovely, wasn't she? with lots of men-friends. I couldn't be more different—perhaps that's why. I mean, I'd be such a safe, unexciting sort of wife, wouldn't I, because he would never need to be jealous of me.'

Mrs Macklin quite rightly took no notice of this diatribe. 'What shall I tell him?' she repeated.

'That I've gone to another job; he'll not want to

know more than that, if he asks. And please don't tell him where I am or about the money.'

Her companion gave her an understanding look. 'No, dear. Now go to bed, you have to be up early in the morning. What about Bollinger?'

Abigail explained about him. 'I don't think he'll worry, not for a little while, and if he comes to see you, if you'll just tell him that I'm working—another case—and that I'll write.'

She said goodnight and went away to pack and then to go to bed and lie awake until it was time for her to get up. The night had been very long. She dressed with relief, had a sketchy breakfast, took Mrs Macklin a cup of tea, wished her goodbye and left the house.

The train journey to Leeuwarden was uneventful. Abigail, watching the flat, wintry fields as they flashed along, saw nothing. Because of her sleepless night she was quite unable to think; wisps of conversation flitted in and out of her tired mind, snatches of things she had said and done in the last few weeks since she had met Dominic, came and went, tangling themselves into a frenzied, half-remembered muddle which did nothing to improve a rapidly worsening headache. She got out at Leeuwarden and a kindly ticket collector sent her to the station café to have a cup of coffee while she waited for the bus, which wasn't due for an hour. There was a map on the café wall, and she studied it, glad to discover that the village she was going to was a long way away from Dominic's home. As far as she could make out, it was on a side road, half way between Leeuwarden and Holwerd on the coast. The side road, according to the map, ended at Molenum, which was the place she was going to. For the first time since she had accepted the job, she wondered what sort of a house she was going to, and what kind of a village it was in.

Molenum, when she reached it, was small; one shop, a post office in the front room of a small house in its main street and a very large church. The landscape was rolling and wide and there weren't many trees. There was a chill, damp wind blowing in from the sea, some miles away, and absolutely no one to be seen. She watched the bus lumber away and went into the shop.

The woman behind the counter was tall and gaunt and middle-aged, dressed severely in black. She stared at Abigail in a disconcerting way which she found a little daunting as she said: '*Dag, mevrouw,*' and then, 'Mevrouw Hagesma?'

The stare melted into a nice smile. The village was so small, probably everyone in it knew she was coming; she smiled back as the woman came from behind the counter and pointed up the narrow cobbled road, past a row of dollshouse-sized cottages, to a house standing alone; it was just as small as the others, but it had a garden all round it. Abigail said '*Dank U*' and picked up her case and started towards it, aware that, as she passed, the spotless white curtains at the little front windows were stirred by invisible fingers. She opened the gate and walked up the narrow brick path and knocked on the old-fashioned wooden door; it had a small square shutter in it which opened to allow an eye to examine her before the door was opened.

Mevrouw Hagesma was tall and gaunt too, and quite old, but her face was kind and her eyes were as bright and blue as a little girl's. It was then that Abigail realised that she would have to speak Dutch, something she hadn't thought about before. She embarked on a few muddled phrases to which the old lady listened with grave courtesy, and then said slowly, her speech thickened by her stroke, 'A friend of Mrs Macklin's is a friend of mine,' and led the way into the living room. She walked with a stick and very slowly and one arm hung, not quite uselessly, at her side.

The room was comfortably furnished and tidy, but the pristine cleanliness Abigail knew was a Dutchwoman's pride was absent. The old lady waved an arm clumsily around her and shrugged her shoulders, and Abigail understood the gesture to be one of apology because not everything was exactly in its place, nor was it quite spotless.

It was surprising how, after those first few minutes, they managed to understand each other. Abigail had a room like a cupboard at the top of the ladder-like stairs—she unpacked her few things and went down again to find Mevrouw Hagesma making coffee. While they drank it, and with the aid of the little dictionary Abigail always carried with her, she found out all she needed to know about the old lady as well as telling her as much as she thought necessary about herself. Mevrouw Hagesma nodded and smiled her slightly lopsided smile when Abigail had finished. 'We shall be friends,' she told her, and although she spoke in Dutch, Abigail understood her very well.

Abigail had expected the days to drag, but surprisingly they didn't. There was so much to do in the little house, and once Mevrouw Hagesma saw that she was a good housewife, able to sweep and dust and polish and not grumble about it, she was content to leave a great deal to her. Not that Abigail allowed the old lady to be idle. She had her exercises to do each day, and her reading, and Abigail was helping her to write once more with her still partly paralysed hand. Mrs Macklin had telephoned several times too and Abigail had longed to ask about Dominic but didn't, and Mrs Macklin didn't mention him.

Each morning, just before dinner time, Abigail took Mevrouw Hagesma for a walk, a very short one, down to the village shop, where she rested for a little while and then back home again. It was a slow clumsy business, but the old lady looked forward to a gossip with Mevrouw Beeksma in the shop and most mornings there were customers there too so that the gossip became half an hour's chat, something which the old lady enjoyed very much although Abigail found the elderly, soberly clad ladies unexciting. They spoke Fries, which made it impossible for her to understand them, and when they spoke to her in careful, slow Dutch, she still had difficulty in understanding them. She got into the habit of wandering round the little shop, examining the crowded shelves, looking at the tins and packets, learning their prices for the sake of something to do, and when she found that Mevrouw Hagesma enjoyed correcting her wild attempts to speak Dutch, she suggested that they should spend a little time each evening struggling with that language and improving her deplorable accent. It passed the long hours before bedtime and the old lady, now that she had something to occupy her mind, began to improve rapidly.

Abigail had been there ten days when Mevrouw Beeksma told her that her daughter had been taken ill and had been taken to hospital in Leeuwarden. Abigail, wrestling with the shopkeeper's pantomime of screwed-up face, hands clasped to back and urgent bendings, tried to guess what complaint the poor girl had. Renal colic, perhaps, or even a slipped disc—she made a sympathetic murmur and listened to Mevrouw Beeksma bemoaning the fact that she wouldn't be able to go and see her each afternoon, because there was no one to mind the shop. If only there was someone to take the place over for an hour or so each afternoon, said poor Mevrouw Beeksma, looking gaunter than ever.

'I will,' said Abigail, not stopping to think.

'*Wel, neen*,' declared Mevrouw Beeksma, and then: '*Waarom niet*?'

Why not indeed, thought Abigail, she had been wanting a job—here it was. For the first week it hadn't mattered too much because deep down inside her she had hoped that Dominic would come thundering after her. But of course he hadn't, and now it was urgent that she should earn some money; she would have to go when Mevrouw Hagesma's daughter came, it would be splendid if she could earn enough money to go straight back to England before that time.

'Three hours each afternoon,' said Mevrouw Beeksma, 'and I pay two gulden an hour.'

Abigail did sums—six gulden a day for six days, that would be thirty-six gulden. She needed more than that, but perhaps she could sell something.

'Yes,' said Abigail.

She was slow that first day. The ladies of the village who came for their groceries had to help her with their change and point out just what they wanted, but Abigail, who considered the job as a gift from heaven, didn't make the same mistake twice. By the fourth afternoon she was managing very well and Mevrouw Beeksma pronounced herself satisfied. 'Another week,' she told Abigail, 'and my daughter will be home.' She smiled and nodded and strode out into the windy street to catch the bus.

It was cold again, just like winter, as indeed it still was. A few snowflakes, blown by the sea wind, settled on the window ledges of the shop. Abigail watched the bus disappear into the empty countryside beyond the village and went back into the shop. She had been working hard all the morning, turning the little house upside down for the weekly clean Mevrouw Hagesma considered absolutely necessary, and today, for the first time, the old lady had helped a little and talked cheerfully about her future, so that Abigail felt heartened by her progress. There had been a letter from Mrs Macklin too, full of messages from Bollinger, who was a little puzzled but quite content to take Mrs Macklin's word for it that Abigail was happy. She took the letter out of her pocket now and read it through as though she might have missed something in it—something, some news of Dominic, but he wasn't mentioned.

She put the letter away with a little sigh, put on the white apron, much too large, which was Mevrouw Beeksma's concession to hygiene in her shop, and got out the stepladder. The apron got terribly in the way and Abigail muttered rudely; it wasn't as though it was necessary—the shop was cleaner than anything she had ever seen in her life, there couldn't be a germ in the place; still, as her employer wished her to dress up in it, she supposed she should. She hitched it up round her pretty legs and climbed the steps.

She had been up there perhaps ten minutes, dusting

bottles of pickles and gherkins and onions, when the door opened, allowing a draught of cold air, a few persistent snowflakes and the professor to enter.

Abigail put the pot of gherkins she was holding carefully back on the shelf, for her hands felt strangely incapable of holding anything. Her heart had leapt, stopped and then begun to hammer at her ribs in a most unnerving fashion. She had no breath; all she could do was to sit and stare down at the top of his head, until he looked up and saw her. They stared at each other for a timeless age before she asked idiotically, 'Is there something you want?' just as though he was a housewife come to buy tea or coffee or a few slices of cheese.

'You,' he said in a rough voice, and went on staring. 'Come down, Abigail.'

Somewhere at some time she remembered she had read that one should always begin as one meant to go on, especially when it concerned matters of the heart. It seemed to her a sound idea. She stayed where she was.

After a silence which she found unendurable the professor said in quite a different voice, 'Please come down, Abby, I want to talk to you,' and when she still didn't move because truth to tell she found herself incapable of doing so, he began again, but this time in a loud rough voice.

'I can no longer sleep because of you, nor can I eat—presently I shall be unable to do my work. It is intolerable that a small mouse of a girl like you can reduce me to this miserable state. Each time that I have sent you away I have racked my brains for an excuse to get you back; I thought at first that I could hold out against you, but I find that there is nothing to hold out against, only gentleness and kindness and honesty and a smile to twist my heart, my dearest darling.'

'You have behaved abominably,' said Abigail severely, 'and I will not be your dearest darling until I know why you did.' She watched the rueful smile touch his mouth.

'I came back from Brussels hell for leather, longing to see you again. I found you with Henk, laughing up at him—you are so pretty when you laugh, my darling—I listened to you talking and it seemed to me that it was I whom you were discussing. I wanted to hurt you then as I was hurt.' He sighed, he went on humbly, 'It has taken me all this while to swallow my pride, for I have to know...'

He was interrupted by the opening of the door. Old Mevrouw Henninga from one of the houses across the street shook the snow off her cap, bade them good day and asked for tea. Abigail had to descend her steps then. She found the tea, served her customer, gave her, for once, the right change and wished her a polite good day, while the professor, not to be outdone when it came to manners, opened the door and closed it after her.

When he spoke he forgot to be humble. 'And why in the name of heaven are you serving behind a counter?' His voice a snarl.

Abigail prudently climbed her ladder again; there was a distinct advantage in being a little above him. 'I'm earning my living,' she explained haughtily.

He glared at her under lowered brows. 'Why here in this back-of-beyond place? Why aren't you in England? I went after you and you weren't there.'

Abigail's heart began to beat its own happy little tune, spreading a tingle of excitement over her.

'I'll tell you why I wasn't there,' she said, and struggled to keep her voice cool and calm and slow. But it came out in an excited babble. 'I had no money—no money to go back to England, and do you know why? Because you haven't paid me—not for weeks,' her voice rose a little. 'You sent me away without references and didn't even bother to ask if I had somewhere to go, just like a Victorian servant girl; for all you cared I might have gone on the streets!'

'On the streets?' he looked thunderstruck. 'My dear little love, what a brute I have been! Can you ever forgive me? You see I could think of nothing else but you and Henk, laughing together—and you are so young. . .' he was leaning on the counter now, looking up at her. 'For years now I believed that I had built myself a new life, a nice safe life in which women didn't matter, in which I could work without getting involved with anyone—any girl. And then I saw you and lost my heart, my lovely girl, but not without a fight. I told myself that you were clever and scheming with your quiet voice and your friendliness and kindness. I fought very hard, my darling, but then I discovered that I didn't want to fight any more. I have used you very ill, haven't I?'

Abigail smiled. 'Indeed you have.' She paused. 'We weren't talking about you at all, only about Henk's latest girl-friend.' She went on primly, 'Listeners never hear any good of themselves.' She frowned quite fiercely at the professor. 'There is something else. I am considered quite old for my age.'

'Abby. . .' The door opened once more and a small boy sidled in and demanded *bischuiten*. The professor, curbing impatience with a visible effort, handed him a packet from the counter, took his money and put it in the till.

'He wants three cents change,' advised Abigail from her observation post, and watched while the professor rang up the till to the manner born and proffered the coins.

'Give him a sweetie,' and when the boy had gone, his cheek bulging with a toffee, she explained, 'It's good business to give the children sweeties when they come on an errand.'

She didn't say any more because the professor was looking at her with such tenderness and love that her breath deserted her. He said now, very firmly, 'Abigail, I have never proposed to a girl on top of a stepladder before, but that's what I intend doing unless you come down.'

He held out his arms and she jumped straight into them; they held her so tightly that she could feel his heart beating under her cheek. Her voice a whisper, muffled by the thickness of his jacket, she said:

'Only Mrs Macklin knew where I was, and I asked her not to tell.'

'And she kept her word. Bollinger and I put our heads together when I got back from England and I went to see her, but all she would tell me was that an old friend of hers needed help until her daughter could go to her.'

She felt his kiss on her hair. 'Abby, my darling girl, if you wish to tell me off I promise you that I will be very meek.'

'Don't be ridiculous!' She looked up into his face, smiling, and he bent his head to kiss her.

'Will you marry me, Abby?'

'Yes, dear Dominic, of course I will.' She would have said more, but the professor's hold tightened so that she had no breath, or almost none, and when she at last essayed to speak, he kissed her silent. It was an enjoyable silence which at length Abigail broke.

'Dominic—wait a minute, there's something important—what about Bolly?'

The professor loosened his grasp very slightly so that he could see her face. 'A useful addition to our household, wouldn't you think, my darling? He's terrific with animals and gardens and, I've no doubt, children too.'

'Oh, he will be pleased—he's splendid with them.'

'Then we must do our utmost to give him every opportunity to be splendid, mustn't we?'

She smiled, and the dimple came and went. 'A bad-tempered little boy just like his father,' she murmured.

'And an adorable mousy little girl just like her beautiful mother.'

They stared at each other happily, contemplating a blissful future, and for good measure the professor kissed her again.

'What shall we do?' asked Abigail, feeling that one of them at least should be practical, but it seemed that Dominic had everything arranged.

'You're coming back with me to Amsterdam, my love. Arie's sister is on her way over to take your place with Mevrouw Hagesma—Jan's fetching her, I'm sure she'll understand when we explain.'

'About Amsterdam,' said Abigail. 'Where. . .?'

'Bollinger and Mevrouw Boot will have everything ready for you—and before you protest, Mrs Macklin is already at my house. You will stay there until I can arrange our wedding, my dearest—in the church in the Begijnhof, don't you agree?'

Abigail nodded, savouring the delight of being loved, indeed her ordinary face had become quite transformed by it so that the professor exclaimed,

'How very pretty you are, Abby,' and since it was obvious that he really believed it she smiled at him with delight and lifted her face for his kiss.

Presently: 'How long do we have to play at shop?' Dominic wanted to know.

'Until the bus gets in at half past four—and it's not playing at shop. I get paid—two gulden an hour.'

The horrified incredulity on the professor's face would have satisfied any girl who might have considered herself to have been badly treated, but Abigail wasn't any girl; she loved him. Looking into his stricken face she remembered that she hadn't yet told him this indisputable fact, and did so there and then, and the professor, holding her with powerful gentleness, kissed her at great length until she reminded him that she should get behind the counter, 'Just in case someone should come, dear Dominic.'

He glanced over her head at the snowflakes whirling past the shop window in a last wintry onslaught before spring made nonsense of them. 'Anyone coming out on a day like this would be mad,' he declared, 'and if they do I will serve them for you, my dearest heart.'

'Well,' conceded Abigail, 'you managed to sell the *bischuiten* very nicely. All the same I just can't stand here. . .'

'Oh, yes, you can,' said Dominic in a voice which sounded so certain of this that she found no point in arguing with him about it, and it was, after all, quite delightful with her head on his shoulder and his arms around her.

'If you say so, dear Dominic,' she said meekly, and kissed him.

From rugged lawmen and valiant knights to defiant heiresses and spirited frontierswomen, Harlequin Historicals will capture your imagination with their dramatic scope, passion and adventure.

Harlequin Historicals... they're too good to miss!